A GOWER STORY

Deborah Fisher

TREGOLWYN

First published in 2001 by Tregolwyn
PO Box 11, Cowbridge
Vale of Glamorgan CF71 7XT

Distributed by the Welsh Books Council,
Castell Brychan, Aberystwyth, Ceredigion SY23 2JB

British Library Cataloguing in Publication Data
A catalogue record for this book is available
from the British Library

ISBN 0-9538688-2-6

Printed and bound in Wales by
Dinefwr Press
Rawlings Road, Llandybie
Carmarthenshire, SA18 3YD

Acknowledgements

Special thanks go to Rebecca Dickinson, Sian Price, Delyth Tovey and Keith Jones, without whose helpful comments this would be a vastly inferior book.

Those who want to know more about the Gower peninsula as a result of reading this novel should have no difficulty in obtaining an up-to-date guidebook. (Regrettably, the 1955 *Guide to Gower* referred to in the story does not, as far as I know, exist.)

For those interested in trivia, I can recommend Edward Gill's *Curiosities of South Wales: a regional guide to the unusual*, published by S.B. of Seaford, East Sussex. (Date and ISBN unknown).

Welsh Words and Phrases

Bach	Little (one)
Bore da	Good morning
Cariad	Love
Chwarae teg	Fair play
Da iawn	Very good, very well
Diolch	Thank you
Diwedd y byd!	Good gracious! (literally: end of the world)
Duw	God
Heddiw	Today
Hwyl	Goodbye
Nadolig Llawen	Merry Christmas
Shwmae?/Sut mae?/ Sut wyt ti?	How are you?
'Stedda lawr	Sit down

Cover photo:
Sunset over Rhossili © Rhys Jones
E-mail: rhys.d.jones@ntlworld.com

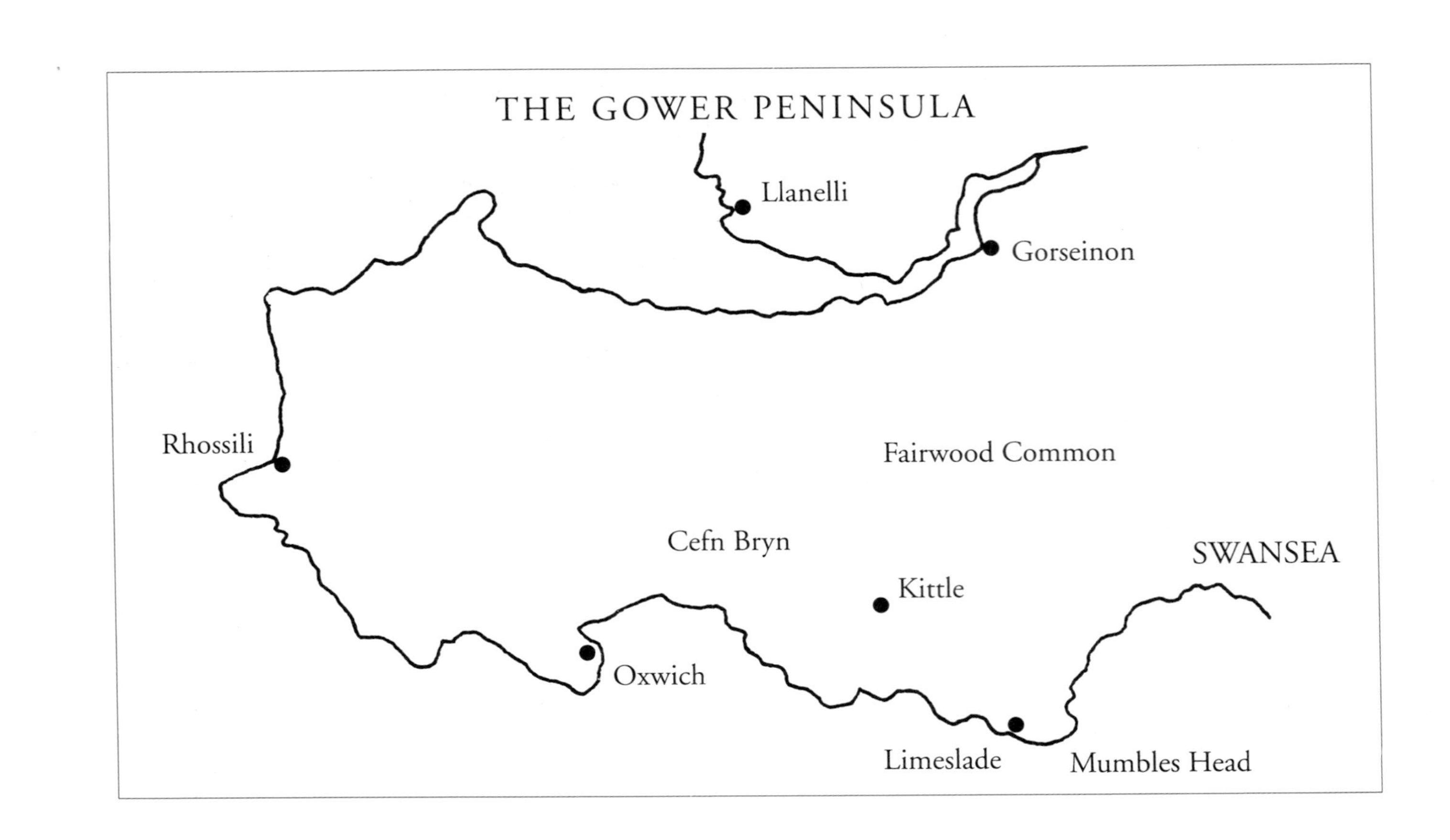
THE GOWER PENINSULA
Llanelli
Gorseinon
Rhossili
Fairwood Common
Cefn Bryn
SWANSEA
Kittle
Oxwich
Limeslade
Mumbles Head

Chapter 1

It was at Welsh class that I first got to know the Sutcliffs.

I had seen them around, before they first appeared at the class, because they were my near neighbours. Tim Sutcliff was a man about my own age, who had just been appointed vicar of the parish. He and his wife, Laura, were both English by birth, but they were making a valiant attempt to fit into our little community. The additional effort of taking Welsh lessons was quite unnecessary, really, as few of the local population knew a single word of their own native tongue; but we Welsh are a funny old nation, passionately proud of our culture even when we can't enjoy it. Their gesture went down well.

For myself, despite having been born and brought up on the Gower peninsula, I had little of the Welsh language. I did a couple of years of it at comprehensive school, and thus picked up a smattering which I promptly forgot for lack of practice. In my thirties, however, I remained very ashamed of the fact that I could speak French almost fluently, and had O-level Spanish, but no Welsh to speak of.

Though the church was close to my own house, it wasn't there that I had seen Tim and Laura, because I had never gone to St Mary's. I was brought up a Baptist, which is very common in this area. Unfortunately (depending how you look at it), the chapel to which my family had always gone suffered from falling attendances, and was eventually sold, the congregation being forced to transfer to one in a neighbouring village.

There's an old Welsh joke that goes something like this. A Welshman is shipwrecked on a desert island, where he remains for ten years without seeing a soul. Eventually a ship does pass, and stops to pick him up. The ship's captain, seeing this weather-beaten man with a long beard and ragged clothes, asks how long he has been stranded there. When the castaway replies that he has been there for ten years, the captain asks what he found to do with his time. The Welshman leads him to the top of a hill, where he proudly points out two wooden buildings.

"See those?" he says. "I built those."

"That's amazing," remarks the captain. "But what are they?"

"Chapels!" replies Dai Crusoe.

"Chapels?" repeats the captain, marvelling at the man's religious devotion. "But tell me, why two?"

"See the one on the left?" comes the reply. "That's the one I go to. And the other one – that's the one I *don't* go to!"

Any Welsh listener – at least in my own age group – will recognise the basic truth behind that little story. There were indeed two chapels in our village at one time, in addition to the church. The Presbyterians bit the dust long before the Baptists, but it's academic, because they've both gone now. Only the Church of England had deep enough roots to survive the onslaught of late twentieth-century godlessness.

Nevertheless, some of the most devout Christians I know would never have dreamed of setting foot inside St Mary's. I had no such qualms. Rather than make the trip down narrow country lanes on a dismal winter morning to get to the nearest chapel, I started going regularly to the village's Anglican church – or "Church in Wales", as we quaintly call it. Having become familiar with Tim and Laura through the medium of Welsh, I made up my mind that one place of worship was as good as any other, and transferred my allegiances accordingly. I didn't go so far as to get confirmed, but to all intents and purposes I became one of Tim's flock.

It was my friend Elvis Jones who had been responsible for starting up the beginners' Welsh classes. They were very informal, and took place on a Thursday evening in our local pub, the Drovers' Arms. In summertime, the pub would be packed out; but from October until Easter the landlord was glad of any extra business. Numbers attending the class were variable, with a few hardy perennials, such as myself, continuing to turn up every week because we regarded it as a social occasion. It got us out of the house, one might say.

Elvis had been christened that way by his parents, hardened old rockers, in the expectation that he would one day become what was then known as a "pop star". They were taken aback when he turned out to prefer Monteverdi to Motorhead and Holst to Buddy Holly. He *was* musical, though, so musical that he became central to the success of St Mary's Church, as its organist and choirmaster.

It was just as well that Elvis's parents had given him an unusual Christian name. With a surname like Jones, he would otherwise have acquired one of those traditional Welsh nicknames. "Jones the Music", probably. Elvis himself professed to be grateful that he hadn't been surnamed Morgan, otherwise he would undoubtedly have become popularly known as "Organ Morgan".

There aren't many churches the size of ours that can still muster a choir with any members under the age of thirty. How Elvis did it I'll never know, but through a mixture of pestering and persuasion he had managed to keep a hold on a number of local children, to the extent that they were prepared to spend an hour a week rehearsing and appear in church on Sunday morning and evening for the main services. Most of them, needless to say, were girls; but there were a handful of boys, who usually stuck with it until their voices broke, giving them an excuse to go and play football instead.

It was one of these boys who was at the root of all the trouble.

Craig Dutton. I can see him now, in my mind's eye, a curly-headed child with a heart-shaped face: what people sometimes call "a pretty boy". At that time, I couldn't have told you his name, but I would have recognised him in the street as being one of Elvis's current batch of singers. He performed no solos, from which I took it that his voice was, at best, average.

I don't remember exactly when or where I first heard his name. It certainly wasn't on that cold evening in late autumn when Tim's wife, Laura, telephoned to ask me to come over to the vicarage as soon as possible. Her tone was urgent, if not desperate, but she refused to go into any detail over the phone, merely saying that she and Tim had something to tell me.

When I arrived at the vicarage, I found I wasn't the only one of the congregation to have been summoned. Clearly, then, this was something to do with the church. There was some important announcement to be made. My heart was in my mouth. Surely Tim wasn't going to tell us that he was leaving?

They had been with us now, Tim and Laura, for five or six years, and in that time the congregation of St Mary's had soared, so that the church, large by village standards, was often as much as three-quarters full on a Sunday morning. Tim had been quick to recognise the contribution made by Elvis and his choristers, and continued to look to his choirmaster and organist to help raise the profile of the parish still further. This would not be a good time for Tim to move elsewhere. On the other hand, I could see that his success at St Mary's might have caught the Bishop's eye. If he were in for a promotion, I would have to try hard to be pleased for him.

Elvis was there before me. I saw his dark head framed in the doorway as I approached. He was talking to Laura, who looked pale and interesting. Her fair hair blew around her face in the evening breeze. The two children, Robert and Caroline, were outside playing. It was dark, and they were wearing mittens and bobble hats to run around the garden. They appeared to have been banished from the house to make way for the adults. Robert was eleven at the time; I can be sure of that, because he and Craig Dutton were in the same class at school. Caroline was younger, about eight years old if I remember correctly.

I smiled at the children as I went past, and they returned my greeting. That was heartening. There couldn't possibly be anything wrong. I had no doubt that leaving the parish would, at their age, qualify as bad news, news they would be quick to broadcast.

There was a little knot of people in the big, flag-floored kitchen. Most of the members of the parish council were there, along with Elvis, myself, and one or two other church stalwarts. Had I thought about it at the time, I would have recognised that we all had one thing in common: we were all staunch supporters and friends of the Sutcliffs. Mrs Bevan, the hubristic and outspoken organiser of the church flower-arranging team, who *was* a member of the parish council, was absent not because she was unable to attend, but because she hadn't been invited. This was Laura's doing, not Tim's.

Tim appeared at the top of the stairs, and called down to his wife to check that everyone was present. Receiving an affirmative reply, he descended slowly, and I had plenty of time to notice how drawn he looked. He was, if anything, even paler than Laura.

I'll admit it now. I was in love with Tim Sutcliff, or at least I had been in love with him. It must have started not long after I met him, and it had continued, on and off, for most of the time I had known him. Fortunately for me, as I look back on it, I had pulled myself together some time before all this happened. Knowing that nothing could ever come of my unrequited adoration, I had made up my mind, a few months prior to the evening in question, that I was no longer going to be silly about him.

The incident that had decided me had occurred one evening the previous winter. When I call it an "incident", I'm exaggerating. If anything, it was a non-incident. That was the whole point. Tim had invited me to come over to the house. He had been working on a history of the village in his spare time, and needed help with editing it and preparing it for publication. Because I knew about books, he assumed I would be the perfect helpmeet.

On that particular evening, I had happened to know that Laura would be out. Tim had said as much beforehand, but in any case I knew it was her evening for W.I. I had never bothered to join the Women's Institute myself, though I'd been along to the occasional meeting when there was a speaker or an activity that appealed to me. This was rare; I've never been any good at jam-making.

Just as Tim was hanging up the phone, after making arrangements for me to come over, he had made some throwaway remark.

"It'll be nice and cosy, just the two of us," he had said; or words to that effect.

Goodness knows why I allowed myself to think he might mean it the way it sounded. A vicar who was considering an extra-marital affair would hardly have been that open about his intentions before he had tested the water.

Let me be perfectly straight about this. I never wanted to have an affair with Tim Sutcliff. My love for him was almost entirely spiritual. It was based on what I then saw as his perfection, as a human being. I admired him. He was, to all intents and purposes, the ideal man. He was gentle and thoughtful. He was courageous and idealistic. He was even quite good-looking. No wonder that an unmarried woman, fast approaching middle age, with nothing much else to base her fantasies on, should have fallen under his spell.

But – and it's a big but – had the unthinkable actually happened, had Tim ever made overtures of that kind towards me, I would have run a mile. Tim would never be unfaithful to Laura, I knew that. That was part of his perfection, part of his attraction. Much as I might have enjoyed fantasizing about it, the reality would have thrown me into total confusion. I couldn't possibly have an affair with Tim.

What I really wanted, I suppose, was for the opportunity to be there, so that I could have the pleasure of resisting it and pride myself on the nobility of my passion for Tim. I wanted to be able to think that he was attracted to me, even though he couldn't do anything about it. On that evening, when we were alone together in the vicarage, I hoped to have my ambitions realised. The children would be in bed, or playing in some other part of the big house, and there would be ample opportunity for confidences. Perhaps Tim would say something, or do something, to betray his true feelings. I would make it clear to him that I was not to be toyed with. At the same time, I would let him know that his feelings were returned.

It seems absolutely ludicrous to me now that I could ever have entertained such a fantasy. Love is blind, they say, and mine for Tim came fully equipped with a white stick and a guide dog. I don't remember exactly what was said and done that evening. All I remember is that I came home in tears, having understood, once and for all, that Tim's feelings towards me were entirely platonic.

Funnily enough, nearly a year later, the village history still hadn't been published. Tim didn't mention it to me again, until I asked him. Then he said that he had asked Laura to edit the manuscript for him. I was hurt. I had to admit it was more his wife's place to carry out such an intimate service for him than mine; but Laura Sutcliff was so scatty that the idea of her editing a book seemed positively outrageous. It was partly my knowledge of Laura's character that had caused me to be so hopeful about the possibility of her husband having some feelings for me, in the first place.

Laura was unbalanced. It wasn't her fault. Being a vicar's wife can't be easy, and she had two kids to bring up and that great big house to keep clean. I suspect, however, that she had always been that way inclined. It was all too much for her. *Everything* was too much for her.

Don't get me wrong, I liked Laura. That was one of the most powerful reasons for not falling in love with her husband, though it didn't cut much ice at the time. She wasn't, in any case, what I would have called a close friend; though I think she may have seen our relationship differently.

We talked often, about Tim and the children. I couldn't offer her any advice on the latter subject, never having had any of my own, but even I could see that it must have been difficult to bring them up to be God-fearing and at the same time able to conform to the expectations of their peers. Laura had once caught Robert performing a mock "communion" over a plate of ham sandwiches, while a couple of other boys who had been invited to tea sat around and laughed. I mean, what can you say about that sort of thing?

Chapter 2

My relationship with the Sutcliffs had been an up-and-down one, with lots of things said and not said; and now here I was, in their kitchen, hoping against hope that they were not going to announce that they were about to leave the district. Love them or loathe them, they were the centre of my social world, and I didn't relish the prospect of getting to know their replacements from scratch.

Tim's expression was solemnity itself as he advanced into the centre of the expectant gathering.

"Right!" he said breathlessly. "Thank you all for coming."

Almost without my noticing it, Laura had thrust a mug of tea into my hand. When I turned to thank her, she put her finger over her lips, shushed me, and pointed to Tim, who, it seemed, was about to unveil the mystery.

"I've asked you all to come here because there's something I feel you should all hear. Something you should all know, that concerns you, as members of this parish. Something unfortunate has happened. Well, when I say happened, nothing has actually happened. I mean, something *has* happened, but it's not . . ."

For a moment, I genuinely thought he was going to burst into tears. The skin around his eyes certainly looked blotchy, as though he had been crying. I wanted to reach out to him, mentally, to help him through the ordeal of making this speech. That it was an ordeal was quite apparent. Tim gave sermons for a living; I had never known him so tongue-tied.

"This is very difficult for me," he stumbled on, "and I hope you'll bear with me. You're my dearest friends and fellow worshippers, and that's why I have to tell you about this myself, before you hear it from someone else. What you'll hear from me will be the truth, and I hope you'll remember that when other people start talking about it. As they undoubtedly will."

"What's wrong, Tim?" asked Mr Samuel, the verger, during the momentary pause while Tim gasped for breath. "What's happened?"

This must be very serious, I realised, if Mr Samuel wasn't privy to any more information than the rest of us.

"I've been accused of a . . . crime," Tim stammered. "A serious . . . offence."

Don't ask me how I knew, straight away, what it was. I simply did.

"Oh, I can't believe that!" scoffed Ray Gough, the head chorister, Elvis's right-hand man. "You must be exaggerating, Vicar!"

Everyone else winced at this insensitivity. Ray probably thought he was being supportive, but he was as good as calling Tim a liar, before he had even started his explanation properly.

"It's no joke," said Tim sharply, regaining control of the situation. "When I say 'crime', that's exactly what I mean. A criminal offence. It's potentially very serious. Before I even begin to tell you about it, I want to assure you all that I am completely and utterly innocent."

"Of course you are!" blustered Ray Gough. "We already know that."

"How can you *know*, Ray?" said Elvis, long-sufferingly. "How can any of us know, before we've heard what the Vicar's got to say?" It was as savage a put-down as I'd ever heard from Elvis.

Ray went quiet.

"Let's not start arguing over this," said Tim patiently, raising his hands in a placating gesture, reminiscent of the sign of blessing that he gave at the end of a service. "Please, just listen to what I've got to say, and if you've got any questions, I'll answer them afterwards. Then you can decide for yourselves what to think."

There followed what I think is called a pregnant pause.

"One of the choristers," said Tim, "has told his mother and father that I behaved towards him in a way that was . . . improper."

This revelation was greeted with a collective gasp. The only ones who didn't gasp were Laura (because she already knew), me (because I'd somehow guessed) and Elvis, for reasons best known to himself.

"Oh, dear God!" exclaimed Mr Samuel, unsuitably. "I can't believe it!"

"Unfortunately," continued Tim, raising his hands again to make sure he was heard above the general babble, "the police have decided to take the matter seriously. I had hoped that no one else would ever need to hear about it. The boy's parents have been remarkably discreet up to this point. But I'm afraid the gloves are off now, and I'm going to have to defend myself against the accusation. I've consulted a solicitor, and it will soon become public knowledge. I'm hoping the press won't decide to pick it up, not just yet, but I can't be sure."

There was a general silence, as people paused to absorb this information.

"When did all this happen, Tim?" asked a lone voice, intruding into the void. I recognised it as my own.

"Olwen." Tim peered at me, across the room. Clearly, he hadn't noticed until now that I was even there. "The accusation was made known to me about a fortnight ago. I'm still not too clear on when the . . . er . . . incident is supposed to have happened. I believe the boy told his parents two or three weeks ago. They decided to come to me first, and confront me with it, an action for which I must say I'm grateful to them. However, when I denied all knowledge of it, they said that, if I wasn't willing to make a clean breast of things, they would report me to the police. The police have now interviewed me, and have said that they feel obliged to take it further. They've interviewed the boy, and they have no reason to think that he's being malicious, so they have to assume that there's something in it."

"Which boy is it?" asked someone else.

"I'm afraid I can't tell you that. I'm not allowed to mention his name. The boy has to be protected, though I don't doubt it will become general knowledge in due course, locally at any rate."

"What about you, Elvis?" asked Ray Gough, rather belligerently. "Do you know which boy it is?"

"I have an idea." Elvis was impassive. "But if the Vicar's been told not to say anything, you certainly won't hear it from me."

"I bet it's that little blighter, Michael Stone," continued Ray, unable to let the matter rest. "Wait till I get my hands on . . ."

"There'll be none of that, Ray," said Elvis, who was being unusually forceful, for him. "Anyhow, I think I'm right in saying that your guess is completely wrong."

"Then who?"

"Now I've already told you, and the Vicar's told you, that it's confidential. If you're going to find out, you won't find out through us. Imagine if the Vicar and I went around telling everybody, imagine what the prosecution would have to say about that in court!"

He was right, of course, but the mention of court sent everyone into a panic. The silence that had been general until now was suddenly broken, with people exchanging excited and anxious comments about the likelihood of the matter ending in a prosecution.

"I know a good barrister," someone was saying. "You know, that chap Evans, lives in Bishopston."

"No, he's moved," said someone else. "Rhossili, isn't it?"

"Please, everyone!" shouted Tim. He had been forced into raising his voice, in order to make himself heard above the hubbub. "Please," he repeated more quietly as the chatter died down. "All I ask is that you accept my word for it that I'm innocent and give me what support you can when people start saying otherwise. My main concern is for the church. I've spoken to the Bishop, and he agrees that it would be wrong to take any precipitate action, so I'm going to continue taking services as normal until the police decide whether or not the matter is coming to court."

"I should bloody think so!" exclaimed Ray Gough, forgetting himself again.

"Language, Ray!" chided Mr Samuel. "Remember where you are!"

Ray went red and quietened down. There were a few more questions for Tim, from other people, but they were mostly the kind which couldn't be answered by anyone except a clairvoyant, such as "What do you think is behind it?" Then Laura made it clear that she wanted everyone to leave, and people started to drift away, still talking it over in twos and threes as they departed down the garden path. I only hoped they would have the sense not to let the children overhear anything.

Elvis and I were the last to leave. By mutual consent, we went to the pub, where we ensconced ourselves in the back bar, the only two customers. We ate two packets of cheese and onion crisps – each – and tried unsuccessfully to avoid a post mortem.

By the end of the week, the identity of the chorister who had accused Tim of molesting him was known throughout the village, simply because he was the only regular member of the choir who was missing from the Sunday services. It was a boy called Craig Dutton, whose father was a doctor.

This last piece of information, though it may not seem relevant, was in fact highly influential in causing individual villagers to come down on one side or the other. Dr Dutton was not the only doctor in the district, or even the most respected; he was nevertheless a doctor, a man who had studied Medicine at university and practised it in the local community for a number of years. He was well known and not disliked. Had he been working class, I suspect it would automatically have been assumed that his son was a malicious liar. Under the circumstances, however, Craig's version of events was given credence by many.

Even though I was expecting it, it came as a shock to hear it being discussed in the village shop.

"There's no smoke without fire," the woman was saying. "These church people like to make out they're so perfect, but they're no better than the rest of us."

I didn't recognise her. She wasn't a worshipper at St Mary's, and I didn't even know her by sight, but my reaction was instinctive. I was trembling even before I had got a word out.

"I don't think you know what you're talking about," I broke in. Both the woman and her interlocutor – Mr Meredith, who ran the shop and was in the process of weighing a bag of tomatoes – turned to me, open-mouthed, as I went on. "No one can say what the truth is until the police have looked at the evidence. How would you like it if someone was spreading malicious rumours about *you*, and people who didn't even know you started talking about you behind your back?"

"Who the f***ing hell do you think you are?" retorted the woman. That took Mr Meredith off the fence and put him on my side.

"Would you moderate your language in my shop, please?" he said quickly. The woman, whoever she might be, evidently wasn't as valued a customer as I was.

She turned to him with a look of unmitigated hostility. "I'll say what I like," she snapped. "It's not right, clergymen going around assaulting children."

"There's no evidence . . ." I started to say, but Mr Meredith raised his hands to silence us both.

"Please, ladies! I don't want any trouble in here. If you want to fight, go and do it outside."

I stood my ground, staring her out defiantly. I won.

"You can keep your f***ing tomatoes!" she screeched at Mr Meredith, storming out of the shop. "And I'm on to *you*, little miss fancy piece!"

To this day, I have no idea what she meant by that. I did, however, apologise to Mr Meredith for causing a scene and, in an effort to make amends, I bought the tomatoes myself, besides a few other things I didn't need.

"What do you think, Miss Harris?" he asked, while he was ringing up the till. "Is there anything in it?"

"No, of course not! You know the Vicar, you surely can't believe he's capable of anything like that."

"No," he echoed, perhaps a little half-heartedly. "No, of course not. I don't want to believe it. It's that poor wife of his I feel sorry for. What must she be thinking? She must be at her wits' end! All the same, to invent a story like that . . . What are kids coming to these days, eh?"

We left it at that.

"Larkhill, 1948," I typed. "vi 269p cloth, index, frontisp, bookpl, 1st ed, very good. £25."

It was no use. I couldn't go on working with this on my mind. I bit the figurative bullet, closed down the PC, put on my coat, and headed for the door. I'd been thinking about it ever since I came back from the shop earlier in the day. I was going to see Laura.

It wasn't entirely a spur-of-the-moment decision. I had deliberately chosen a time when Tim would probably be out. He tended to go visiting on Tuesday afternoons; I knew that, because it was the day he normally chose for visiting the old lady who lived next door to me. At the moment, I wasn't sure I could face seeing him. I only hoped he hadn't given up his visiting routine as a result of recent events. As I set off for the vicarage, I was filled with misgivings.

A long, winding lane connects our village with the main road. At its narrowest point, it forks, the right-hand fork leading down towards the church and the other widening into an almost suburban-looking street, where the village shop stands opposite the telephone kiosk. My family home lies beyond the church and the vicarage, tucked away in a deceptively capacious cul-de-sac.

I was born on Gower, and I've lived here almost all my life. In those thirty-eight years, I've seen a lot of changes, but the place remains fundamentally the same. Wildly beautiful by comparison with most of England, the landscape is unusually tame by Welsh standards. Most of the population of the peninsula resides in small villages, remote in winter and congested with tourists in summer. Not exactly a recipe for comfort, but I'm content. Sometimes I hear my neighbours complaining, but I don't see many "For Sale" signs.

Our village is less troubled by tourists than most, and is near enough to the city of Swansea to enable me to do the bulk of my shopping in a giant supermarket, rather than the village stores. Some of the older people aren't so mobile, and have to rely on local services. Others, who nominally live in the village, actually spend half their lives commuting and only get to enjoy the scenery at weekends. The thing that makes me stand out from most of my neighbours is that I work from home.

My business is dealing in second-hand books. It isn't a particularly lucrative pastime, but it saves me from having to trek into Swansea every morning in the rush hour to earn my crust. Most of my business is done by mail order, but in this day and age I have acquired a web site, which I constructed myself with the aid of – you've guessed it – a book. It was surprisingly easy.

Books have always been my passion. Even in the days when I had an ordinary office job and was employed by someone else, I spent a lot of my time buying and selling books. The buying came first, of course. It was only when I ran out of room to keep the books that I started selling them. I reasoned that, since I couldn't afford to buy any more and had nowhere to put them anyway, the best thing to do was to get rid of those I could manage without and use the money to buy others that I really wanted.

Before long, I had become quite expert on the subject of books and their bindings. I could tell just by looking at them whether they were likely to be valuable. It doesn't always work; some of the tattiest books I've seen have raised the highest price from customers. However, in general, the better a book's condition, the more you're likely to get for it. After doing a bit of book dealing on the side for some years, I eventually decided to give up my day job and do it full time. By now I had read up on the subject, and had acquired reference works that would help me recognise which editions were the most sought-after. I had learned all the jargon.

Two things finally decided me to go into business on my own account. One was that my parents got fed up with village life and moved to sheltered housing in Swansea. Unlike me, they had been born in the city. They had always, sneakingly, missed its hustle and bustle. Once the Baptist chapel closed down, they had no reason to stay in the village. Moving back into town had enabled them to get rid of the car. One thing they didn't miss, at their time of life, was the hassle of driving.

They left me with the family home, to do with as I thought fit. My elder sister, Sian, had long since married and moved away to Newport, so I only had myself to please. It was a few months before it dawned on me that what would make me happy was to give up my regular job and work for myself. Then the office where I was working decided to get rid of a few people, and I had the chance of a small voluntary redundancy settlement, which was all the incentive I needed. You might surmise that I was going through an early mid-life crisis, but I've never regretted the decision.

By converting the garage into a stock room, I managed to find space for lots more books. I was already known locally as something of an expert, and people often asked me to find them particular titles; all I had to do was start taking the exercise seriously. I took a couple of courses, run by the local authority especially for owners of small businesses, and suddenly I was self-employed. A bit frightening at first, but I soon got used to it.

Occasionally, I come by a book that's worth hundreds of pounds. The profit I make on such finds helps tide me over, and enables me to keep the business going. Small profits on cheap books are my bread and butter.

By the time I set out for the vicarage that afternoon, I had gone over the whole thing in my mind several dozen times, and I was still none the wiser. Not being personally acquainted with Craig Dutton, I felt unqualified to pronounce on his truthfulness or otherwise; but, like Mr Meredith, I found it went against the grain to believe that the accusation had been made, by an eleven-year-old, out of pure malice. There must be more to it. There must have been some mistake.

I tried desperately to imagine situations where Tim's words or actions could have been misinterpreted as an attempt to seduce. Nothing came readily to mind. An accidental brushing up against the boy in the vestry, perhaps, while they were both changing in readiness for morning service. Tim always came straight from the vicarage, already in his cassock, but the boys and girls would need to put on their white surplices before entering the choir stalls. They normally put them on over their everyday clothes, though, and there would be no real reason for Tim to be there while they were doing so. Perhaps *after* the service . . .

Reluctant as I was to raise the subject with Laura, I felt I needed to speak to her. She would, no doubt, bring it up herself. She always did, with anything that happened to be troubling her, and goodness knows there was no shortage of things that did.

"Olwen!" she exclaimed, answering the door to me. "I dread opening the front door these days. I never know who it's going to be. It's a relief to see a sympathetic face."

I was afraid to ask who all these unwanted visitors were. The police, no doubt. The press, quite possibly. And perhaps all kinds of other "well-wishers". Coward that I am, I was rather glad when she chose not to elaborate on her initial statement.

"It's a pity Tim's not here at the moment," she said. "He wanted to ask a favour of you."

"Anything," I replied, meaning it sincerely. "Anything at all. Just say the word."

"We can talk about that later. Have you got time for a cup of tea?" She evidently thought I had come specifically to see Tim.

"Actually," I said, following her into the kitchen, "I came over to see how you were. How are you coping?" I couldn't bring myself to be more precise.

"Oh, I go from day to day, you know." She ran a hand through her lank, untidy hair.

It was the kind of thing people often say when they've suffered a bereavement. This situation, if anything, was worse. The uncertainty alone must be mind-blowing, I thought. I couldn't even comfort her by suggesting that time would be a great healer.

"What about the children?" I asked, bringing to the fore a question that had been bothering me. "Do they know what's going on?"

"That's the worst thing, Olwen!" she cried. "The other kids are saying all kinds of things to them at school. I wanted to keep them away. I went to see the headmistress, but she said, better not, better carry on as normal. She's told their teachers to keep an eye on things as far as they can. But it's difficult, in the playground. And you know, Craig Dutton is in Robert's class."

Until she mentioned it, it hadn't occurred to me.

"That must be terrible!" I exclaimed. "For you, and for the Duttons too, I suppose."

"Yes." The mention of the Duttons didn't appear to have upset her – no more than she had been upset before, at any rate.

"Are – were – Robert and Craig friendly?" I probed, ashamed of myself for asking questions, assuaging my guilt by telling myself that it might help Laura to talk about it.

"Not particularly. Not enemies, though. I asked Robert about it, before he knew what had happened. Tim and I have had to sit them down and try to explain it all to them since then. They don't understand properly, but we've at least reassured them that it's not true. We said it was all a mistake, and the police were going to find proof that Daddy was innocent."

I took a gulp of tea. It was far too strong for my taste, but perhaps an overdose of caffeine wouldn't come amiss at this moment. I noticed a half-empty bottle of sherry, standing on the worktop, and thought of asking for some. It would be rude, but no ruder than it was of Laura to keep it to herself.

"And what *are* the police doing? Have they said any more?"

"Not much. They've taken a statement from Tim. They give the impression it's going to be a long, slow process. It might be months before anything else happens, they said."

"Oh, surely not?" I was shocked. "Don't they realise the effect it's having on everyone?"

"They say they do, but they can't go any faster, apparently."

"What about Tim? Has he got any idea what led up to this? Does he remember anything that might shed light on it?"

Laura shook her head sadly. It was surprising, to me, that she wasn't reacting more violently; but she was a woman who expected Fate to be unkind to her at every opportunity, and took it for granted that things would go wrong. Furthermore, I knew, from past experience, that her mood could swing rapidly from one extreme to another.

"He says he can't think of anything. He says he's racked his brains, but he's quite certain he's never . . . touched Craig. He barely knows the boy. Elvis does everything with the choir, as you know. Tim only sees them at morning and evening service."

"It's so horrible," I exclaimed, not thinking my words through. "I mean . . . a boy."

"I'm glad it's a boy," said Laura matter-of-factly.

I was speechless.

"If it had been a girl," she elaborated, "there might have been some smidgin of doubt in my mind. But with it being a boy, I know full well there *can't* be anything in it. Tim's never been like that."

She didn't need to explain what she meant by "like that". Nevertheless, I tried to ignore the implications and continue with superficial conversation.

"So he's no idea at all what prompted it?"

"He says not."

I noticed how the phrase "he says . . ." came at the beginning of each reply. Laura had doubts, of some kind. Perhaps they weren't actually doubts about Tim's innocence, simply doubts about the boy's motivation. Like me, she found it hard to believe that the whole thing was made up.

Having given her as much support as I felt was possible, with so many unknowns, I left in good time to avoid seeing Tim himself. Quite why I was avoiding him, I couldn't have said, unless it was the thought that I knew him well enough to be able to tell when he wasn't being completely honest. Yet the other night, when we had all been gathered in the kitchen listening to his protestations of innocence, I hadn't had the slightest doubt that he was telling the truth. Nothing had happened since then, to make me change my view.

Chapter 3

I don't publish my home address over the Internet, or in the press; I've always used a Post Office box number for advertising and correspondence. When you rent a PO Box, you can still choose to have all your mail delivered to your home address. It costs a bit extra, but it saves me the cost of the petrol I would use in making a daily trip to the nearest sorting office, which is some distance. The box number merely gives me the security of knowing that I'm not likely to get any cranks coming to the door.

Despite these precautions, word gets round, and I have the occasional personal caller. Here was one now, if I wasn't mistaken.

He was an immaculately-dressed, middle-aged man, and he was getting out of a silver BMW, which he had considerately parked to one side of the entrance to my drive. As he approached the front door, he cast a surreptitious and rather contemptuous glance at my shabby old mini van, standing in the drive. I noted also that he was carrying a briefcase. A serious collector, by the look of him, who had found me as a result of personal recommendation.

Not displeased at this intrusion, which gave me a chance to interrupt my housework, I opened the door before he had arrived at it.

"Miss Harris?" he ventured, extending his right hand.

"That's me. What can I do for you?"

"My name is Charles Cornwell. I'm the Reverend Sutcliff's solicitor."

He proffered a business card, which I took and glanced at. It proved nothing, except that he anticipated being challenged by some of the people he called on.

Apparently unperturbed at my failure to invite him into the house, he remained on the doorstep, regarding me calmly as I sized him up. I've always mistrusted men in suits, particularly navy blue suits. Something was persuading me to make an exception for this one.

He was, I guessed, in his mid to late forties, with rapidly-greying, wavy brown hair. His face was thin and serious, but there was an air of unforced amiability about him which went beyond the accustomed urbanity and practised charm of the professional lawyer.

"I wonder if you'd be willing to talk to me," he added.

I liked that. Not, "Can I talk to you?" but, "Will you talk to me?" He wanted a conversation; he wasn't intending to give a lecture.

Nevertheless, I felt uneasy about the reason for his visit. "I suppose so," I said grudgingly. "Come in. Excuse the mess."

There wasn't much of a mess, actually, or not as much as usual. I had more or less finished the vacuuming, and all the ironing had been put away. A few magazines were scattered around the place, and there was a ring on the glass top of the coffee table, from where I'd thoughtlessly put my mug down earlier in the morning.

"Sit down," I said, moving *Current Archaeology* off one of the armchairs. I realised, after he had obeyed, that I should have made him sit on the sofa, facing the window, so that the sun would be in his eyes instead of mine. To avoid squinting at him, I took the other armchair.

"What was it you wanted to talk about?" I asked, while I was making up my mind whether to offer him a hot drink.

He put down his briefcase on the floor in front of him, opened it and took out a notebook and pen.

"Do you mind if I make some notes while we talk?"

"That depends what it's about, Mr Cornwell."

He smiled. It split his face like a sunbeam coming out of the clouds. "Of course. Perhaps I should say that the Reverend Sutcliff himself gave me your name and address. Normally I would have telephoned before calling, but since I've come straight from the vicarage, it seemed like a good opportunity to try and catch you at home. He seemed to think you were likely to be in."

"I work from home. I'm almost always in."

"Ah." He nodded thoughtfully, obviously puzzled by the statement. "Good. You're a . . . a bookseller, I believe?"

"That's right. But I run my business by mail order."

"Oh, I see." The smile flashed across his face again, but didn't stay there. "I was a bit slow off the mark there, wasn't I?"

I stood up. "If this is going to take any length of time, I think I'd like a cup of coffee. Could I get you one?"

"That's very kind."

I could tell he wasn't bothered one way or the other. He accepted coffee from anyone who offered it, simply out of politeness. Under the circumstances, he could make do with instant.

Being on my best behaviour, however, I gave him his drink in a cup and saucer. Thanking me, he stirred it, then put it down on the floor by his feet. Somehow I knew he wasn't going to forget himself enough to kick it over by accident, so I resisted the urge to push the coffee table closer to him.

While I was in the kitchen making the coffee, Mr Cornwell had brought out some papers from his briefcase, and was looking over them. I caught sight of my own name, scribbled on a yellow post-it which was stuck to the top sheet.

"How much do you know about the Reverend Sutcliff's current . . . situation?" he asked suddenly.

I shrugged. "Not very much. Tim told me he'd been accused of some kind of indiscretion with one of the choirboys. Craig Dutton."

"You know the boy?"

"Not really. I've seen him at church, obviously. I know which one he is. But I don't have much to do with teenage boys, as a rule."

It came out sounding like a joke, which wasn't what I had intended. Charles Cornwell didn't laugh.

"I'll come to the point, then, Miss Harris. The Reverend Sutcliff has suggested you as a suitable person to act as a character witness, if it comes to a court case."

I gasped. "Is it likely to come to that?"

"We hope not." He looked directly at me, his dark eyes grave and concerned. "But we need to be prepared for the worst. I hope you understand."

"Of course I do!" I snapped. "We're not all congenital idiots round here, you know."

He held my gaze for a few seconds. "I'm sorry if I sounded patronising. I meant . . ."

"No, *I'm* sorry. It's just that Tim and I are close friends. And Laura, of course." It sounded like the afterthought it was. "The whole thing's come as a bit of a shock."

"Yes, I'm sure it has. But I feel we have good grounds for confidence about the outcome. It's just that it may take some time to get it all ironed out."

He looked at me, expectantly. I looked back at him, equally expectantly.

"May I ask you one or two questions?" His pen was poised, hovering over his notebook. He had barely touched his coffee. "How long have you known the Reverend Sutcliff?"

I was thrown by the way he kept referring to Tim as "the Reverend Sutcliff". I always called him "Tim", as did most of his parishioners. Children called him "Vicar Sutcliff" or simply "Vicar", and so did non-churchgoing locals.

"I've known Tim – and Laura – since they came here, which is about five years ago, I think."

"Six and a half years, according to them," he corrected.

"In that case, six and a half years. I've always lived here, and I met them the day they arrived."

"The actual day?" He sounded sceptical, and I could understand why.

"I remember it clearly. The vicarage is very near here – as you know. I was out for a walk, and I saw the removal van outside. They were in the process of bringing in their belongings, and I stopped to say hello. I felt I ought to welcome them."

"That was the first time you'd met them?"

"Yes. I believe Tim had been down here before that, to get used to the parish and the church, but I'd always missed him."

I went on to explain how Tim and Laura had joined Elvis's Thursday evening Welsh class at the pub, shortly after their arrival, and I had got to know them better through that than I would ever have had the opportunity to do simply by attending Sunday church services.

"Surely Elvis will be a character witness, won't he?"

Mr Cornwell pursed his lips. "I'm not sure. He may be too closely connected with the matter, being responsible for the choir. Some people might say he was biased. You'll be a better bet, being unconnected with the church, except as a parishioner."

"Actually, I'm not a parishioner."

"Oh?"

"I'm a Baptist. I'm not even allowed to take communion at St Mary's. I just go there."

"I see." It was obvious that he didn't, but a more detailed explanation wouldn't have added anything to the facts, so I let it go.

He asked a few more questions about me, such as how long I'd been in business on my own account; and he double-checked that *I* didn't have a criminal record.

"I hope you understand," he said again. This time I withheld the snappy answer. "I have to ask. It would be embarrassing for everyone if something came out later."

When he had drained his now-cold coffee cup, out of sheer politeness, and left my house, I felt somehow deprived. In my time as a self-employed trader, working from home, I had become rather isolated. Opportunities to meet interesting new people face to face were few and far between. I restored my good humour by reminding myself that Jessica would be coming soon. That would brighten things up a bit.

My niece, Jessica, is my sister's eldest daughter. For some years now, she's been coming to stay with me for lengthy periods, during her school holidays and latterly her vacation from university – Oxford, no less. The terms there are very short, and she was due to turn up at my place at the end of the first week in December.

Jessica, I should explain, had an ulterior motive for visiting me. It wasn't just that she found me pleasant company. In the run-up to Christmas, I could use an extra pair of hands to pack up all the Christmas orders, and I paid her to help me, besides giving her free bed and board. It was a mutually beneficial arrangement. I got cheap Christmas help, not to mention the social contact she offered. As for Jessica, she got a bit of extra money, a break from her parents, and a chance to visit friends on the Gower and in Swansea, of whom she had quite a few. Working for her auntie had to be preferable to a temporary clerical job at the DVLC.

Today was my housework day, and having spent as long as I could justify in finishing my coffee, I soldiered on with the job of clearing up the magazines and wiping over the table-top to get rid of that ring. I washed up the two coffee cups, then went upstairs, to look over the spare room.

It was a bit soon to be making up the bed in preparation for Jessica's arrival, so I contented myself with shampooing the carpet. The bed would, of course, need airing before she came. I looked through the linen cupboard to see what suitable sheets I had, and smiled as I came across the Paddington Bear matching set that I had bought for one of her visits – or maybe it was for one of her sisters – years before, when they were little girls who had barely started school.

Now they were practically grown women, all three of them. Jessica, the eldest, was the most attractive, and my particular favourite. That was probably because she was the one I had first got to know. When the other two came along, and Sian and my parents were busy babying them in turn, I bonded with Jessica. We shared the feeling of being left out of things, and we were alike in many ways. She even looked a little like me, though she was fortunate in not having to wear glasses. They had been the bane of my life, since I acquired them at the age of ten.

At that age, I hadn't been familiar with Dorothy Parker's witty saying about men not making passes at girls who wear glasses. All I knew was that the male half of my primary school class labelled me "Four Eyes" the minute I got back from the optician's with my new specs. Over the years, I learned to cope with the teasing, mainly by developing a nice line in sharp put-downs. Boys don't like to be made to look stupid, and it took a long time for me to find anyone who saw through that façade, to the sensitive girl underneath. It was a shame, because at that age I'd had a lot to give. There wasn't much left of it, now. My feminine emotions were withering away, for lack of use.

Leaving the Paddington Bear sheets where they were, I got out a more suitable set, with a floral design, and transferred them to the airing cupboard. I did a bit of dusting, just the areas that had been particularly neglected since Jessica's last visit. Then I went back downstairs and started writing out a shopping list, trying to remember all the things she liked best to eat.

After a few minutes, I recognised this as a displacement activity, designed to take my mind off Tim Sutcliff and his personal problems. But what else could I do?

Chapter 4

Depression had descended on me like the proverbial black cloud. Colourless, perhaps, rather than black. Christmas this year promised to be a dismal occasion, even with Jessica for company. How many people would stay away from the special services, simply because they doubted the innocence of their vicar? Would it end up with only half a dozen of us standing up for Tim and Laura?

It was astounding how quickly some could turn their coats, once they had listened to other people's poison. Even Ray Gough no longer seemed as certain as he had of Tim's spotless character. Now that he knew which of the choirboys was making the accusation, he was less inclined to accept that there was nothing in it. Dr Dutton had delivered one of Ray's three kids, in a January blizzard when he couldn't get his wife to the hospital. Dr Dutton's son was bound to have been well brought up.

I had at last spoken to Tim, on the day after Mr Cornwell's visit to my house. I had finally come to my senses and realised that I owed it to him not to avoid his company.

We had been so close in the past, Tim and I. Like brother and sister, if nothing else. It grieved me that I should have failed to recognise how important my support would be to him, in these circumstances. Tim needed me. He needed me all the more because of Laura's state of mind.

"Laura's a tower of strength," was almost the first thing he said to me, when I walked in through the vicarage door. Somehow I doubted that the tower would remain standing for much longer.

Laura herself wasn't looking too good. Hardly surprising, but what I mean is that she looked even worse than she had when I'd talked to her a few days before.

I was in haste to change the subject. "I came to tell you that I've seen your solicitor – Mr Cornwell, is it? I've told him I'll be only too glad to act as a character witness, should you ever need one. Though, of course, it won't come to that. He seems very confident that it'll all be sorted, in the end."

"In the end!" repeated Laura emphatically, slamming down the earthenware teapot so hard on the wooden table that I was afraid she would smash it.

"Thanks, Laura," said Tim mechanically, referring to the provision of tea. "I could do with a cuppa right now."

It was like Tim to make light of his own problems, but I had never seen him look so distracted as he did now – apart from the other night, when he had been addressing us about the situation. He had borne up well at the Sunday services, acting as though nothing had happened, taking as his text the Parable of the Sower from St Luke's Gospel. It wasn't something that could be easily misinterpreted; but he was likely to have to choose his topics carefully from now on. "Suffer the little children," would be out, for a start.

Laura said nothing more, but went upstairs, ostensibly to check on what her own children were up to.

"I'm sorry I haven't been round before now," I said, when she had left the room. "I wasn't sure you'd want to talk to anybody."

"I don't, particularly," said Tim. "But I make an exception for you," he added.

"How's Laura bearing up?" I asked. "She doesn't look very . . ." I had been going to use the word, "happy", but that clearly wouldn't have been appropriate.

"Up and down," he replied. "It's hit her very hard."

"That's quite understandable." I had been about to follow up with some tactless remark along the lines of, "I wouldn't like to be in her shoes". There were two things wrong with that. Firstly, I wouldn't have minded being in Laura's shoes if it had meant being married to someone like Tim Sutcliff. Secondly, I was sure that, however horrific the situation, I would have been able to cope with it a lot better than she was doing. Complacency like that just *has* to come before a fall.

"She's rather distressed today because something unpleasant has happened," Tim added.

It took me a moment to understand that he was talking about something new, some other misfortune that had come on top of the police investigation into his private life.

"Someone vandalised the garage last night," he said. "They sprayed a message on the door, in red paint."

"I didn't notice anything."

"No, you wouldn't have. I got someone round to paint over it, first thing this morning, as soon as I noticed it myself. I didn't want the children to see it. Not that they would have understood."

"What did it say?"

"'The Vicar is a paedophile'," he replied, as though it were the most common phrase in the English language. "They spelt it wrong, of course," he added.

"That's terrible!" I was indignant rather than upset, remembering the woman in the village shop and marvelling at how ready people are to believe the worst. "No wonder Laura's upset!"

"You'll be a friend to her through all this, won't you, Olwen?" Tim was looking at me appealingly under his fringe of thinning gingery hair. "Whatever happens to me, you'll stand by Laura, won't you?"

"Of course I will." I wondered what was behind the plea. It didn't matter. I wouldn't be doing it for Laura's sake, really, I would be doing it for Tim's. He was probably only too aware of that.

It was all I could do to restrain myself from asking him for further details of Craig Dutton's accusations. Hoping that he would volunteer the information himself, I played for time by telling him everything that Mr Cornwell had said to me, such as it was. Tim listened and nodded and thanked me, but didn't reciprocate.

After a while, I got up to go. It seemed to me that Tim was rather relieved to be able to draw the conversation to a close. He clasped my hand, a gesture he had only ever made in the church porch after a Sunday service, and reiterated that my friendship was very important to him and to Laura.

As I was leaving the vicarage, I was shocked out of my reverie by the sight of Mrs Bevan, flower-arranger-in-chief, advancing up the path towards me, from the direction of the church.

"Good afternoon, Miss Harris," she said. "Is the Vicar at home?"

This unaccustomed condescension on her part floored me, so

that I barely had time to stammer out a positive response before she launched into her spiel.

"We must all rally round, now. Rally round, that's what we must do. I'm sure the Vicar and Mrs Sutcliff can count on you, can't they?"

"Er . . . yes."

"Such a lot of nonsense. Who's been putting ideas into that little boy's head, that's what I'd like to know? I blame television. He's probably seen some programme, one of these crime things, no doubt. Why can't they stick to Agatha Christie? Miss Marple, that's what I used to like. You never heard anything about child abuse in those days. And why? Because there wasn't any, that's why! It's all been dreamed up by the newspapers, to give themselves something sensational to write about."

Silenced by the sheer illogicality of this tirade, I decided not to mention that Agatha Christie had actually written a book on the theme of child abuse. I merely nodded and agreed with Mrs Bevan.

"I've been talking to Mr Jones," she resumed, "and I think the best thing for us to do is to organise a campaign. Don't you think so? We must show our support for the Vicar and Mrs Sutcliff. Not forgetting the children, of course. Such a lot of nonsense! As if the Vicar would . . . oooh!" She shuddered theatrically. "It doesn't bear thinking about, does it?"

I shook my head. It had crossed my mind to tell her about the vandalism at the vicarage, but I decided against it. Tim could tell her himself, if he so chose.

"I'm going to talk to the Vicar about it now," she announced, "and I'll be calling on you in due course, to get your input." I found myself smirking at her use of a phrase she had undoubtedly picked up from one of the newspapers or television programmes of which she was so contemptuous. She didn't seem to notice my wholly inappropriate amusement, as she walked away towards Tim's front door.

Meeting Mrs Bevan like that had put me in an unaccountably good mood. It was nice to know that I wasn't alone in my support for Tim, though I knew he would never go along with the idea of a campaign, in the usual sense of the word. Whatever her motives (and I had no doubt that self-aggrandisement was one of them), Mrs Bevan was welcome to join in the group effort of protecting the Sutcliffs from their false accusers. The woman, for all her faults, knew the meaning of Christian charity. She didn't even seem to be blaming Craig Dutton.

I wished I could be as charitable. I had, by now, spent some considerable amount of time wondering what had led up to this situation. Unlike Mrs Bevan, I was disinclined to believe that Craig's strange conduct was due to something he had seen on television.

Okay, so my own experience of bringing up children is non-existent. My understanding of their behaviour is limited to second-hand knowledge of my nieces, Jessica and her two younger sisters, Tammy and Kelly. But I do know one or two things about children; I'm not quite as out of touch as Mrs Bevan.

Eleven-year-old boys are quite capable of wickedness. One of the most notorious British trials in recent years boasted, as its defendants, two ten-year-olds who had confessed to a crime so horrible that it made many grown adults physically sick just to think about it. Craig Dutton was perfectly capable of having made up the whole story as some kind of joke, thinking nothing of the misery he was likely to cause the Sutcliff family.

What led me away from that last explanation was the way Tim himself, and Elvis, who knew the boy well, both kept saying that it was out of character. That made me think that the parents must be at least partly to blame.

Dr Dutton wasn't my GP, thankfully. On the rare occasions when I needed medical attention, I went to a different practice. I wasn't even sure what Dr and Mrs Dutton looked like. They weren't regular members of the congregation at St Mary's. To the best of my knowledge, only Craig and his younger brother had ever come to church.

Craig's brother, like Craig himself, hadn't put in an appearance since the word got out of what Tim was alleged to have done. Not that it was clear exactly *what* Tim was alleged to have done.

As I was driving past the vicarage, the following morning, on my way out of the village, a silver BMW passed me in the opposite direction, taking the bend rather too fast, and slipped in through the gates of the Sutcliffs' drive. I caught only a glimpse of Tim's solicitor, Charles Cornwell, at the wheel. He wouldn't have seen me; and if he had, he wouldn't have remembered me.

It was time for me to make one of my occasional excursions to the public library. Our village wasn't large enough to have its own branch, though a mobile library called once a week. That was enough to satisfy most of the villagers' pretensions to culture. Those who worked in Swansea joined one of the central libraries. Others, such as Elvis and myself, went to the nearest proper branch library, about five miles away, for our reading matter. When I was making the trip, I usually gave notice to the old lady next door. Sometimes, if she felt well enough, she would come with me. Nine times out of ten, she would just give me her reader's card and ask me to try and find something in large print, or a talking book, that she hadn't already had out.

The reason I was going to the library today was quite different. This was business. I had an arrangement with them. Like most public libraries, they couldn't afford to buy as many new books as they would like. Nevertheless, they had an awful lot of surplus stock. Books don't last forever, especially library books. Every so often, the library would root out all the stuff they no longer wanted, either because it was too tatty or because it was deemed obsolete.

The criteria which the library service uses to decide which books are to be withdrawn from stock are not the same as an individual would use. For example, certain authors are considered to be "old-fashioned" and it is believed that people no longer wish to read them. The borrowing figures may appear to bear this out; but it's surprising how many people contact second-hand booksellers looking for works by those very same "old-fashioned" authors.

My arrangement with the local library was that I came along every so often and took away the stuff they didn't want. Depending how I was fixed myself at the time, I would either pay them for it or offer them replacements, books in good condition that I had acquired from other sources and didn't think I would be able to sell through my usual channels. It worked much better than you might imagine. Invariably, I would find a volume or two among the library's discarded stock that I had been specifically asked for by a potential customer. The library, for their part, couldn't lose, because they ended up either with "new" stock or a bit of cash to bump up their book-buying budget.

It was a fine, crisp winter's morning, and the lanes looked bright and neat. There was still some colour in the trimmed-back hedgerows, despite the trees having lost their leaves. By the time I got to the library, I was in quite a cheerful mood. The lone librarian on duty, Mrs Hodges, waved to me as I entered, from behind a queue of people waiting to have their books stamped, and pointed towards her office. There, on the table, was one measly cardboard box. I took it out to the van.

They didn't have much for me today. They were waiting till after Christmas to go through their stock. They just wanted to get rid of a few bits and pieces. Most of it was rubbish. Some of it, even if it was in lousy condition, could potentially be repaired by a skilled bookbinder (which I was not). I doubted that there would be anything in this box that I could find a home for.

I went back into the building, where Mrs Hodges was just dealing with the last candidate for book stamping.

"Sorry we haven't got much for you today, Miss Harris, but I wanted it out of the way before Christmas. I hope you don't mind."

"That's okay," I sighed. "I've got plenty of room. Only I may not have time to look through it for ages, if I get the usual rush of last-minute orders."

"Now tell me," she said, leaning across the counter and putting her face close to mine, so as not to be overheard. "What's all this about your vicar?"

News travels fast, and far. Tim's story hadn't got into the press yet, but it was only a matter of time.

"It's all a storm in a teacup," I said, hoping I sounded more confident than I felt. "There's no truth in the rumours, I'm sure. But people believe what they want to believe."

"All the same," she said, "you have to wonder, don't you?"

Sensing that Mrs Hodges was on the verge of saying something we would both regret, I forestalled her by recounting the story of the woman who had sworn at me in the village shop. That effectively deterred her from continuing in the present vein, and she said only that she was terribly sorry about the trouble, and that I was to give her regards to both the Vicar and Mrs Sutcliff when I saw them. She was quite sure that it would all turn out to be nothing, in the end.

Words like “hypocrite” and “busybody” buzzed around in my mind, all the way home.

Chapter 5

Business seemed slow, considering how close it was to Christmas. Perhaps it was all in my imagination. There were orders. There were enquiries to be dealt with. I simply didn't feel like getting down to it.

Jessica would be coming in a day or two. The prospect of her arrival was the only thing that gave me any reason to be cheerful.

The ring of the doorbell roused me from another doleful mood, at least for the time it took to get up and answer the door. Through the window I caught sight of a silver BMW parked outside. On the doorstep stood Charles Cornwell.

"Miss Harris," he said. "Remember me?"

"Mr Cornwell. Won't you come in?"

I hadn't expected to see him again so soon. There must have been further developments in Tim's case.

"It's not about the Sutcliff matter," he said, taking the wind out of my sails. "I'm looking for a book."

"You've come to the right place," I remarked, intending humour of the most feeble variety. "Was it a particular book?"

"Not really."

This wasn't as surprising as it might sound. There are a lot of people who go in search of "a valuable book", as opposed to a specific title, usually for one of two reasons. Either they are looking for a way of making money, and don't realise how difficult it is to find a book that will make a worthwhile investment; or – and I suspected this was the case with Mr Cornwell – they want something that will look nice on their bookshelves, something they can use to impress their visitors. "Look at this!" they will enthuse, showing off the gold-tooled leather binding. "It's a first edition, you know."

If that was what Charles Cornwell wanted, he had rather come down in my estimation. At our first meeting, I'd noted one or two things about him. Although he had a trace of a Swansea accent and the friendliest of faces, he seemed a cut above your average local lad, even your average solicitor. I suspected him of having come from a prosperous family, who had perhaps sent him away to boarding school.

"It's a little embarrassing," he explained. "I'm not sure exactly what it is I'm looking for. It's for my sister-in-law."

His face was tilted downwards, so that he was looking up at me from under his dark eyelashes. He was no longer the successful professional man, in command of the situation. It was an appealing look, a little boy lost. I wondered how many women fell for it.

"Tell me more," I said.

"She loves books. She has some favourite authors. I never know what to get her for Christmas, but I had a brainwave. I thought I would ask you if you had something – you know, something special – that would suit her. Something that would make a unique present. I wondered, do you have anything that's been signed by the author?"

"A famous author, you mean? I've got plenty that have been signed by nonentities."

He beamed that face-splitting smile again.

"Preferably an author she's heard of."

"Would you like to come through, Mr Cornwell? You can see for yourself."

"Thank you. And my name's Charles." As if I hadn't remembered.

It wasn't often that I invited a visitor into my former garage. I know exactly what's in there myself, and I don't like things disturbed, so I never let anyone browse at will. For one thing, it's difficult to get adequate insurance for the kind of thing I deal in, and the stock is constantly being replenished. I mentioned before that I don't often hold books of high value. When I do, I try to make them difficult for the opportunist thief to find, by placing them randomly on the shelves. They are the only items not shelved in alphabetical order; but of course, I know exactly where to find them.

"Good heavens!" exclaimed Charles Cornwell, looking around him in wonder. "What a little treasure chest!"

I was pleased that he appreciated that much, even if he didn't understand the true worth of my book-stock, which consisted not in its monetary value, but in the unique provenance of every volume.

I take good care of my stock. When I had the garage converted, I also installed a de-humidifier and temperature control, to maintain the condition of the books. I check them all, individually, from time to time. If I come across anything I don't think I will ever be able to sell, I put it to one side. When I've accumulated a boxful of such lost causes, I take it to a car boot sale. That way, I usually get rid of a few, and the rest go to Oxfam. Then I replace them with things I think I *can* sell.

"The only thing I can think of, off the top of my head," I said, going to the shelves and taking out a volume, "is this Howard Spring. He was from Cardiff, you know."

"Howard Spring?"

Though I tried to disguise my disgust at his ignorance, the effort was in vain. My twitching eyebrow had already given me away.

"I don't have much time for reading these days," Charles added apologetically.

"He was a very popular novelist in the 'thirties and 'forties," I explained. "His best-known book was *Fame is the Spur*. You might have seen the film, with . . ."

". . . Michael Redgrave," he finished. "I think I know the one. He's a politician, he cheats on his wife."

He stopped short, struck dumb by his own indiscretion. I put the book down, without looking at him.

"Unless she happened to be a fan of his, it probably wouldn't grab her anyway," I said. "The best thing would be . . . poetry?"

"Poetry," he repeated, for all the world as if he'd never heard the word before. "I think she likes poetry."

He was watching my every move. I felt his eyes on me as I crossed to another set of shelves and picked out a thin volume. I was loath to offer it to him; I had been saving it for myself.

"There *is* this," I said. "It's not signed, but it's a first edition, and in beautiful condition. Charlotte Mew."

"I don't think . . ." he began.

"She's nowhere near as well known as she deserves to be," I interrupted, before he could betray his ignorance again. "I don't blame you for not having heard of her. But they are lovely poems. Women's poems."

"When was she around?" he asked, taking the book from me and handling it with care.

"She died in 1928. Suicide."

Charles almost dropped the book.

"Don't worry," I said sarcastically. "It's not catching."

"Why did she?" he asked, still looking through the pages as if they might contain some clue, and frowning a little as he scanned the lines of verse. I felt certain he was, like me, short-sighted.

"I'm not really sure. She suffered from ill-health. Perhaps she was in pain. She certainly seems to have been a troubled soul."

He glanced up at me. "Something tells me you don't want to let this book go."

Once again, I was astonished by his perceptiveness.

"I can't afford to get sentimental about my stock," I said. "It's my living. But you're right." I took the book out of his hands. "I am fond of this one." I replaced it on the shelf.

"Tell you what," I continued quickly. "I'll look out for something for you. There's still plenty of time before Christmas, and I'll be getting catalogues and spending a lot of time on the web. I might come across something suitable. Of course, it would help if you could tell me what kind of thing your sister-in-law likes."

"I'll try and find out. I'll grill her."

We laughed.

"And what sort of price range are we talking about?"

"Oh . . ." He made a sweeping motion with his hand, as though it were helping him to think. "Let's say, anything up to fifty pounds."

I shouldn't have been surprised, but I was. "Your sister-in-law must be very special."

"She and my brother have been very good to me, since my divorce."

I'm available, he was saying. It was exactly what I'd wanted to hear, but I still didn't feel comfortable. Neither did Charles, by the look of him. We were both blushing madly. I turned away.

He made no move to leave. There was no alternative but to offer him a drink.

"Thank you." He smiled. "It's very cold this morning. A coffee would warm me up nicely." He couldn't have been conscious of the double entendre.

I went into the kitchen to make it, still thinking about the former Mrs Cornwell. Questions were racing through my mind. How long had they been married? Were there any children?

"I hope I didn't embarrass you," came his voice from behind me, "by talking about my personal circumstances."

I whirled round, to see him standing by the kitchen door.

"Sorry," he added. "Did I startle you?"

"No," I lied, continuing with the coffee-making in the hope that he wouldn't notice my trembling hands.

"And . . . *did* I embarrass you?"

"Why should you think that?" There are times when I'm very good at evading a question. This wasn't one of them.

"No reason. I suppose what I really mean is, I embarrassed myself and I'd hoped you hadn't noticed."

"If I didn't notice at the time, you're rather drawing attention to it now, aren't you?"

Why did my voice sound like a steel blade? Charles didn't take offence. Perhaps he knew exactly what was going through my mind. There was potential danger, potential rejection, in this encounter.

"It was a long time ago," he continued. "Sometimes I forget that I was ever married."

"Really?" I was deliberately keeping my back to him.

The kettle came to the boil.

"Why don't you go and sit down?" I said. "I'll bring the coffee in, in a moment."

"Couldn't we have it out here? There's actually some winter sunshine permeating into this kitchen. It seems a shame to waste it."

Relenting, I sat down by the breakfast bar, and gestured him to the stool opposite me. I still didn't dare look him in the eye. He was so poised, so assured. Even his embarrassment was more attractive and, somehow, more *confident* than my own strident attempts to laugh it off.

"How long ago was it?" I found myself asking, as I passed the mug across to him.

"About fourteen years."

"And how long were you married?"

"About six. Have you ever been married?"

"No," I admitted. "Isn't it obvious?"

He shook his head. "I wondered. Not that it's any of my business."

"Will it be relevant to my suitability as a character witness for Tim?"

He glanced at me appraisingly, wondering whether or not to laugh. "No," he said. "Marital status isn't a cause for concern these days. Even for a woman."

"That's just as well." I pushed the sugar bowl toward him, remembering that he took half a spoon.

He was smiling to himself as he picked up the teaspoon. I wished I found it as easy to read his thoughts as he apparently found it to read mine.

"Have you got any children?" I asked.

"No. We would have liked to, but it never happened. We thought we couldn't have any. But Deirdre managed it easily enough when she re-married, so perhaps it was something I wasn't doing right."

Now he *did* look embarrassed.

"I mean," he laughed shyly, "perhaps it was my fault, in some way."

He cheated on her, I thought. He had an affair.

There was no way I could ask a question like that, and he was hardly going to volunteer the information.

"Anyway," he went on, sensitive to my embarrassment, "it's all in the past. No use crying over spilt milk, as they say."

In the act of pouring, I spilled the milk. He laughed.

"Dear me, did I cause that to happen by talking about it, I wonder?"

"I shouldn't think so," I blabbered, reaching for a cloth and mopping it up quickly. "It's just that I'm very clumsy."

"Now I know for a fact *that's* not true. I've just watched you handling those books, remember?"

"They're my substitute children," I said drily. "Touch them at your peril."

It was at that precise moment that the telephone rang. The caller was one of my contacts in the book-selling world, wanting to know what I had by Howard Spring. The kind of coincidence that does sometimes happen in real life.

By the time I'd completed the call, Charles had finished his coffee and was putting on his outdoor coat.

"Thank you very much for the coffee," he said, not looking at me as he buttoned up. "I ought to go now. I have an appointment in half an hour, and it's on the other side of Swansea."

My disappointment must have been very obvious, but I stopped myself from blurting out anything silly, along the lines of, "You must call again some time."

"I'll call again some time," he said, and smiled. "If that's all right," he added.

"Don't forget to let me know about the book," I said.

"The book?"

"For your sister-in-law. Let me know what she likes."

"Ah, yes. Of course."

Ah, yes. Of course.

Chapter 6

"Bore da," said Elvis, as I let him in through the back door. "Shwmae?"

"Da iawn, diolch," I lied.

Elvis liked to make me practise my Welsh at every opportunity, but my progress was slow and we were limited to basic conversation. (If *I* had said "Shwmae" instead of "Sut mae", he would have told me off for sloppy pronunciation.) We switched quickly to English when there was anything complicated under discussion, as there was now.

"What's the latest?" I asked, knowing that Elvis wouldn't have been here if he hadn't had something to tell me.

Elvis, like me, was often around the village during the daytime. For years, he had lived with his disabled mother. This prevented him holding down a regular job, so he taught music at home, mostly in the evenings. Piano and singing. You would have thought that looking after the choir and playing the organ in church would have been a busman's holiday, but Elvis didn't mind, because music was what he really loved. All he really loved, apart from his mother.

I'll never forget him, at her funeral, crying as if his heart would never mend. Emotional at the best of times, he seemed to have gone to pieces. Yet an hour later, at the wake, he was laughing and joking with his friends over whisky and cheese straws. It's good to have that kind of release mechanism, the one that tears provide. Other men keep it in, thinking that it makes them somehow stronger. Elvis knew better.

Without his mother, he no longer had any need to stay at home, but he didn't immediately go looking for a more financially rewarding occupation. The only thing he could realistically have done was teach, Music or maybe Welsh. The schools around here are always looking for Welsh teachers.

A comprehensive would have been anathema to someone like Elvis, though. He could never have coped. The shortage of facilities would have frustrated him to death. Thirty teenagers, forced to attend his classes when their interests lay elsewhere, would have made mincemeat of him.

On a one-to-one basis, he was fine. He had his private pupils eating out of his hand. In church, it was different again. The choir got paid every time they sang at a wedding, or in a special concert. That was one of their main incentives for continuing to belong, because Elvis wouldn't let them perform if they had missed too many rehearsals. How much they got for their public appearances depended on what the bride and groom could afford, or what the concert was in aid of, but it was never less than a couple of pounds. Elvis made up any shortfall out of his own pocket.

If Elvis had been a different kind of man, I might have fallen in love with him instead of – or as well as – Tim Sutcliff. However, he wasn't your average man. He never talked about his personal proclivities, but I suspected that women weren't among his preferences, if you take my meaning.

That wasn't the subject under discussion at the moment; it never was. We were talking about what Elvis had dubbed "the Sutcliff situation". It might have made a good film title.

"I've been hearing things," he said.

"Ringing in the ears?" I suggested, making light of it, as I filled the kettle and plugged it in.

"I've heard more of the story. Craig Dutton's version of events."

"From a reliable source? Dare I ask?"

"From Craig's dad, as it happens."

"Never!"

I sat down opposite him. When Elvis came for coffee, we always had it in the kitchen. Nothing to do with sunshine, just habit. Elvis was about as different from Charles Cornwell as a man could possibly be.

(Yes, Charles Cornwell was still there, at the back of my mind.)

"How about a drop of scotch in here?" asked Elvis mischievously.

"It's only eleven o'clock!" I protested.

"I know, but it's bloody perishing out there."

I gave in gracefully, for fear of having some information withheld from me if I failed to come up with the goods. As an afterthought, I added some scotch to my own coffee as well.

"God, aren't we decadent!" he exclaimed, slurping his first mouthful with relish, followed by a satisfied gasp.

"Come on, Elvis, give!"

"All right, all in good time, bach." He put down his mug, and rubbed his hands together. "Duw! Freeze the balls off a bloody brass monkey!" When he was satisfied that his circulation had been completely restored, he clasped his hands together, like a politician about to deliver a party election broadcast.

"It's like this, see. I was going past the health centre yesterday night, about half-past five, and I saw Dr Dutton coming out. He couldn't avoid me, so I fell in with him, and I started making polite conversation. So far, so good. He didn't want to be rude. When we got to his car, rather than let him get in, I kept him talking. 'Elvis,' he says, 'I don't mean to be discourteous, but under the circumstances, I don't think I should be seen talking to you'."

"He said that?"

"He did. I came back quickly at him. 'Don't treat me like a criminal,' I said. 'I'm very concerned for Craig. He's one of my best singers.' That's not true, actually, but I had to say it. Anyhow, he looked a bit shamefaced, then he said, 'Look here, Elvis, this is a terrible thing for my family, and I'd be grateful if you'd be discreet about it'. So I said, 'Listen, Doc, I've got no quarrel with you. All I want to know is what really happened. The police have questioned me, but I can't help them because I don't know a dang thing about it. How could I have been so blind as to have that kind of thing going on, under my own nose, when I'm supposed to be responsible for the choir?' Well, he seemed to take my point."

It went on in that vein. What Elvis had discovered from his conversation with Craig's father was that the incident was alleged to have taken place at a charity concert at the church hall, back in September.

"That's earlier than Tim suggested, when he told us about it," I remarked.

"Yes, it is, isn't it?" mused Elvis. "But it seems it was a couple of weeks before the boy said anything to his parents. And when he did, it sounded a bit strange."

What Craig had told his father, when he eventually plucked up courage (that was how Elvis put it, and I chose not to point out to him that it doesn't take a lot of courage to tell a brazen lie), was that he had put his hand in the Vicar's pocket.

"In his pocket?" I echoed, in bewilderment.

"That's what he said, apparently. And when his dad asked him why he did it, Craig said, 'He made me'."

I wriggled about on my stool. "Does that make any sense to you?" I knew what I was thinking, but I wanted to hear Elvis's reaction first.

He looked at me curiously. "The obvious interpretation to put on it is that Tim asked Craig to . . . you know . . . bring him off."

I wasn't blushing yet, but I got up and walked around the kitchen a bit, just in case I should need to hide my face. Elvis pushed his mug across the table towards me, hoping for a refill.

"Asbestos mouth!" I scolded, pleased to be able to change the subject, albeit momentarily.

"What about a drop more scotch, as well?"

Making tutting noises, I retrieved the bottle from the top of the cupboard. Drinking scotch before midday would be a good excuse for having red cheeks.

"Have you noticed, Laura likes a drink recently?" I asked.

"Laura? Yes, now you come to mention it. Don't blame her, either. I don't think it'll do her any harm. Probably keeping her sane, at the moment."

Reluctantly, I returned to the subject in hand.

"So that – what you said earlier – that's what the police think, is it?"

Elvis shrugged. "How should I know what the police think? All I know is what I'm telling you, what Dr Dutton said."

"Why are you telling me?"

"Because I want to know what you think."

I sat down again, and looked across at him. "There must be other explanations."

"Of course there are. I can think of a few. But I haven't quite told you everything yet."

I waited.

"Craig says that Tim gave him money."

This was too much.

"No. Elvis, no, I can't believe that. Maybe Tim gave him the money, for some other reason, and Craig just thought he was being asked to do something in return. Or maybe after Tim gave him the money . . . Yes, that's it! *After* Tim gave Craig the money, Craig was looking for a way of explaining it, and he made up the story about the hand in the pocket."

At this suggestion, Elvis looked even more sceptical.

We compared notes for over half an hour, ending up with two explanations that we both felt were distinctly plausible. The first was that Craig had been trying to take, or steal, something out of Tim's pocket – perhaps his coat pocket, hanging up on a hook – and Tim had caught him in the act. I favoured that theory, because it explained why Tim was so reticent about the whole incident. If the boy had been trying to steal, Tim might have felt obliged to cover the whole thing up, even if it meant taking the rap for something he hadn't done.

Elvis was as unenthusiastic about this first theory as I was keen. He knew the boy well enough to be able to say that "thieving" was as uncharacteristic of him as was telling lies. He could imagine that the boy might have tried to take something out of Tim's pocket – a sweet, or something like that – and been caught in the act, but he hardly thought that would constitute the kind of theft that Tim would react to, or that needed to be covered up for. I had to concede that point.

The bit about Tim "making" Craig do it also militated against theory number one. (This was always assuming that Craig's story was based on some real-life incident, and not complete fantasy.) The other theory we came up with was that Craig had been told, by Tim, to go and get something out of his coat pocket – again, while Tim was not wearing it – but had reservations about the action, thinking that it somehow constituted stealing, and had later felt obliged to unburden himself to his parents. This made little sense to me, but Elvis felt that Craig was the kind of boy who might well make a mountain out of a molehill.

Then there was the additional element of the money. Elvis hadn't been able to ascertain how much money we were talking about. It might have been anything from ten pence to ten pounds. Knowing Tim's financial position to be insecure, anything more would have been out of the question, whatever service he might have been asking Craig to perform.

I suggested that Craig might have been told to take something out of Tim's pocket, had found some loose change in there, and had taken it along with whatever he had been asked to fetch. Here again, the problem was that Tim had denied having any memory of any event which might throw light on the subject. He would surely have remembered if some such event had occurred.

"Unless, of course, he noticed that the money had gone, guessed that Craig had taken it, but chose to say nothing about it," I said eagerly. "That would be just like Tim."

Elvis said nothing.

There were other variations on the theme, but those two basic versions of events were the best we could come up with that morning. Neither of them was particularly convincing to us, knowing the main protagonists as we did; but either might be effective in swaying a jury, if, God forbid, it came to that.

Elvis's information had, in some ways, heartened me. My worst fears had been put to rest. At least now I knew that Tim wasn't accused of having raped the boy, something I would have found impossible to believe but difficult to stop thinking about. This was an altogether less serious matter – serious enough, but not earth-shattering.

Yet, in its very triviality, it became more real. Tim Sutcliff wasn't the sort of man who went around making brutal assaults on small boys, but was he capable, in a moment of madness, of persuading a boy to help him work off his sexual frustrations? Did Tim even have sexual frustrations, I asked myself. There was no reason to think that his sex life with Laura, inadequate as she might be in other ways, was less than satisfactory. They did, after all, have two children. Consequently, there was no reason to think that he had engineered a situation of the kind hinted at by Craig, simply in order to satisfy a momentary need.

If Tim had been looking around for a way of venting his

frustrations, I thought, he wouldn't have needed to look far. There was me, for a start. He must have known how I felt about him, yet he had never made the slightest move in that direction. His behaviour towards me, and (as far as I knew) towards every other available woman in the parish, had always been above reproach. It was inconceivable that he would have turned to a child for that kind of relief, even in his direst need.

We had racked our brains for other solutions.

"It couldn't have been some kind of game, could it?" I suggested. "Tim playing some kind of game, making the boys guess what was in his pocket by feeling it, or something like that?"

"Bit of a dangerous game, that would have been," observed Elvis, correctly.

When we had explored all the possibilities we could think of, and Elvis had drunk up his specially-fortified coffee and gone home, I continued to brood over it. There was one thought in my mind, one thing which I felt would help me understand the situation better, and that was to speak to Laura Sutcliff again.

I was on the verge of setting out for the vicarage several times that afternoon, and didn't. How could I possibly approach Laura with questions about her sex life? It would have to be led up to very cautiously, and even if I could think of a way, perhaps I wouldn't achieve a result.

Furthermore, I would have to choose a time when Tim was absent, not listening in on our conversation. The children, too, would have to be out of the way.

Soon, I had run out of time for any such expedition. At four o'clock, I was due to collect Jessica from Swansea railway station.

Chapter 7

Some miracle caused the train to arrive bang on time, and Jessica, as usual, didn't disembark alone. She had a knack of picking up someone of the opposite sex whenever she needed one, as she did, on this occasion, to help transport her luggage.

It didn't matter to Jessica whether the man was young or old, fat or thin, tall or short, good-looking or hideously ugly, as long as he was fit to play the role required of him. This one very nearly didn't make the grade. He was huffing and puffing fit to burst, as he manhandled her heavy cases along the platform and through the station concourse. Every time he halted, winded, to recover his strength, my niece would smile at him bewitchingly, and he would struggle on for another few yards.

He looked relieved when he saw me, apparently thinking that I intended to relieve him of some of his burden. Instead, I took Jessica's small hold-all out of her hand, kissed her, and led the way across the little footbridge to the car park.

My mini van is useful for several reasons. It is small enough to manoeuvre and park easily, but at the same time it has enough capacity to transport any amount of personal luggage, or more often, boxes of books. The fact that there are only two seats is no disadvantage, because it means, as in this case, that I have a good excuse for not giving a lift to people I don't like the look of.

We took our usual death-defying route, down the vehicle ramps to the floor where I'd parked, avoiding the urine-scented stairs and the lift which never works. When the baggage was loaded up, I made my apologies to the weakling, and left it up to Jessica whether to let him have her telephone number.

We got home before five, and I started immediately on the tea, while Jessica took the bags up to her room – no, I didn't offer to help – and began unpacking. While I was mashing the potatoes, the front doorbell rang.

"I'll get it!" shouted Jessica, thundering down the stairs like a baby elephant.

After a moment, I heard a female voice in the living room, and peeped out to find Laura Sutcliff there. When she saw what I was doing, she apologised and made a move to leave. I pressed her to sit down and eat with us, but she said she couldn't stop long, and besides, Tim would be wanting his own dinner.

Laura was looking for someone to take the kids off her hands for a couple of hours, that very evening. She had to go out – she wasn't specific about where – and she didn't want to leave them with Tim, because he was "up to his eyes in it". What exactly "it" was she didn't reveal, but I surmised it was something to do with the Dutton business.

"He's very depressed," she added. "I thought it might be better for the children to be with someone else."

She meant Jessica. My niece had babysat for the Sutcliffs several times, during her stays with me, and the children, like everyone else who met her, adored her good-humoured liveliness. Laura had known Jessica was coming this evening. She didn't like to ask, on the first night of her stay, but . . .

"I'd love to see them," said Jessica.

I was grateful for her readiness to help, not least because I saw that she genuinely didn't mind being taken advantage of, on this occasion. We hadn't talked properly about the Sutcliffs' awful situation. Jessica knew only the bare bones, and it was probably for the best. There was no danger of her letting any cats out of bags while the kids were in our house.

We arranged that Laura would drop Robert and Caroline at our door in an hour's time, and collect them at about nine. Then she left, and we settled down to eat.

The Sutcliff situation was the most sensational piece of news I'd ever had to offer Jessica when she came to visit, but I was reluctant to dwell on it. In view of Elvis's original warning to Ray Gough about the prosecution's likely strategy, I thought it best not to mention the details I'd heard from him. This was despite the fact that they had come straight from Craig's father and were therefore more likely to be true than any other version of events Jessica might get to hear in the village.

I took a foolish pleasure in talking about Charles Cornwell, when Jessica asked whether Tim had a good solicitor.

"He seems very capable," I said. "He's called here once or twice. He wants me to be a character witness, if it comes to court. But he doesn't think it will."

"It's coming to something," Jessica remarked, "when vicars need character witnesses. Couldn't they get someone from the church? An archbishop or someone?"

"They want someone impartial," I explained. "Charles seemed to think I'd be suitable."

That "Charles" had slipped out without my thinking. Jessica didn't pounce on it.

"I'm sure you'll be very good," she murmured reflectively. No doubt her mind was on something else by now. Boys, probably.

"Are you going out with anyone at the moment?" I asked, grateful for the opportunity to switch subjects and deflect attention from my own romantic leanings.

"No one special," she replied. That meant that the young man she was really keen on hadn't asked her out yet. Even in this day and age, girls still seem to wait for boys to make the first move.

The only other thing I had to tell Jessica was that a special social event would shortly be taking place in the church hall. A poetry reading had been arranged by what was laughingly called the Cultural Society. This in fact consisted of Elvis and a couple of other like-minded individuals (including, I have to admit, me) who had shouldered the responsibility of introducing the village residents to the finer things in life, including music and literature.

The Cultural Society wasn't an official body, but it was always referred to in conjunction with any such events that were organised. In the run-up to Christmas, Elvis had come up with something special – a recital by a young poet whose parents were distant cousins. It was the best we were likely to get, since we didn't have any funds to pay for visits from celebrities. Elvis had assured me that The Poet, apart from being very personable, was a rising star in the Welsh literary firmament. Personally, I had never heard of him and doubted that I ever would again.

Unimpressed by my announcement, Jessica declared that she would go along with me, "for company", if she could find nothing better to do, but reminded me that she had a lot of assignments to complete during the vacation, and she really didn't think she would be able to find the time. After all, I wouldn't want her academic work to suffer, would I?

Robert and Caroline arrived as scheduled, and we set about finding diversions for them. Robert was unusually quiet, which was only to be expected, but Caroline's behaviour was perfectly normal. She couldn't have had much idea what was going on.

I suggested a game of Monopoly, which went down like a lead balloon. Then Jessica suggested that the children help her unpack, which was welcomed with whoops of delight. I didn't see much of them for the rest of the evening. When Laura arrived to pick them up, it was difficult to persuade them to come downstairs.

"I hope they haven't been any trouble," she muttered.

"No trouble at all," I answered truthfully. "To be honest, I've barely seen them. They've been helping Jessica unpack, and no doubt trying on some of her clothes."

"Not Robert, I hope," said Laura. I was glad to see her sense of humour hadn't completely deserted her.

I hastened to reassure her that Jessica would no doubt keep Robert occupied with the traditional male task of transporting things.

Laura accepted a cup of tea, while we waited for the children to come down. I was glad to have this opportunity of talking to her, as I'd intended to do earlier in the day.

"I expect you're wondering where I've been," she volunteered, as we sat down in the kitchen to enjoy a few more moments' peace and quiet.

It was true, I had been wondering; but I hadn't intended to ask. That would have seemed rude.

"Anywhere nice?" was the best I could find to say.

"In a manner of speaking. Don't tell anyone, but I've been going to group counselling."

"I see. Well, that's . . ." I groped around for a suitable response.

"You won't mention it, will you?"

"Of course not." In any case, I suspected I was the last person in the village to find out. "How long have you been going?"

"A few months."

That did come as a surprise. My turn on the grapevine should have arrived long before now.

"It's a great help, at a time like this," she went on.

"It must be." I hesitated. "What made you start going, in the first place?"

"The doctor suggested it, when I went to try and get Prozac."

I felt suddenly overwhelmed by guilt. Where had I been, where had Laura's other friends been, that she couldn't turn to us for help and advice when she needed it? I had always known she had problems, but I had never really bothered to try to persuade her to talk about them.

"I've been like this for years," she went on. "It's the first practical thing anyone's ever been able to do for me."

If there had ever been a good time to get her to talk about her relationship with Tim, this was it, but I held back. I still wasn't sure that she wasn't blaming me for not giving her the support she had needed in the past.

"I'm sorry," I said, trying to put a soothing note into my voice. "Perhaps I should have been more observant."

"Oh, I'm not blaming *you*, Olwen," she smiled, putting out a hand to touch mine. "You've always been a good friend to me."

I was glad she thought so, even if it wasn't true.

"What . . . Do you mind me asking, what started it off?"

"No one particular thing. I've always found it hard to control myself, in certain situations. I've always had these black moods. Tim's been a saint, putting up with me."

"But you seem happy enough, the two of you."

"Oh, we are! In ourselves, I mean."

She fell silent again, and I started to wonder what the phrase, "in ourselves", signified. Did it, perhaps, mean that their intimate moments were satisfactory, that they were happy together when there was no one else around to throw a spanner in the works? I hoped so.

There was no opportunity to delve deeper into Laura's psyche, because the children came thumping down the stairs, with Jessica hot on their heels.

"I'm wearing make-up, Mummy!" announced Caroline, proudly.

She was indeed. The entire contents of Jessica's cosmetic bag, by the look of it.

"I'm sorry, Laura," said Jessica. "I meant to wipe it all off before you arrived."

"That's okay." I noted how easily Laura took Caroline up on her lap and stroked her hair. For all her shortcomings, she didn't lack a mother's natural tenderness. "Aren't you pretty? Like Miss World."

"What's Miss World?" asked Robert, petulantly. He was clearly jealous of the attention his sister was getting.

"Don't they have it any more?" asked Laura, turning to me.

"Not on TV," I replied. "And a good thing too."

Jessica immediately contradicted me, saying that they had revived it recently, but that it wasn't like it had been when she was little. That made me feel my age. After Laura and the children had left, I felt emotionally and physically drained, and decided to go up to bed. Jessica said that she would probably be up "in a few minutes". I knew that she seldom retired before midnight, and I was certainly fast asleep before she ever set foot on the stairs.

Chapter 8

One of the first things Jessica wanted to do was to go Christmas shopping. That meant another trip into Swansea, the following day. I couldn't refuse, since she pleaded that she hadn't yet bought presents for her mum and dad and younger sisters, but I insisted on her getting out of bed at a reasonable hour, despite the late night, because I hate crowds and I wanted to get in and out of town before lunchtime. (I had done most of my own Christmas shopping, by mail order, back in October.)

Jessica had other ideas. Things went according to plan, to begin with. Getting up early was no problem for her, given the incentive, but once we got started on the shops I could see that there was no prospect whatsoever of our being home in time for lunch. We'd be lucky if we got back for our evening meal. It was Saturday, not a working day, but I was in the habit of spending Saturday morning opening and dealing with the mail, which might well contain orders and enquiries. That wouldn't be done much before bedtime, I could see. I was already writing the day off, mentally.

The problem was clothes shops. There are too many of them in Swansea. All the major department stores, with their multiple "Ladies' Fashion" sections, and then the individual chains, Top Shop and Dorothy Perkins and New Look and you name it, we've got them all.

When we went to look round the first one or two, I didn't bother to complain. Reminding Jessica gently that the ostensible reason for our visit had been to purchase Christmas gifts for her immediate family, I allowed her a little leeway. The girl worked hard at college. She deserved a bit of a break during her vacation.

By half past eleven, when we'd been in six or seven different clothes shops and hadn't even made a start on the Christmas present shopping, I was getting restive, and I put my foot down.

"Jess!" I said firmly. "This has got to stop. Your sisters will end up with nothing in their Christmas stockings at this rate. Now come on, let's get down to it."

Jess looked at me appealingly, and I started to understand why men found her so irresistible. "There's plenty of time for that, Auntie Olwen. After all, there's about three weeks to go before Christmas. It doesn't have to be done today."

She had conned me, as usual. It wasn't as if she was actually buying any clothes, either. She just liked trying things on. It was odd how two members of the same family could have such different attitudes to shopping. Don't get me wrong, I'm as keen on shopping as the next woman, but I like to do it when it's quiet in town. If there's one thing I hate, it's trying things on in shops. I especially loathe it when there are lots of other people there and you have to queue up for the changing rooms – or worse still, change in a communal area with lots of teenagers eyeing your midriff bulge with amusement. (At least, I always imagine they are.)

Soon, I knew, Jessica would start trying to persuade me to buy some clothes for myself. She had already put out feelers in that direction. I wasn't so cynical as to think that she hoped I would fork out for some smallish item for her when I was buying something big for myself (though of course I was a soft touch). No, I think she genuinely regretted my appearance, and wanted to smarten me up a bit.

"You're bound to be going out to one or two parties at Christmas," she said, when we were in one of those shops – River Island, I think it was – looking through the racks of glittering evening wear. "You'll need something special to put on."

"I haven't been invited to any parties," I retorted, "and I'm not likely to be. I've got all the clothes I need, and I'm not going to buy any today."

"You must be going somewhere!" she protested. "Don't Tim and Laura usually have a Christmas party?"

The annual vicarage get-together consisted of sausage rolls and crisps provided by the parishioners and eaten in the vicarage kitchen, washed down with soft drinks and the odd bottle of someone's home-made wine. It was hardly an occasion for sparkly evening gowns. Besides, I somehow doubted whether there would even be a get-together this year.

"I don't think . . ." I began, and stopped.

It was the boys who caught my eye, as they passed the entrance to the shop with their parents. I had seen them both at church, many times. Jessica was still admiring the party togs, and didn't notice me drift away towards the shop doorway.

So that was Dr Dutton, and Mrs Dutton presumably. These were the people who had caused so much heartache, or rather their son had. I didn't recognise either of the parents, though I must have seen them around the village at one time or another. They were a good-looking couple, younger than I had imagined. The doctor had fair hair. He was very tall, and walked with a slight stoop. His wife was tall, too, for a woman, but dark-haired. Her pretty face was spoiled by a pout; but as I watched, he said something to her, and her expression changed as she laughed.

How dare they laugh? That was my first thought. How dare they laugh, when Tim and Laura were in such a terrible state over what had happened?

Then I looked at the boys. The younger one appeared happy enough, running around, stopping to look covetously at the toys in the window of the Early Learning Centre, waving his arms in the air unselfconsciously. His elder brother was another matter. Craig Dutton didn't look like a boy who was taking any satisfaction in the trouble he had caused; quite the opposite.

That far-away look might have been his normal expression. I somehow doubted it. I tried to steel myself against him. He might have an angelic appearance, but the most heinous crimes have been committed by little boys with curly hair, as I reminded myself. Yet I felt, instinctively, that this was not the face of a mischief-maker.

The Duttons didn't notice me. Even if they had, I doubt they would have recognised me as a friend of the Sutcliffs. They were going about their business as normal, which was all that could have been expected. It's what I would have done, if I'd had children of my own and one of them had got into this kind of scrape. (That was putting it mildly, I reflected.) It must be almost as traumatic an experience for them as it was for Tim and Laura.

The parents had stopped laughing now, and I detected the strain behind Mrs Dutton's sulky look. Poor woman, I thought. Even if the whole thing is a lie – *especially* if it's a lie – the poor, poor woman.

"Auntie Olwen, what are you doing?" Jessica had finished looking at the spangled party clothes, and was standing beside me.

"Nothing." I might have pointed out the Duttons to her, but there seemed little purpose in that. "Let's go to lunch," I said.

We managed to find a self-service restaurant, in one of the big stores, that still had free tables at a quarter past twelve, and Jessica insisted that I sit down while she went and fetched the food. By this time, I was faint with hunger, not to mention despondency, and I didn't hesitate to take her up on the offer.

I watched the entrance anxiously, for fear that the Duttons might appear. I didn't think I could bear to see them again. That chance encounter had completely unsettled me. I tried to analyse my reasons.

For one thing, I had been wondering about their domestic life. They looked a normal enough family, but you could never be sure what lay beneath the surface. I'm not sure what I had expected. Dr Dutton, being a GP, was bound to be vaguely respectable. What I had hoped for, I suppose, was to see some signs of internal friction, something that would have led a boy like Craig to make up such a story about Tim. Logic proclaimed that he should have been one of two things: either a spoiled brat, running wild, without even a child's sense of morality; or a cowed, unloved child, brought up by a stern father and a self-absorbed mother. The kind of child who wanted to draw attention to himself. Today I had seen, with my own eyes, that Craig Dutton was getting no pleasure from that attention.

I thought about little else for the rest of the day. The afternoon's torture continued, with Jessica dragging me into every shop that sold clothes or accessories or cosmetics. We did, eventually, buy one or two Christmas gifts, but I didn't get my usual enjoyment out of the exercise, now that my mind was on other things.

When I got home, there wasn't much post, but there was a message on the answerphone from a woman in Limeslade. She had got my name out of the yellow pages, and wanted me to come over there and have a look at her father's book collection. He had died earlier in the day.

I was pleased about that – not the old man dying, obviously, but the opportunity to go through his books. Most of my best business is done that way. It's far more likely to result in a spectacular find than any book sale. Moreover, it would get me out of the house, prevent me from brooding over Tim.

As it was only ten minutes since the bereaved woman had rung, I called her straight back and offered to come down to Limeslade at her convenience. We agreed on the following Monday. In fact, she would have been happy for me to come down there on Sunday, if I hadn't put her off. It seemed like indecent haste, but she explained that she had come down from Wrexham and was going back there immediately after the funeral. She wanted the house cleared out by then, if possible. She was putting it up for sale.

The following day, Sunday, I looked forward to seeing Tim at morning service. Jessica, unusually, agreed to come with me. She admitted that this was partly out of curiosity, because she wanted to see how Tim was looking, in view of his current troubles. I didn't castigate her for this piece of thoughtlessness. Jessica was a good girl, but she was young. When she got to my age, she would start to think more deeply about the implications of a situation like this, for all concerned. For the moment, it wasn't to be expected that anything short of a nuclear holocaust would make a lasting impression on her.

The previous day's shopping trip hadn't been a complete waste of time, because I'd managed to buy some laverbread in Swansea market. As I recalled, it was one of Jessica's favourite delicacies, and it's not easy to come by in Newport. Impossible in Oxford, unless you're willing to eat the tinned variety.

English visitors, when they first hear the term, "laverbread", usually expect it to be some kind of fruit bread, like bara brith. They often get a nasty shock when they see it for the first time. It's black and sticky and looks something like the insides of a Dalek in the early black-and-white episodes of *Dr Who*. The "laver" is the seaweed which is boiled up to make laverbread. You prepare it for eating by forming it into little cakes, using flour or (if you prefer) oatmeal. Then you fry it, generally with bacon. It makes a nice Sunday breakfast, now and again.

A lot of people like to eat cockles with their laverbread. Like the laver, the cockles are gathered from Gower beaches, and you can get those in Swansea market too. Neither Jessica nor I has ever liked them much; it takes a lot of vinegar to make them palatable, in my opinion.

Tim seemed on reasonable form, during the service. He picked a neutral sort of text for a sermon, as I had hoped.

The choir was out in force. As far as I could see, the only absentees were the two Dutton boys. Of course, it was Advent now, a popular time. Holly and poinsettias festooned the window sills, and we were singing carols. The boys and girls always enjoyed that. Looking more closely, I noticed that there was someone else missing: the head chorister himself, Ray Gough.

Apart from that, the congregation didn't seem down on a normal Sunday morning. Any falling off caused by people believing the stories and wanting to ostracise Tim as a result was made up for by others coming to church out of sheer nosiness or, just possibly, a desire to offer moral support.

Whichever the true motive, many of the new faces were offering verbal sympathy as they shook hands with Tim in the church porch, following the service. There was quite a queue building up. Jessica wanted to wait, but I side-stepped the little crowd of people and went on towards the lych gate.

"Don't you want to speak to the Vicar?" asked Jessica in consternation.

"No need to bother him now. I'll go straight round to the vicarage. I often call there after morning service, so Laura won't be surprised to see me. I want to check if she's okay."

It was unusual for Laura and the children to miss morning service, and I had to assume she was keeping them away deliberately, just in case there was any unpleasantness.

She looked washed out. I was disappointed as much as anything else. She had seemed so on top of it all when she called to collect the children from my place, after her group therapy session. I should have known it was too good to be true. It was only to be expected that a few hours back in that dank old house should have returned her to square one. She didn't have anyone to talk to.

Over the hill came the cavalry. In other words, me. From now on, I was going to "be there" for Laura. Tim had specifically requested it, but even if he hadn't, our conversation of the other night would have alerted me to the fact that she needed help and that I had been remiss in not offering it sooner.

Considering what a desperate state she was in, Laura didn't look all that pleased to see us. To be sure, she was in the middle of cooking Sunday lunch, but then she always was when I called there after morning service, and she never usually minded. I had been known to pitch in and help with the potato-peeling.

Jessica was immediately pulled into the house by the children, and was made to go and look at Caroline's new Barbie, a present for her recent birthday. Doing my best to take Laura's lack of enthusiasm in my stride, I launched into my repertoire of feeble good humour and comforting remarks. She barely smiled. After ten minutes or so of this, I was on the verge of giving up and going away when she said something quite startling.

"You know what the worst thing is, Olwen? Tim's not even allowed to know what it is he's supposed to have done!"

"Not allowed to know?" I echoed. "How is that possible?"

"Well." She put down the vegetable knife, to my relief, and pressed her hands against the draining board, kneading its edge between her fingers as though to punish it for existing. Her knuckles were white. "They say the whole matter is under consideration by . . . whoever it is, and the details can't be revealed until they've come to a decision, otherwise it might help Tim with his defence."

I was more than perplexed, I was flabbergasted. "But surely that's the whole point? A man's innocent until proven guilty, so they say. How is he supposed to defend himself if he doesn't know what he's supposed to have done?"

"Quite." She was about to continue, when the door creaked open and Tim himself entered. He wasn't alone. Elvis was with him.

"Elvis has just come to pick up the note of the hymn numbers for that funeral on Friday," said Tim, apparently seeking a balance between the spirit of total dejection and his usual cheery Sunday-morning manner.

Elvis greeted me with a quick cuddle, and went into the study with Tim.

"Don't say anything to Tim," warned Laura quickly. "I don't want him to know I've been discussing things with you." As she turned away, I thought I caught a whiff of alcohol on her breath. But who could blame her if she'd been enjoying a nip of the cooking sherry while everyone else was at morning service?

Trying not to be offended by Laura's last statement, I called Jessica to get ready to come home, as the Sutcliffs would obviously be settling down to their lunch soon. Elvis, who had been in the study for no more than half a minute, shouted to me to wait for him. This surprised me. I had expected him to be in conference with Tim for a little longer.

When Elvis saw Jessica, he let out a yelp of delight. He had always had a soft spot for her, ever since she was a little girl, and for some reason she felt the same about him. Tim acknowledged Jess with a sad smile. She, to my relief, didn't refer to the unfortunate circumstances, but acted as though all was normal in the Sutcliff household.

The three of us left the house with minimal formality, knowing that we would see Tim, if not Laura, again at evening service. In view of what I had just been told, I badly wanted to talk to Elvis, but he and Jessica were chattering away nineteen to the dozen, and I couldn't get a word in edgeways. I was forced to invite him to have lunch with us, an invitation which he accepted with alacrity.

Elvis had been to Sunday lunch (and other meals) with me on many previous occasions, but I had tried to make sure it didn't become a regular arrangement. That kind of commitment can become very wearing, however close a friendship. Sometimes I would go into Swansea on a Sunday and take my parents out to lunch, or be entertained by them at their little retirement apartment. Mostly, though, I was happy to eat alone.

In honour of Jessica's arrival, I had bought a chicken for today's lunch, so it wouldn't be difficult to stretch the meal for a third person. All I needed to do was to prepare a few extra vegetables. I was a bit late getting the bird in the oven, but I had one of those quick-roasting contraptions that meant it only needed about an hour, and the food would be ready by two o'clock. We weren't exactly starving, after our special breakfast of bacon and laverbread. Any hopes I might have had of getting a few minutes alone with

Elvis before lunch were soon banished, when Jessica started showing him snapshots of Oxford and describing her college's Christmas celebrations.

Elvis was particularly fascinated by the idea of an Oxford Christmas because of the musical aspect. He wasn't a hick from the sticks; he had visited Oxford many a time. He had even heard the famous Magdalen College choir, singing from the top of the tower on a May morning. There was still, however, a special glamour attached to the concept of Oxford music that made him sit, with his chin in his hands, listening raptly to Jessica's description of the *Messiah* she had attended, at the end of term, in Christ Church Cathedral.

"God, I wish I'd been there!" I heard him say, and smiled to myself as I peeled a few extra carrots.

Elvis knew his talents were wasted on St Mary's, but it would have taken more than money to tempt him away from Wales or, more specifically, Gower. After his mother's death, he had been offered a job in Llandaff which would have given him both status and a salary double what he made as a piano teacher. He had turned it down without a second thought, because he couldn't contemplate moving house.

It wasn't just about the music, either. Elvis felt he was serving the community, keeping its children out of trouble while indoctrinating them with a love of music. No wonder he was so concerned to find out the truth about Craig Dutton.

The chatter continued all through lunch and out the other end, until, after pudding and coffee, I was forced to be brutally frank and tell Jessica that I wanted to speak to Elvis in private. She went meekly into the garage to start sorting through the box of stuff that I'd brought home from the library the previous week.

Elvis didn't seem overly anxious to know what was on my mind. I'm sure he had a rough idea, in any case.

"I take it this is about the Sutcliff situation," he said, when Jessica was safely out of the way. "Or is it that you want me to yourself? Can't stand the competition for my affections, eh?"

I replenished our coffee from the percolator.

"I suppose you noticed Ray Gough was conspicuous by his absence this morning," he went on, sounding quite cheerful about it.

"I did notice. Surely it wasn't anything to do with this business?" Elvis nodded slowly. "But I thought he was one of Tim's most vociferous supporters."

"Bloody turncoat," muttered Elvis. "He had the nerve to send me a note saying he wouldn't be able to attend rehearsals between now and Christmas because of pressure of work. He knows how strict I am about not letting people sing in the services unless they've attended rehearsals regularly. Anyway, what was it you wanted to ask me? Or tell me?"

"I'm in a bit of confusion," I said. "I wondered if you could shed any light on it. Laura told me, this morning, that Tim doesn't know what Craig is accusing him of. Is that possible?"

Elvis nodded. "He *didn't* know, not exactly, until a few days ago. He does now."

"You're not going to tell me that you told him yourself?"

"Of course I bloody did! I couldn't go around concealing knowledge like that, could I?"

"Then how come Laura doesn't know?"

"Come on, woman, use your loaf!" He made a pretence of tapping my head with the teaspoon. "Hello? Anyone home?"

I tried not to laugh. "Seriously, Elvis. What's going on? I don't understand any of this."

"I'm not surprised really. It's difficult enough for me, and I'm a man." He gurgled noisily with laughter, then leaned forward confidentially. "As I understand it, in cases involving child abuse, Social Services don't let anyone know anything about what's been said until they're good and ready. Don't ask me how a person's supposed to deny the charge when they don't even know what it is. That bit doesn't make any sense to me, but it's all to do with protecting the child and so on. All Tim got told was that Craig had accused him of interfering with him in some unspecified way – which of course Tim strongly denies."

"But Tim said the Duttons had gone to him in person, before they ever reported the matter," I objected.

"Not quite accurate." As usual, Elvis was some distance ahead of me. "What actually happened was that Craig said something to someone at school, and the other kid told one of the teachers. This is hearsay, and I don't know the full story, but I gather the teacher felt obliged to do something about it, and asked for advice. The advice they got given was to speak to Craig's parents, to see whether there was some simple explanation. Craig's parents ended up being interviewed by a social worker and, not surprisingly, they were very upset."

Elvis went on to explain that, once a case of this kind had come to the attention of a social worker, it takes on a momentum of its own. Dr Dutton had been warned not to reveal any details of the accusation to anyone else, including Tim. He had then rung Tim and outlined the problem, mistakenly believing that there would be no further action on the part of the authorities unless he so chose. Because Tim had flatly denied Craig's accusation, whilst refusing to offer any logical explanation for it, and because the doctor preferred not to believe that his son was a liar and trouble-maker, he reported back to Social Services that he wanted them to take the matter further.

What he hadn't understood, at this stage, was that there was already no going back. The teachers had no choice in whom they chose to inform. It had already been decided that Tim had a case to answer, and the authorities were already involved. Tim himself hadn't understood the likely consequences when he spoke to Dr Dutton, or even afterwards when he found himself being interviewed by the police. He thought that, as long as there was no firm evidence against him and he continued to deny everything, he couldn't possibly be charged. He soon found out how wrong he had been.

This was the point at which I felt obliged to challenge Elvis.

"Why would Dr Dutton have told you what he told you, if he'd been warned to keep his mouth shut?"

Elvis wasn't put off by the question. On the contrary, he had obviously given it a great deal of thought. "That's the six million dollar question, Olwen. It seems to me that the good doctor has got cold feet. He doesn't want his family dragged through the courts, the talk of Swansea and Gower. Even if what Craig said was true, they wouldn't want it broadcasting. When I made my approach, he must have realised that I was a close friend of Tim's and would repeat back to him everything that was said to me, but he still went ahead and told me. My guess is that he's hoping it will help Tim to think up a good excuse when he's finally confronted with the evidence. Such as it is."

"But Tim hasn't told Laura . . ."

"No, of course not! For goodness' sake, you can see the state she's in, as it is! She doesn't need any more aggro. Tim's keeping it from her. The fewer people that know about it, the better."

It was typical male logic. Keep the little woman protected from the big bad facts, otherwise she might get upset and throw a wobbly.

"Elvis, this is nuts!" I protested. "Laura needs to know this."

I described to Elvis how relieved I'd felt after hearing what Dr Dutton had told him, how it had helped me to know that Tim wasn't being accused of some kind of savage rape of a minor. Then I remembered what I had thought afterwards, how much easier it had been to believe Tim capable of this act as described by the boy. And I wondered if Laura Sutcliff would have the same doubts about her husband as I had found within myself.

"There we are, you see!" said Elvis. "It's not quite so simple as we'd like to think, is it? Do me a favour, Olwen, don't do anything rash, and don't tell anyone what I told you. It won't do any good, and it might do harm. It's up to Tim what he tells Laura."

For the moment, I conceded. The information had been given me in confidence, and I don't like to betray a trust, however righteous the motive.

Chapter 9

Limeslade Bay was looking as grey and fierce as it always does in winter. The tides are deceptively dangerous, and even at the height of summer there have been cases of drowning, usually when people have walked out to secluded spots under the cliffs to sunbathe and then found themselves cut off.

You could hardly describe Limeslade as a place in its own right. It's just one of a string of little bays festooning the southern coast of the peninsula, most of them more attractive and more popular than poor old Limeslade. Watercolour views of the bays abound, littering every other shop in Swansea – Three Cliffs Bay, Langland, Caswell, Oxwich and so on – but you never see one of Limeslade.

It took me about a minute to find the house, which stood out among the holiday homes and student lets by virtue of its lack of outward adornment, combined with the presence of two people and a vehicle in the driveway.

"Mrs Roberts?" I assumed that the small, dark, woman with the pointy face, standing by the car, was the one who had phoned me.

"Ro*barts*," she corrected, looking less than pleased.

"Sorry!" I apologised quickly, glancing down at the note in my hand. "Can't read my own writing! I'm Olwen Harris." I handed her my business card, which she pocketed without looking at it. Silently, she led me into the sad little house.

"I don't know what you'll make of all this stuff," she said, showing me into what had presumably been her father's living room.

I could understand her point of view. The books had taken over.

"Wow," I said. "He was fond of his books, wasn't he, your dad?"

"You could say that." She didn't smile. "After Mam died, he hardly ever went out. Just sat here, reading. Goodness knows what for. I think he was doing some sort of research. At least, that's what he called it. He was going to write a book, only he never got round to it."

After glancing at one or two titles, I didn't need to ask what the subject of the old man's planned masterpiece had been.

"Was he a war veteran?"

"He was at Dunkirk," she said. "He knew Wynford Vaughan-Thomas. They used to meet up regularly."

Wynford Vaughan-Thomas was not only a well-known travel writer and TV personality, but had also been a war correspondent, one of the first to report back from the front line at the climax of the Second World War. The French awarded him the Croix de Guerre. If this man had been his contemporary . . .

"How old was he?" I asked. In situations like this, I always try to show an interest in the deceased as well as in the books. In this case, I didn't have to pretend; I was genuinely interested.

"Eighty-three," she replied. "You might say he had a good innings. But he never got over losing Mam."

For a second, I thought she was going to cry. She wasn't as hard-faced as she had seemed at first.

Mr Robarts had followed us into the room, but was taking no part in the conversation. He stood over by the window, looking out onto the bay, hands in pockets.

"I just want all this stuff taken away," said his wife. "I don't want to see it again. Can you take it with you, now?"

I hesitated. "I don't think I've got room for all of it in the van. And we'll need to agree a price. I'll have to have a closer look at what's here before I can make you an offer."

"How much do you think?" she urged. "Fifty? A hundred?"

At these words, Mr Robarts had turned away from the window, and was studying my face.

"Steady on, Val," he said. "Some of these might be valuable."

"Oh, who sodding cares?" she retorted angrily. All was not well between this couple, that much was evident. Whether it was normal for them, or whether it was just the emotional upset, I couldn't tell.

"Could you give me half an hour or so to look around?" I asked. "Then I'll make you an offer for the lot, if that's what you want."

"Fine," said Val Robarts sharply. "Fine. I'll go and make a cup of tea."

"You're right," I said, to her husband, when she had left the room. "Some of these could have some value. Military history is a very specialised field, and I'm no expert. I really ought to consult someone."

He came over to me, hands still in his pockets. "Poor old bloke," he said. "He never had a lot of fun out of life. We used to come down and see him, after Val's mother died, but he never had much to say, so we more or less stopped coming, until he got ill the other day. He was only in hospital a week. I think he was glad to go, in the end."

"A shame he never finished his book, though," I remarked, leafing through a well-thumbed volume on the history of the Spitfire.

"Don't think he even got started. He left it too late. If you're going to do something like that, you need to do it while you're young."

I tended to agree.

Sooner or later, I had been expecting to hear from that solicitor again. It's not easy to explain why. A woman knows when a man is "interested". Charles Cornwell was sending out all the signals. Nevertheless, it went against the grain for me to believe that someone like him could have felt that kind of attraction for someone like me.

Why not? Was there anything wrong with me, any reason why a man shouldn't be interested? Nothing specific. I suppose, for my age, I was looking fairly good. Jessica said so, anyway. I kept reasonably fit, went for walks, didn't overeat. I didn't wear make-up very often, and I didn't smoke or drink to excess, so my skin was good. My hair wasn't even beginning to go grey. I wear glasses, but so do lots of people in my age group.

It wasn't that I thought I wasn't fit to be seen. It was more to do with the kind of man Charles was, or rather, the kind of man I took him to be. He had been around. Whatever the circumstances of his divorce, however innocent or guilty he might have been, he would certainly have been involved with other women in the fourteen years since he ceased to be married. As for me, I hadn't had a serious relationship for goodness knows how long – I literally couldn't remember. Unless, of course, you count Tim Sutcliff.

One of the reasons for my celibate lifestyle was that, since I gave up my office job, I seldom met any men. Working for myself had been intended to free me from the claustrophobia of the office environment. In many ways, the result had been the opposite. Theoretically I was free to come and go as I pleased, yet I always seemed to be in the house.

Apart from the odd book sale, and one-off trips like the visit to Limeslade, the furthest I ever went was to church or to the shops. The kind of men I met there were not such, or were not in such a situation, as to encourage familiarity, let alone romance. Despite the unemployment problem in South Wales, you don't see many men below retirement age walking their dogs in the daytime, not on Gower. There was Elvis and there was Tim, both equally ineligible, and that was about it.

I told myself that I was happy with things as they were; but I couldn't deny the void in my personal life. That I felt it to be a shortcoming was evinced by the swiftness with which I had become attracted to Charles Cornwell. It had taken all of five minutes.

That the attraction could have been not only instant, but mutual, was something I was afraid to accept. I wasn't yet at the stage where I expected anything to come of it. When I saw him coming up the path, that Tuesday morning, I was neither thrilled nor particularly hopeful. There could be some quite innocent explanation. Perhaps he was coming to tell me the date of Tim's court hearing, when I would be called upon as a character witness.

Not wishing to seem too eager, I took my time about answering the door.

"Oh, hello!" I greeted him, trying to sound surprised as I gestured him into the living room. "I was just making coffee. Would you like one?"

He saw through my pretence, but accepted the invitation with apparent willingness, offering no explanation for his presence until the drinks were poured and we sat in the kitchen, just as Elvis and I had done the week before. Once again, it only served to reinforce the contrast; there was nothing about this man that reminded me of Elvis.

It was early. Jessica was still in bed. I prayed she wouldn't suddenly appear, in a skimpy nightie, while Charles was in the house.

"I came to say that I've changed my mind about the book," he said, after the briefest exchange of pleasantries. "I'll take it, after all."

I put down my cup with a rattle. "The Charlotte Mew book?"

"Yes. On second thoughts, I decided I might as well."

"I'll go and get it," I said, beginning to rise from my stool.

"Plenty of time for that," he countered, touching my arm lightly to prevent me.

It was nice, having my arm touched like that. There was nothing overtly suggestive about it, yet it made me feel – how can I put it? – as though he knew me intimately. It was as though we were becoming friends, not mere business acquaintances.

At the same time I was disappointed that he had chosen to take the book after all, especially in view of the comment he had made, last time, about being able to tell that I wanted to keep it for myself. In an effort to excuse him, I reminded myself how I had protested that I couldn't afford to get sentimental about my stock.

"I thought perhaps you'd come about Tim's case," I said, returning to my drink.

He failed to respond, raising his cup to his lips, continuing to watch me over the rim.

"Have there been any further developments?" I asked. "Do you know yet, whether it'll come to court? Have the police said anything?"

He lowered the cup, while deciding how to answer.

"Don't think me rude," he said, "but . . ."

"I'm sorry!" I gasped. "It's all confidential, isn't it? You're not allowed to say anything, except to your client. I shouldn't have asked."

"It's quite all right," he said. "You are concerned in the matter, after all. It's simply that I must be careful not to reveal anything that might have a bearing on the case, and of course my client's confidentiality must be preserved."

"I understand. It's just that I've been talking to Elvis – Mr

Jones, the organist – and we came up with a couple of theories about what might have happened." I felt myself flush. "I don't suppose you're interested in the ideas of a couple of amateur sleuths who aren't even in possession of the full facts."

The sunbeam smile came out again. "On the contrary, if you have anything to contribute, I'd be glad to listen. Sometimes the solution to a problem comes from the most unexpected sources. As long as you let me reserve the right not to comment on your ideas."

So I told him. I outlined the theories Elvis and I had discussed, a few days before, sitting in that very spot. Naturally, I kept quiet about my darker fears. The purpose of the exercise was to help prepare a defence for Tim. It wouldn't have done to test Charles Cornwell on the question of his client's innocence.

After listening attentively to my wittering for a good ten minutes, with nothing but the occasional nod, Charles pushed aside his cup and saucer, and looked at me intently.

"You've been busy," he commented.

I waited for something more.

"Some interesting ideas there," he went on.

"But no use to you?"

"I didn't say that. Only . . . do you mind my asking how you knew what Craig Dutton had said about the incident?"

I probably blushed, but I was too confused to realise it. It dawned on me that, in my eagerness to impress Charles Cornwell, I had been very indiscreet. In many ways, I was no better than the rest of the loose tongues in the village.

"Did the Reverend Sutcliff tell you?" he persisted.

"No. Not a word. But there's . . . talk."

"Do you normally pay any attention to gossip?"

I thought about it for a moment. "Yes, sometimes. I mean, I take it with a pinch of salt, but there's usually some grain of truth in it. Don't you find that?" Even as I said it, I was conscious of my own inconsistency.

He smiled weakly. "Perhaps."

"I'm not asking you to tell me whether . . . the person who told me had the facts right. I only want to help Tim. That's my only motivation. Please believe that."

Did I sound as desperate to him as I did to myself?

"It concerns me a little that this story has got out," he said. "The details should be kept confidential, as far as possible, until the court hearing – if there is one, which I still hope there won't be. The more that becomes generally known, the more difficult it will be to prevent it coming to court. Can you see that? So it's vital that gossip be discouraged – even if it's the truth."

"Of course," I agreed meekly. I could hardly go on to ask the burning question: had Charles Cornwell already known the facts? I had assumed that he would have heard them by now, from Tim if no one else. Tim might choose not to confide in his own wife, but he would surely have told his solicitor anything that was likely to assist in formulating a defence.

Sensing that he had inadvertently hurt my feelings, Charles cast about for a way of making amends.

"I'm really very grateful to you for confiding in me," he forged on. "And I do think there may be something in your ideas. May I think about them, for a while?"

I nodded, getting up to clear away the cups.

"I'll get you your book now."

We went into the garage. It was a gloomier day than on his previous visit, and I had to turn on the light in order to locate the Charlotte Mew.

He took it from my hands. "It's a very attractive volume," he said. "Very . . ."

"It's a first edition," I said, though I knew I had already told him that once. "That's all."

He looked up, startled by the rancour in my voice. He should have understood its cause. Having remarked, himself, on how reluctant I was to let the book go, he was asking for it, to give away to some stranger. My heart softened towards him as I thought of the possibility that he had not felt able to wait, to see me again, and had asked for the book merely as an excuse to return to my house. A lesser transaction could have been conducted over the telephone. Come to that, so could this.

Turning away, I asked if he would like the book wrapped, any special way. I don't do gift-wrapping as a rule, but if someone asks for it, I attempt it.

"*I so liked Spring last year,*" he read, to my back, "*Because you were here.*"

"That's one of my favourite poems," I said. The tear in my eye had caught me unawares.

"It's lovely," said Charles, reading it through, silently, to the end. It didn't take him long. "Does it remind you of someone?"

He still hadn't answered the gift-wrappíng question.

"No one specific," I said. "Maybe someone I haven't met yet."

I turned to look at him. The smile parted his lips with an unaccustomed slowness.

"Who knows?" he said. "There's no need for wrapping. I'll take it as it is. How much do I owe you?"

"I'm afraid it's fifteen pounds," I replied, still half-hoping he would change his mind again.

"Seems a bargain."

"I doubt you'll find it cheaper. There are more important things in life than money. At least I know it's going to a good home."

"Oh yes, I'll look after it."

"I thought you were going to give it to your sister-in-law?" I challenged.

"I may," he conceded, looking uncomfortable. "But I'd still like you to look out for something else for her. Something more . . . obvious."

Was he, perhaps, intending to keep Charlotte Mew for himself? I hoped so.

"It'll give me a reason to call and see you again," he added.

"Do you need one?"

I was surprised at myself, giving him such a brazen come-on.

That incredible smile cracked through his face again. "We'll see."

A creaking board on the landing told me that Jessica was getting up. Water was running in the bathroom. Charles looked up at the ceiling, anxiously.

"I'm sorry, I thought you lived alone."

"I do. That's my niece. She's staying with me for the Christmas holidays."

The look of relief was unmistakable. "I'll look forward to meeting her. Only I'm afraid it'll have to be another day."

By the time Jessica came downstairs, he had gone.

"Did I hear someone at the door?"

"Now, Jess, how can *I* possibly know whether *you* heard someone at the door? There was someone at the door, if that's what you mean, and he's been and gone."

"Who was it?"

"It was Charles Cornwell. Tim's solicitor."

She grunted acknowledgement.

"When you've had your breakfast, Jess . . ."

"I don't eat breakfast."

I sighed, just as I'd heard her mother do. She wouldn't have said that if there had been any laverbread left.

"Then you can get down to some work straight away. I want you to sort out that other box of stuff in the stock room. I brought it back from that house in Limeslade. It's mostly military history, but there are probably a few old novels in there as well. Keep an eye open for anything signed by the author."

Chapter 10

It was a couple of days before I saw Charles Cornwell again. By the time I did, my world had fallen apart.

Meeting Aubrey Bantoft was only the start of it. If I'm honest, the good mood I'd been in when Charles left my house the previous morning had soon dissipated, and it was my own doing. It all really started when I asked Jessica to go into the stock room and start sorting through that box of books.

After due consideration and a couple of calls to specialist dealers, I had offered Val Robarts three hundred pounds for the contents of her father's library. She had practically bitten my hand off. It turned out she had two younger brothers, and she was determined that they were not going to get their hands on anything. The house and contents, as far as I could make out, were likely to be left jointly between the three of them, but Mrs Robarts was anticipating the reading of the will.

To do her justice, I don't think she was trying to pull a fast one on her brothers. She simply wanted to realise the assets as quickly as possible. She was afraid that, once the rest of the family arrived, they would start making difficulties and would try to prevent the sale of their father's effects. I got the distinct impression that her brothers weren't as short of money as she and her husband were.

I had no more than a momentary concern about the possibility of the books not being hers to sell. These things often happen in the wake of a death. The family starts squabbling over who gets what's left, and before you know it, none of them are on speaking terms. In a way, I was doing them a favour by removing the problem. By the time anyone raised a question mark over the matter, they were hardly likely to come running after me to get the stuff back. There would be other things to fight over – the house, for a start. Assuming there was no written inventory in existence, no one would be able to remember, let alone prove, what books the old man had owned.

I had no intention of taking advantage of the family's misfortunes. I had spoken the truth when I said that I wasn't an expert on military books. Mrs Robarts had a key to the house, so I treated her as the owner of the collection, and it was her own choice to close the deal quickly, rather than waiting for me to call in one of my contacts in the trade to take a look. Under the circumstances, I made the fairest estimate I could of the market value of the books, and deducted one-quarter as my profit margin. Amongst other things, I needed to cover my petrol costs; it was going to take at least two trips to shift that lot.

Ten minutes after I had given Jessica her instructions, she was still lounging around in the living room, showing a marked reluctance to begin. I could almost see her brain working overtime, trying to come up with a way to stave off the inevitable moment when she had to start on the allotted task.

"I've been thinking," she said. "You know what you and Elvis were saying the other day, about the police not telling Tim what he's supposed to have done?"

"Jessica, that was private! You weren't supposed to be listening!"

She didn't blush. There was very little that was beyond the pale, as far as my niece was concerned.

"I wasn't listening! I just caught one or two snatches, that's all. Don't worry, I won't tell anyone. I don't know anyone around here to tell, in any case."

"You know the Sutcliffs, and I'd be grateful if you would make sure you don't give the impression that Elvis and I have been gossiping about them."

She grinned. "Even if you have."

For once, I didn't share the joke. "It's not funny, Jess. There's a lot at stake here. A whole family's welfare, for a start." I suppose I was all the more upset because I recognised the basic truth of her remark.

Looking pensive, she sat down at the table opposite me, interrupting my work once again.

"You believe the Vicar's innocent, don't you?" she said.

"Of course! I've known Tim a long time. He would never . . ."

"People do awful things, Auntie Olwen. Even priests and people you'd never think . . ."

"Jessica!" I cried. "I thought you were on Laura's side. You shouldn't listen to all the tittle-tattle you hear around the village. A lot of people are jealous of Tim."

"I don't mean it like that." Her voice was soft, and her eyes full of concern – for me, not for the Sutcliffs. "Of course I don't want to think that the Vicar's done anything wrong. But I've got a friend who's a social worker, and she's always telling me stories about cases she's dealt with."

"That's all they are, Jess. Stories. It may be that some priests do . . . bad things, but that doesn't mean that everyone who's accused of child abuse is guilty. Look what happened in Cleveland . . ."

I paused, realising that she was probably too young to remember.

"Families can be destroyed, Jess," I said gently. "Idle gossip and well-meaning interference. They can do permanent damage, make people doubt their own husbands and wives, come between children and their parents. I don't want to see that happen to Tim and Laura."

"No. I love the children, you know that. But it would be better, wouldn't it, if it turns out that the Vicar *is* guilty, for him to be found out and stopped at this stage, before any other innocent children suffer? And if he did do it, then he doesn't deserve to have such a lovely little family, and Laura would be better off without him."

I couldn't fault her logic. She simply didn't understand. She was too young.

"Don't let me hear you saying things like that!" I snapped. "Now go and get on with some work. What am I paying you for?"

Flashing me a hurt look, she got up and went slowly into the stock room. If she'd had a tail, it would have been between her legs. I tried to get on with the accounts, but my mind wouldn't focus on the figures. The whole episode, coming on top of my little tête-à-tête with Charles Cornwell, had put me off balance.

Later in the morning, when I took in the elevenses, I apologised for speaking so harshly. Jess can be very sensitive, but she's also resilient, thank God. She knew I hadn't meant to be unkind. In an effort to make up for our little quarrel, I pulled up my chair alongside hers.

"I'm sorry I blew my top."

"That's okay, Auntie Olwen." Her tone was submissive. She had obviously been brooding over it for the past half an hour. "You made me realise that I was shooting my mouth off about things I don't really understand. And for what it's worth, I don't think Laura's husband is guilty. I don't know him very well, but he doesn't seem to be the type."

I sighed, wondering what on earth Jessica would know about the "type" of man who goes in for child abuse.

"What was it you were going to say, anyway?" I asked. "Before I chewed you out, you were going to tell me something, or ask me something, about what Elvis and I were saying on Sunday."

"Oh yes! About the Vicar not having been told what he was supposed to have done. I've heard about that before, from my friend. It's quite normal, apparently, in these cases. It doesn't mean they've got strong evidence against him. It doesn't mean anything. It's just what they do."

I pondered. "As I said to Elvis, it doesn't seem right to me."

Jessica thought for a moment. "Nor me."

We sat there, victims of collective depression, until we had finished our coffee and Jessica's favourite song came on the radio. Things went downhill from there on.

It was, ironically, Mr Samuel who introduced me to Aubrey Bantoft, when we bumped into one another outside the church, next day.

"Morning, Olwen. I was just showing Mr Bantoft the church. Have you two met?"

I had no idea why Mr Samuel should expect me to have met this tall, distinguished-looking man in a smart suit.

"De-*ligh*-ted!" said Mr Bantoft, in an exaggerated drawl, offering me a limp handshake. Bent as a corkscrew, I thought to myself.

I don't usually think things like that. I've had numerous gay friends and acquaintances in the past. And then there was Elvis. It was just the mood I was in at the time. What happened after that was probably the punishment I deserved.

At the time, and for half an hour or so afterwards, I had no idea who Bantoft was. Mr Samuel continued giving him the tour of the church, and I accompanied them to make sure he got his facts right. Mr Samuel had a tendency to go off at a tangent, and I considered myself something of an expert on the history of St Mary's. Although I'm a Baptist by upbringing, I've always had an interest in church architecture. Any work on the subject that shows its face in a used book sale can be sure of being snapped up, if I'm around.

I pointed out all the interesting features that Mr Samuel missed out, and Aubrey Bantoft oohed and aahed with the air of someone who appreciated Art and Architecture with capital As. The stained glass was, according to him, "out of this world", and the carved stonework was "stupendous". Personally, I found his enthusiasm, well-merited as it was, a little over the top.

When he'd had a good look over the church, we went outside, where I pointed out the battlemented tower to Mr Bantoft.

"It's typical of Gower. Most of the churches in this area were built around the thirteenth century, and the church was the villagers' only place of refuge in times of trouble."

"Re-ally?" drawled Mr Bantoft. "That's *fas*cinating!" It was an almost perfect impersonation of The Queen.

Having concluded the tour, the three of us walked through the graveyard in the direction of the vicarage. I expected the two men to head off up the street towards Mr Samuel's house, while I continued on my way to see Laura. To my surprise, they followed me, and I took it that Mr Samuel had undertaken to introduce his guest to the Vicar.

Laura answered the door, and appeared unfazed by the sight of the three of us together. Tim, emerging from his study, greeted us warmly, and it became apparent that he and Mr Bantoft, if not exactly on familiar terms, had met before. The trio of men went into the study together, and Laura invited me to have tea with her in the living room.

I hated that room. The kitchen, bare and unattractive as it was, at least had a measure of warmth about it. It had windows, for a start. The living room had a window, admittedly, but it looked out onto a stone wall, no more than six feet away, so there was a dearth of natural light. The furniture was second-hand and shabby. I didn't know how Laura could bear to live with it.

Accepting my mug of tea from her hands, I sat down on the

settee, which had enough give in it to keep a flag-seller going for hours.

"Is Mr Bantoft some friend of Mr Samuel?" I asked.

Laura looked puzzled. "I don't think so, particularly. He's a lawyer."

"But Tim's already got a good lawyer!" I complained. "Mr Cornwell. Surely he's not going to change solicitors, at this stage?"

My protests were based on my belief that Charles Cornwell, whose professional expertise I had never had cause to test, was the most efficient solicitor in the universe. Fortunately, Laura hadn't noticed me colouring up.

"No," she explained. "Mr Bantoft is Mr Cornwell's partner. Mr Bantoft has handled a case like this before, so Mr Cornwell asked him to come over and talk to Tim, to see if there was anything else that could be done to expedite things. He's got a lot of good contacts, apparently."

Various cynical thoughts crossed my mind. My relief on hearing that Charles was to continue as Tim's legal representative was tempered by the knowledge that his partner, being an expert in this type of case, might try to muscle in on his territory, giving Charles no further excuses to visit the village.

Laura and I went on to discuss the latest developments, of which there had been none. There was no news about the impending court case. Indeed, Tim had not yet been formally charged with anything. The Director of Public Prosecutions, or whoever was responsible for the decision, had not yet made up his or her mind about the force of the evidence against him. When it came down to it, the word of one eleven-year-old boy, however good that boy's reputation, was hardly likely to be enough to convict a vicar with an equally spotless record.

The possibility that Tim's record might not be spotless never occurred to me at the time. There were enough odd thoughts going through my mind, without that. Much, much later, I would learn that Tim had a conviction for possession of an illegal substance, going right back to his student days. It hadn't prevented him from being ordained as a priest, nor would it have affected the court case. Previous convictions are not normally admissible as evidence, even when they are for similar offences. All the same, it was just as well I didn't know about it at the time.

"It's going to be a miserable Christmas this year," Laura moaned.

I wished I could say something to comfort her on that score, but I tended to agree that Christmas would, for her, be miserable. I forbore from mentioning my own plans for the festive season. On Christmas Eve, I would drive Jessica up to Sian's and, by the time we arrived there, Sian herself would have met my parents off the train and brought them to her house. (They couldn't travel with us, because of the shortage of seats in the van.) As usual, I would have to share Jessica's bedroom for a couple of nights. Kelly and Tammy would sleep in together, and my parents would have what was normally Kelly's room.

Uncomfortably crowded it might be, but it would be fun. On Christmas morning, some of us might go to chapel, if we felt energetic enough. Although the girls were past the Father Christmas stage, there would be lots of present-opening. Weeks earlier, I had bumped into my mother doing her shopping in the Quadrant Centre in Swansea, and she had shown me what my father would be getting in his stocking. My own gift was still a surprise.

The only thing wrong with a family Christmas, as far as I was concerned, was the feeling that I was borrowing someone else's family for the day. Okay, Sian was my sister, and we were close. Mum and Dad were my parents. But Sian's husband, and her children, didn't belong to me, and they would have been justified in resenting my intrusion on that most important day of the year.

Mr Bantoft and Mr Samuel remained closeted with Tim for the whole of the time I was at the vicarage, and I didn't see Tim himself again for a couple of days. When I got back to the house, Jessica told me there had been a phone call from a Mr Cornwell. Resisting the urge to ring back straight away, I looked through a catalogue that had come in the morning's post, in the hope of coming across something to suit his sister-in-law. As luck would have it, there was a signed Daphne Du Maurier that I thought might be right up her street. It would be just as well to have something to say, when I called him back.

"Did he say what he wanted?" I asked Jessica, wondering whether it was about Tim that he was ringing or about the book.

"No. He wouldn't leave any message. He just said he'd try again later."

"I'll ring him back."

"He said not to. He said he'll be tied up in meetings, and he'll get back to you when he's got a spare moment."

I felt deflated, unreasonably so. It was absolutely natural for a professional man to give priority to his paying clients during the working day. I had no reason to suppose that the call was significant. Charles might well have forgotten my existence by the time the last of his meetings was over.

In an effort to take my mind off him, I picked up a couple of books which had slipped to the floor when I moved one of the boxes from Limeslade. How long had Mrs Robarts said it was since her parents went to live down there? The *Guide to Gower* looked as if the old man might well have bought it when he first arrived in the area. Lifting the faded cover with its once-garish artist's impression of the Worm's Head at Rhossili, I turned over the yellowing flyleaf to find that it was dated 1955.

If I have a specialism at all, as a bookseller, it's what they call "Welsh interest" books. It happened more by accident than design. Because I'm based in Wales, my contacts would try me first when they were looking for something about Wales or written in the Welsh language. Some such requests come from as far away as Australia. The Welsh diaspora is not insignificant; but I didn't foresee myself being able to sell this particular volume readily.

Most people would take the view that a guidebook is useless once it's out of date, but for the student of popular history, it can still pack a lot of interesting information. For example, this book told me that "the cockle-women, wearing their traditional hats, may be seen on the beach at Penclawdd, gathering shellfish to sell at Swansea market". I wasn't completely sure that you could have seen those hats, even in 1955, but it conjured up a picture of the past that appealed to me. It also mentioned the donkeys the women used to transport their catch back to the shore in panniers. I happened to know that those had gone out of use relatively recently.

Leafing on through the book, I found that it repeated the myth of the Red Lady of Paviland.

"In 1823," I read, "an English archaeologist named William Buckland discovered the skeleton of a woman, painted with red ochre, in a cave on South Gower. Buckland, a clergyman, believed the remains to date back to the great flood mentioned in the Bible."

Ho ho ho, I imagined the author saying. How gullible folk were in those days! The last laugh was on him. In 1955, he could hardly have foreseen the revolution that would take place in archaeology through the advent of radiocarbon dating. When a scientific approach to the problem became possible, it was discovered that not only was the "Red Lady" a man, but the skeleton was much older than anyone had previously dared hope (about 26,000 years old, in fact), making it one of the earliest known human inhabitants of the British Isles.

This old guidebook was fascinating. Had we been less busy, I could have spent hours looking at it, but I needed to get back down to work. I put the book on one side, along with the other volume that had fallen off the pile, ready to take upstairs for future bedside reading.

My valued customer didn't, in fact, ring back. At five o'clock I gave up on him, and started to think about what we might have for our evening meal. When the phone rang, just after six, I expected it to be Sian, waiting for cheap rate to get in touch with her daughter.

"It's for you, Auntie Ol." Jessica passed the receiver to me, and took over the task of watching the potatoes come to the boil.

"Olwen?" Charles Cornwell's cultured tones sounded even more delicious over a telephone wire than in real life. "I hope I'm not disturbing you. I meant to get back to you earlier in the day, but I've been terribly busy."

"That's all right. I'm glad you called back, because I've located a book you might be interested in. I'd have to order it for you, but you should get it in time for Christmas, and it's reasonably priced."

I told him what it was, and he sounded quite enthusiastic. He hadn't, as yet, had much chance to ask his sister-in-law about her preferences, and he was only too conscious that Christmas Day was looming nearer and the postal system would soon be getting very congested.

He asked if I could confirm how long it would take to get hold of the book, and I promised to ring him the following day, after I had spoken to the dealer who was offering it for sale. After I had put down the receiver, I remembered that it was Charles who had phoned me in the first place. Clearly, there had been no particular reason for this call, other than the pleasure of making contact.

As you can imagine, I was on cloud nine for the rest of the evening. Jessica didn't comment, but I'm sure she noticed my unusually sunny mood. It lasted well into the next morning, when I called the dealer to find that the Daphne Du Maurier was still available and he could get it to me quickly. Everything was going so smoothly that it couldn't last. I rang Charles back.

At first, the receptionist said she didn't think he was available, but then I heard a minor commotion at her end, and Charles came on the line.

"Olwen? Good morning. Nice to speak to you again so soon." Sincerity rang out.

I told him that I had arranged to get *Rebecca* for him at what I thought was a good price, and he said he would call in to collect it. I said I would probably have it by the end of the following week, and he said he hoped to see me before then.

The following morning, I found myself constantly looking out of the window. Every time a car came past, I would glance up in the hope of it being the silver BMW. Luckily, Jessica was absorbed in what she was doing, and didn't notice how jumpy I was. How she would have laughed, to think of her Auntie Olwen acting like a silly schoolgirl with a crush on the head boy!

I knew it was too soon for him to get in touch again, but I couldn't stop thinking about him. The morning dragged terribly. At lunchtime, the phone rang. Jessica passed it to me.

"It's the school," she said, twisting her lovely face into an expression that attempted to convey both puzzlement and distaste. She looked like a constipated chimpanzee.

Equally baffled, I took the receiver, and found myself speaking to the head of the local primary. All became clear when she explained that my number was on her list of alternatives for use in case of emergency, and she had a problem with Robert Sutcliff. Then I recalled Laura asking me, a few years before, if I would mind her giving my number to the school. They have to have someone to contact if a child gets ill, as was the case now. The

Sutcliffs didn't have any relatives living locally who could stand in for them, and they knew I was usually at home during the day.

The head teacher, a Mrs Barnes, asked if I could possibly come down to the school and collect Robert. He had been sick a couple of times in class, but they had been unable to raise Tim or Laura on the telephone. They really felt Robert ought to be at home, or at least in some familiar domestic setting. There was no difficulty about Caroline, who would come home on the bus at the end of the afternoon, as usual.

I agreed readily. It was a welcome interruption to my vigil at the window, and after all, what are neighbours for? I thought nothing of the fact that they hadn't been able to contact the Sutcliffs. It was one of Tim's days for visiting, and Laura had probably gone shopping. As I passed the vicarage, I looked out for signs of life. Unlike most of the villagers, the Sutcliffs actually kept their car in the garage when it wasn't being used. The freshly-painted garage door was closed, so I couldn't tell whether the car was there or not.

Chapter 11

It only took ten minutes to get to the school, which was in the next village. Many years had passed since I last had occasion to visit a primary school during the day. I must admit I was a little shocked, on entering, to see how like a high-security prison it had become. The doors were locked, and there were buzzers and closed-circuit TV cameras. The sign beside the main entrance, which read, "Parents are always welcome in our school", sounded like a bad joke.

You have to be so careful these days. I could understand why all these precautions were necessary, but it made me sad. Whatever happened to innocence?

The woman who answered the door, apparently the school secretary, had a friendly enough smile.

"Mrs . . .?"

"Olwen Harris. I've come to collect Robert Sutcliff."

"Oh yes. He's in with Mrs Barnes. Come through."

Now I began to understand why Mrs Barnes had been so keen for Robert to be taken home. The afternoon session of school had started, and the other kids were back in their classrooms, but Robert was sitting on what might have been called an easy chair, in the head teacher's office. In his case, the chair was more like an instrument of torture. He sat stiffly, obviously on his best behaviour under the eye of the head, unable to relax and probably terrified in case he should have another bout of nausea and throw up all over her carpet. That possibility was probably bothering her as much as it was bothering him.

Robert was in the top class of primary, the same class as Craig Dutton, and had turned eleven earlier in the autumn. He was a big boy for his age, which probably saved him from any danger of bullying, but that didn't mean he was tough. Laura was always saying how highly-strung he was, and on this occasion he looked it.

Mrs Barnes thanked me profusely for coming to fetch Robert. I asked for a few details of what had happened, so that I could relay them to his mother when I tracked her down. It seemed he had started to complain of feeling sick during morning play, but had soldiered bravely on until just before lunch, when he was sick while standing in the dinner queue. My first thought was that it must have been very off-putting for the rest of the children who were about to enter the dining hall. Recalling similar incidents in my own childhood, I smiled to myself. No doubt the rest of the boys were even now describing, in graphic detail, exactly what it had looked like.

Robert followed me obediently out to the van, and strapped himself into the passenger seat. He was still very pale, and I hoped he wouldn't repeat his earlier performance while we were on the way home. The van might be old and tatty, but I didn't fancy driving it with the smell of vomit hanging around, not to mention the job of sponging down the upholstery.

"How are you feeling now?" I asked anxiously.

"A bit better." He was putting a brave face on it.

I found it hard to relate to Robert. Caroline, being a girl, was easier. We had been all girls in my family, and my sister had three girls, so boys were quite alien to my experience. Rather than make forced conversation, I concentrated my attention on getting him home as quickly as possible.

There was still one question I felt obliged to ask. "Do you know where your mum and dad are, Rob?"

He said nothing, but shook his head, forcing me to take my eyes off the road for a second.

"I expect your dad's out visiting," I ventured, thinking that it was not at all likely that Tim's visiting round would coincide with lunch, and wondering if he had gone into Swansea to see his solicitor. "Did your mother say she was going anywhere today?"

He shook his head again.

What I really wanted to ask, of course, was how things were at school. I might not be much good with children, but I didn't want to think that this little boy was going through hell and had no one to stand up for him, or that he was making himself physically sick with the fear of what each day would bring. Mrs

Barnes hadn't referred to the Sutcliff situation, and it was hardly my place.

I rambled on, regardless. "I think we'll stop off at your house first, and see if your mum and dad are back. If there's no one in, we'll go back to my house and Jessica can keep an eye on you, okay?"

He brightened up a little at that prospect, but still said nothing. I pulled up the van outside the vicarage, and we walked up the drive together, Robert trailing a little behind me, as though he felt it was the adult's place to do any explaining that might be required. I rang the bell twice, but there was no response. Knowing that the back door (which, perversely, was at the front of the house) was the normal way of gaining access, it occurred to me to try it, but I hesitated because of Robert's presence.

Seeing me glance towards the kitchen door, he stepped forward and turned the handle. The door wasn't locked, and we went inside. There was no sign of life, apart from a newspaper lying open on the table.

"Laura?" I called. "Tim? Anyone home?"

I glanced at Robert again. He looked back at me, uncertain of his ground.

"She might be lying down upstairs," he said. "She does that sometimes."

"Shall I go and look?" I don't know why I was asking him. It was probably just a vague feeling that I shouldn't make free with his parents' house without his permission.

Robert was hardly likely to argue the toss with an adult. He merely nodded.

"You stay here," I instructed. "Why don't you get yourself a glass of milk or something? It might make you feel better. I'll just nip upstairs and see if your mum's awake."

Robert obeyed, but I could see that my nervousness was transmitting itself to him. He sat down unhappily at the kitchen table, and pretended to be interested in the newspaper.

If ever there was a candidate for a haunted house, the vicarage was it. Ghosts, I imagine, steer clear of the clergy, but all the same I wouldn't have liked to be in that house on my own at night. It was just too damn big. The stairs creaked under my feet. That was all to the good. With a bit of luck, Laura, if she had fallen asleep, would hear my footsteps and come to the top of the stairs to see who it was.

I knew which bedroom was Tim and Laura's. I'd been in this house many times, and had helped Laura by taking coats upstairs when she had a lot of visitors. The Sutcliffs weren't troubled by any intrusion into their personal space; they couldn't afford to be. The vicarage belonged to the Church in Wales, and its incumbents had so many callers that they couldn't hope to keep the rooms in pristine condition, even if the house hadn't been old and dilapidated to start with.

All the same, it was with a certain reluctance that I knocked on the bedroom door.

"Laura? Are you there? Laura? It's Olwen."

There was no response. I knew I couldn't possibly enter without an invitation. I was about to turn around and go back downstairs, when I heard a sound, like a little moan, from inside.

"Laura!" I raised my voice. "Laura? Are you all right?"

The moaning sound was repeated, more loudly. Without a second thought, I opened the door and went in.

Laura lay on the bed, scrunched into a little ball – a foetal position. It was freezing in there, and I wondered why on earth she hadn't got under the blankets. Her eyes were closed, but she was twitching and making quiet noises, as though locked in some unpleasant dream.

My eyes were drawn to the bedside table. On it was a half-empty bottle of wine, and beside that a smaller bottle, of tablets. I didn't look at the label; I simply rushed towards the bed, caught Laura by the shoulders and shook her violently.

"Laura! Laura! What have you done?"

To my relief, she began to rouse herself immediately, but her eyes were slow to open, and she still looked woozy.

"Ol . . . Olwen? What . . . What are you doing here? What's the matter?"

"I might ask you the same question!" I sat down on the bed, pulling her upright. "Laura, what have you done?" I gestured towards the contents of the bedside table.

She looked confused, but unconcerned. "What? I don't understand." Her speech was slurred, and the smell on her breath was unmistakable.

"Laura! Get a grip!" I wasn't sure that I was addressing that command to the right person, but I persisted in shaking her shoulders, desperate for a response that would show me I had nothing to worry about.

She began to shiver, and looked around her, frightened, as if she didn't recognise where she was.

"I was only sleeping, Olwen," she said. "I was only sleeping! What are you doing here? Why are you in my bedroom?"

Explanations, I realised, were in order.

"The school phoned me. Robert wasn't feeling well, and they wanted to send him home, but they couldn't get an answer from you."

"Oh! I was asleep!"

Ignoring that self-evident remark, I continued, hoping that the flow of words would bring her back to her senses. "They had my number, for emergencies, so they rang me and I went over and fetched him. But there was no one downstairs. Where's Tim?"

"He's . . . gone out."

Feeling unreasonably irritated by what was a perfectly truthful reply, I resumed my tirade. "Come on, Laura, snap out of it! Robert's downstairs. What am I going to do with him? You've been drinking, haven't you?"

She could hardly deny it, with the bottle there beside the bed.

"I . . . just wanted something to help me sleep, that's all."

"And those tablets? How many have you taken?"

"None! Well, not since this morning. They're my anti-depressants. The doctor gave them to me."

"Oh." I reflected for only a moment on this statement. "I'm sure you're not supposed to drink alcohol with them, are you?"

"There's hardly any alcohol in that." Averting her eyes, she gave a silly little laugh. "It's somebody's home-made wine that they gave us ages ago. Rhubarb, or something."

I reached for the bottle. It was an effort to decipher the handwritten label. "Elderflower, I think. But it is wine, and you shouldn't be drinking it if you're on medication."

"No, I suppose I shouldn't," she said meekly. "I'd better get up."

She made a feeble attempt to raise herself from the bed. I doubted her ability to tackle the stairs. There was no way I was going to let Robert see his mother in this state.

"Don't panic," I said, more gently. "Look, I'll take Robert over to my house. Jess will keep an eye on him, and then I'll come back and check on you, okay?"

"I'm fine, really," she protested.

"Yes, I can see that," I lied, "but you need a bit of time to come to yourself. I'll take Robert for an hour or so, and bring him back when the school bus is due. In the meantime, make yourself a cup of tea or something, and I'll be back in a few minutes to see if you're okay."

She nodded. As I left the bedroom and returned to the kitchen, I felt an intense dislike for myself. Why I should feel so guilty I didn't know. All I had done was to act like a good neighbour, looking after the child, showing concern for the mother. The trouble was that I hadn't done either of them with any real feeling, still less any practical result. Robert was only eleven, and I should have been able to say or do something to comfort him, instead of palming him off on my niece. As for Laura, she obviously needed help, but all I had been able to think of, when I rushed into that bedroom, was how inconvenient it would be if I had to call an ambulance and have her taken to hospital.

Later, I felt differently. Robert showed no signs of agitation when I told him that his mother was resting and he could come back to my house and see Jessica. Jess looked a little surprised when the two of us arrived back, but made no complaint at being asked to keep him amused for an hour or so, while I went back to talk to Laura.

I also figured out where Tim was. The funeral cortège was just departing, as I hustled Robert back into the van. The hearse emerged from behind the trees and trundled past me on the road that swept around from the churchyard, followed by six or seven other vehicles. Tim was sitting in one of them; he didn't see me. He had probably been with the family of the deceased for most of the morning. They would be on their way to the crematorium now, probably Morriston, so they would be gone for a good long while. Laura had time to get herself together before her husband came home.

When I returned to the vicarage, she was sitting by the kitchen table, sipping tea and looking almost normal. I felt a fool for rushing back. My instincts had obviously been mistaken. Nevertheless, it seemed only wise to double-check that she hadn't been in any danger. I would never have forgiven myself if I had ignored a cry for help.

The wine bottle stood, empty, on the draining board. Seeing my expression when I noticed it, Laura was quick to reassure.

"I poured the rest down the sink," she said matter-of-factly. "It was disgusting, anyway. I only drank it because I was having difficulty relaxing."

"How often do you do that sort of thing?"

She studied me for a moment or two before attempting a reply. "Sometimes," she said, uninformatively.

"Laura," I said, "I hate to ask this, but those group therapy sessions you've been going to . . ."

"Group counselling," she corrected.

"Whatever. It is a proper medical thing, isn't it, not Alcoholics Anonymous?"

Her eyebrows shot up to meet her wispy fair hair.

"What would I need Alcoholics Anonymous for?" she exclaimed. "I'm not an alcoholic!"

"No," I soothed. "No, of course you're not."

"There's no need to take that condescending tone with me, Olwen! I'm not an alcoholic, and I'm not a child either!"

The note of bitterness was unexpected. I had, I realised, deserved it. Her reaction to my interference was much as my own response would have been, had someone else taken it on themselves to come into my house and start giving me unwanted advice.

"I'm sorry, Laura," I said. For once, I was wholly sincere. "It's just that, when I found you like that, I thought for a minute you'd . . . you know."

Her blue eyes widened. If her face had been a little chubbier, she would have looked like a china doll, her perfect features permanently startled.

Laura was, now that I came to look at her properly, extremely beautiful. Her face had perfect symmetry, and she had a marvellous bone structure. These days, she always looked tired and harassed, but I wondered that I had never noticed, until this minute, just how attractive she was. I had known her for years, and I had simply never seen it. Perhaps I had been too busy looking at Tim.

"Do you seriously think," she said, "that I would do a thing like that, with two children to bring up?"

I felt well and truly told off.

"I'm sorry," I repeated. "It's just that, with all that's been going on, no one could have blamed you if you were tempted. And people sometimes . . . so I'm told . . . do it as a kind of cry for help. They don't really mean to kill themselves, they just want to . . ."

". . . draw attention to themselves?" she finished. "That's your considered opinion, is it?"

I was shocked by her sarcasm. Laura's mood swings were legendary, but I had never heard this kind of thing from her before. On the contrary, I had always thought that she valued my opinion.

"Listen, Olwen," she continued. "I won't say I'm not grateful to you for seeing to Robert, and I know you meant well when you came upstairs, but really . . . You're not a parent yourself, nor ever likely to be. How can you possibly know what a mother feels?"

"I . . ."

"Tim thinks a lot of you," she went on. "He's a man, he admires you because you've made your own way in the world, but he doesn't see how much *easier* it is for someone like you, with no one dependent on you. I appreciate everything you've done for us, all the support and so on, but there are things you don't understand about a married couple. You can't possibly know what it's like to have children to care for."

Hearing the truth, so baldly spoken, I was cut to the quick. I said nothing, just looked down at the table. It was turning misty in front of my eyes.

"I'm sorry I interfered," I said, getting up quickly. "I'll bring Robert back later."

I cried all the way home. Part of it was pain and anger, brought on by Laura's outburst. How long had she been thinking those things about me? If she had been a hundred per cent, she never would have said them. She would just have gone on thinking them, which would have been worse. At least now I knew what she thought, what the pair of them thought. Tim must have felt much the same. Although she had said he admired me, I sensed that the matter must have been discussed between them, more than once, with Tim standing up half-heartedly for me and Laura pointing out all my weaknesses. God knows, there were enough of them.

When I got back to the house, I went straight upstairs, asking Jessica to take Robert back to the vicarage at half past three. I lay down on the bed, staring at the ceiling, still blinking back the tears. In half an hour, I had gone from being a strong, sassy woman, who had no time for wimps like Laura, to a pathetic middle-aged spinster who could understand neither children nor their mothers and really had very little to live for.

I heard Jessica go out, and some time later I heard her come back. Presumably, she had been passing the time of day with Laura. I hoped she hadn't any inkling that we had quarrelled. After another half hour or so, she started on the tea, clanking a few pans and dishes around in the kitchen; then she called up the stairs to me.

"Auntie Olwen? Is an omelette all right? I thought you'd want something quick, if you're going out tonight."

There was a pause.

"What are you doing up there? Are you all right?"

I emerged from my room. The tears had dried up, and I suddenly felt hungry, recalling that I hadn't got round to having lunch before I went out to fetch Robert.

"What was that, about going out?"

"You are, aren't you? Isn't it that poetry reading?"

In all the excitement, I had totally forgotten about the event Elvis had organised, not to mention that fact that it was scheduled for that very evening. Had it been any further afield than the church hall, I would certainly have cried off, but it wasn't often I got a chance to attend a cultural event so close to home, and my non-attendance would definitely be noticed.

Jessica refused to change her mind about coming. I had to admit to myself that I wanted her with me only for moral support. The Sutcliffs would probably both be there, and I didn't think I could face either of them at this moment. At least Elvis would be on hand.

Having taken the trouble to have a shower and change into a skirt and blouse, I began to feel more human again. By the time I had eaten Jessica's (unexpectedly fluffy) omelette, I was almost looking forward to an evening out. It would help to take my mind off things – and there was no shortage of things I needed to forget about.

The first person I saw when I walked into the church hall was Laura. She avoided my eyes, and turned to talk to Mrs Bevan, the woman she disliked so intensely but whose company was still, apparently, preferable to mine. Luckily, there were no spare seats close to them. Elvis caught my eye next, but he was engaged in an animated dialogue with a young man who, I guessed, was The Poet. The chairs had been arranged in a kind of horseshoe. I found a seat next to Mr and Mrs Samuel, and sat uncomfortably, waiting for them to notice me and include me in their conversation.

At last, there was a general quietening down, and Elvis and The Poet moved to the centre of the room. Elvis gave a brief introduction, and then sat down, too far away for me to attract his attention.

The Poet was in his mid-twenties, and a bit of a looker. He had wavy black hair, and the kind of blue twinkly eyes that get women going. Girls, I should say. He was far too young for me. It occurred to me that Jessica would be very disappointed when I told her what she had missed.

His poems were another matter. Some showed flashes of insight, others were trite and clichéd, but all of them were in the so-called "free verse" that lazy people prefer to employ when indulging in "creative writing". That's fine for schoolchildren, but at his age he might have been expected to have picked up a few tricks of the trade. A spot of alliteration, or a few well-placed metaphors, wouldn't have come amiss.

He talked, between readings, about the contemporary poetry "scene", in which, by all accounts, he was a prime mover. Being a local boy, he had cashed in on every grant and award available from the Welsh Arts Council, Welsh Books Council, Academi Gymreig and goodness knows what other official body with money to chuck around. You had to hand it to him, he might not be able to write good poetry but he was no slouch at publicising himself.

Good luck to him, I thought grudgingly. When he called for questions at the end, I was tempted to throw in a few spicy comments designed to show up his ignorance of real literature, but I restrained myself. After all, wouldn't that merely have shown *me* up as exactly the kind of self-important meddling bitch that Laura Sutcliff had accused me of being?

I contented myself with asking The Poet whether he would agree that there had been a major resurgence in the popularity of poetry in the past ten years. Mr Samuel, seated alongside me, looked at me approvingly and muttered something to his wife. No doubt they were impressed by my eloquence. In reality, I was once again trying to make myself look more important than I was. I doubted that Laura Sutcliff was impressed. She had seen through me, to the lonely, unworldly person underneath the varnish.

The evening had, at least, had the effect of giving me something other than myself to concentrate on. Lousy as the poems were, I had been temporarily carried away by The Poet's rendition of them, gazing at his blue, blue eyes and crisp black hair. While he was framing his reply to my question, I found myself thinking that he reminded me a little of Charles Cornwell.

Ridiculous, I realised, even before the thought had time to register. Apart from the twenty years' age difference, he was really nothing like Charles. The problem was that everybody and everything now reminded me of Charles Cornwell. It's one of the best-known symptoms of being in love. For pity's sake, I had only spoken to the man about four times! If I was going to go all gooey over him on such short acquaintance, what would it be like when I'd known him for six months?

But that, I reasoned, was an even more foolish thought. In six months' time, Charles Cornwell would no longer be around. He wouldn't even remember my name.

Chapter 12

Following the poetry reading, there was sherry and mince pies in the church hall, handed around by the "members" of the non-existent Cultural Society.

"Where did these come from?" I asked Elvis as he approached me, plate in hand.

"Sainsbury's," he replied. "We warmed them up in the micro-wave. Have a drink!"

Mindful of that afternoon's events, I declined. Elvis went away, looking slightly offended. I felt guilty, but I would have felt worse if I'd broken my resolution to pass a whole day without the assistance of alcohol. Whatever else I might be, I was determined that I wasn't going to turn into a lush, like Laura Sutcliff.

Who happened to be standing at my elbow.

"Hello, Olwen," she said, an artificial smile pasted onto her face. "How did you enjoy the reading?"

"It was . . . interesting," I said. "And you?"

Tim, I noticed, was not with her. He had probably taken advantage of the need for someone to look after the children this evening.

"I thought it was remarkable," she replied. "It must be wonderful to have that kind of talent."

"Mmm." I realised that Laura, in common with half the women in the room, had spent more time looking at The Poet's face than listening to his mediocre verse.

"Olwen . . ." I knew, from her tone of voice, roughly what she was about to say. "I'm sorry about all that earlier. I wasn't myself. It was very kind of you to go and rescue Robert, and I really am grateful. Tim and I, we're both very grateful for everything you've done."

"I've done nothing," I cut in.

"Yes, you have, you've been wonderful. I don't know what you must think of me. You probably think I'm an unfit mother."

"Of course I don't." And it was true, I didn't. If nothing else, Laura was an extremely capable mother. I was the one who wasn't fit to be a mother, or a wife, or anything else requiring womanliness.

We seemed to have patched up our quarrel. Laura, as I now realised, was feeling at least as bad about it as I was, probably cursing herself for opening her big mouth, even though she had spoken the truth. As for me, I wasn't going to forget what had been said overnight, but in time it would cease to matter. I would try, I really would try, to turn over a new leaf. I would start by believing Tim when he said he hadn't done anything to deserve the accusations made against him by Craig Dutton.

Next day, I was in a more sturdy frame of mind. There was nothing left that could go wrong, or so it seemed. I didn't spend the whole morning looking out of the window for Charles Cornwell. I got down to some real work.

The sight of the hearse had reminded me that I was due to make my final trip to Limeslade, to pick up the remainder of Mrs Robarts' father's book collection. I always felt guilty when I was called on to carry out this kind of task. Tim had once told me, when I voiced this feeling to him, that I should consider myself fortunate to have this opportunity of helping the bereaved family.

It was true that, on more than one occasion, I had gone away empty-handed after giving the family free advice on how to dispose of the books – either because they weren't worth anything, or because they were too valuable for me to assess properly. In the latter case, I might get something out of it by passing on the details to a contact in the trade, who would return the favour at a later date. In the former case, all I got was a warm feeling.

When I got to the little house overlooking the bay, only Mr Robarts was there. His wife had gone to visit some other family member, and he'd been left behind to supervise me and help with the heavy lifting. A box of books can present a problem to someone my size; I often find myself having to kick-slide the box along the floor, or even empty it a few books at a time and re-pack it later.

"I'm not sure I'm going to get all these in the back of the van," I said, surveying the pile of boxes in the middle of the now bare living room floor. "I must have underestimated the amount."

"No," he explained. "We found a few more things in the attic. Nothing about the Second World War, just a few dusty old odds and ends, but we thought you might as well have them. You never know . . ."

I nodded, trying to look grateful. I could just imagine the kind of stuff he meant. Sorting it out would make another nice little job for Jess.

I did manage to get everything in the van, just. A couple of the smaller boxes had to go on the passenger seat. Not a very secure position; I would have to drive slowly to make sure they didn't fall through the windscreen when I stopped at traffic lights. I took a last look around me before shaking hands with Mr Robarts and saying goodbye. Limeslade still looked grey. Just as well, really. It wouldn't have done for the weather to perk up just as Mrs Robarts' poor old dad was taking his leave of the place.

I had already come to feel quite close to the old man. Through his books, he was almost more real to me than his daughter and son-in-law. What a shame that the collection he'd accumulated over the years had to be broken up like this. On the other hand, at least I could be fairly confident that such specialised books would go to people who were genuinely interested in them and would use them and refer to them. I had been surprised that Val Robarts – or at any rate, her husband – hadn't wanted to keep anything for sentimental reasons. Presumably they weren't great readers. Some people aren't.

I was back home by midday. After lunch, I walked over to the vicarage, to do my duty by Tim and Laura.

This time, it was Tim who came to the door. "Laura's nipped out for a bit of shopping, Olwen, but I'm glad you called. Come in and hear the latest."

I entered the kitchen to discover that we weren't alone. Elvis was sitting at the scrubbed wooden table. He grinned sheepishly.

"Shwmae, Olwen, cariad."

Something told me Elvis was here with a purpose, probably to find out what was going on in the matter of Craig Dutton. From Tim's greeting, it sounded as if there had been a development. It was possible that Tim had asked Elvis over specially, to hear about it. If that was the case, I felt rather hurt that I hadn't been invited along as well. Then I remembered that Elvis was the church organist and choirmaster, whereas I was only . . . me.

"You may as well know, Olwen. Dr Dutton's been on the phone to me again. He says he doesn't think he can allow Craig to give evidence against me in court. He says it would be too distressing to the family."

I sat down slowly, steadying myself with a hand on the edge of the table.

"Does that mean it's all over?"

"Oh no, not by a long chalk! I've been talking to Charles Cornwell this morning. The law protects children in cases like this. Charles says there are all kinds of ways round it. Video evidence, and so on. He's consulted Aubrey Bantoft, and Aubrey doesn't think we've heard the last of it. If the powers-that-be think there's something in it, they'll press the Duttons to let Craig's interview with the social worker be used as evidence. I'm not sure that the parents have the final say in the matter, anyway."

The mention of Charles's name had startled me. It must have been a busy morning for him. Aubrey Bantoft's name also started to have a resonance in my mind. Mr Bantoft was, if I hadn't lost my powers of observation, a man who was familiar with the ways of other men. He might have some personal reason for taking an interest in a case like this. He might be popular with the local gay community as a legal representative because he understood them, and there would obviously be times when someone was, rightly or wrongly, accused of indecent assault and needed to avail himself of Bantoft's services.

It crossed my mind to ask Tim how he had first come by Charles Cornwell as his solicitor. It might be pure coincidence, but it seemed fortunate that he had become the client of a firm with one partner who was expert in such matters. That was as far as I took that line of thought, for the moment.

The three of us chatted for a while, about life in general. Elvis was optimistic about Tim's chances of being completely vindicated as a result of Dr Dutton's reluctance to let Craig give evidence. The boy, he thought, would be petrified at the thought of repeating his story in public. Whatever his motives for making up the tale of the assault, he must have thought better of it, and would probably make a poor showing in front of a court hearing, either in person or on video.

In that case, Tim argued, why had the police ever taken the complaint seriously? They had already heard what Craig had to say, weeks ago. If there had been some cause for believing his version of events then, why would they let it go now?

Perhaps, Elvis said, the police hadn't heard Craig's account at first hand. Perhaps they had only had it relayed to them by Craig's father and mother, or perhaps the parents had always been there, prompting him, when he told the story previously. Now that he knew he would be on his own, talking to a social worker or, worse, a judge, he might be panicking about it. Elvis knew Craig, he reminded us, and the boy wasn't an out-and-out bad 'un. Elvis had always wondered how he intended to carry it off, when it came to the crunch.

I found myself wondering what Tim meant when he referred to "Craig's version of events". Tim had always said, up to now, that he had no idea what Craig was talking about when he told the story of the assault. Although Tim must, of necessity, know more than he was saying, he had assured everyone that he recalled no incident of the sort Craig was describing and had no idea what had sparked off the accusation. But that was back in the time before Elvis had found out the full details from Dr Dutton and relayed them to Tim. Presumably Tim had remembered something now.

At last, Elvis got up to go. I made no move to accompany him, though he had clearly been expecting me to. He raised an eyebrow when I stayed put, sitting at the table, and I thought he was about to change his mind about leaving. Then he moved towards the door, with one last look at me and a "See you, Olwen".

Tim offered to make a fresh cup of tea, then came and sat back down with me. The questions were buzzing in my head.

"You're lucky to have someone like Ch – like Mr Cornwell as a solicitor."

He gave me a look I found impossible to interpret. "Yes, I suppose I am. He seems to know what he's doing."

"How did you find him?"

Tim smiled slightly. "Through Alan Samuel, actually. Apparently they were at school together."

I was incredulous. "Mr Samuel and Charles Cornwell? Good grief! I had Mr Cornwell down as a public schoolboy."

He laughed at the idea. "Oh no. Bishop Gore, I believe. Alan's a few years older than Charles, of course."

I felt the need for a change of subject, and began to explore the concerns which had occurred to me earlier.

"Tim, I hope you don't mind if I ask, but have you remembered anything more about what happened with Craig?"

"What happened with Craig? Nothing happened with Craig!" He was on the defensive.

"No, I know that. I don't mean that." I felt very tactless, not to mention very silly. "It's just that earlier on you said 'Craig's version of events'. That sounded as though you had a version of events of your own."

"Well, I do. Nothing happened."

"Nothing that Craig could have misinterpreted?"

"Nothing at all."

I was reluctant to mention the "hand in the pocket" story, for two reasons. Firstly, I still wasn't sure I was supposed to know about it. Secondly, I was just too embarrassed.

If I was embarrassed, how much worse must it have been for Tim. There were two spots of high colour in his cheeks. He sighed, and leaned forward over the table. "Olwen, you do believe in my innocence, don't you?"

"Yes, Tim, I do. There's no doubt in my mind." I felt obliged to say it, even if it wasn't the gospel truth. I owed Tim that much. It wasn't exactly a lie, either. My doubts were not about Tim's basic innocence. They were about whether he was telling me everything. And after all, why should I expect him to? It wasn't as if I was his wife.

"I heard . . ." I continued. Tim frowned. It wouldn't be wise to let him know where I'd heard it. "Someone said that Craig is claiming the assault happened after the charity concert, in September. Is that right?"

"That's what Craig has apparently said, yes."

"But you still can't remember any incident, anything that might have made Craig think that you meant him some . . . harm?"

Tim shook his head, without meeting my eyes.

"The thing that confuses me, Tim, is that you don't seem to be ready to condemn Craig as a liar."

He got up from the table. The tea had been given ample time to brew. He swilled out our mugs under the tap, before re-using them. He got the milk out of the fridge, and replenished the sugar bowl from a packet in the wall cupboard. The whole process took several minutes. I deliberately said nothing in the intervening period. It would have seemed too aggressive. I still hoped that he would tell me everything voluntarily, when he was ready.

Putting down a mug in front of me, he sat down again and resumed his previous position, leaning forward, elbows on the table. He spread out his hands in front of him, examining his fingernails which were, as always, clean and unbitten.

"I was at the concert, as you know," he said. There was no tremor in his voice, no sign of nervousness. "Afterwards we had that party. We called it a 'celebration'. Why does the church have to be so uptight about the idea of its members having a good time? Anyhow, we had the celebration. I was there, Craig was there, most of the choir were there, as I recollect. Even Craig's parents were there. They'd been to see the concert. You were there, weren't you?"

"Yes, I was."

"Then surely you must realise, there was no *opportunity* for me to do anything to Craig! How could I? And why would I? With my hand on my heart, Olwen, I swear to you that I did not harm that child in any way. Do you believe me?"

"Yes, Tim, I believe you!" I was angry with him, in a way, for testing me like this. I was also extremely relieved to hear him deny the charges in a way I found, finally and irrevocably, acceptable.

"Good." He forced a smile onto his face. "Now drink your tea, because I'm going to have to throw you out shortly. I've got a sermon to write, and it's going nowhere at the moment, with all the social calls I'm getting."

It wasn't like Tim to be sarcastic. I had pushed him close to the limit, I thought, or maybe Elvis had done the ground work before me and I had tipped him over the edge.

"I'm sure everything will be all right, Tim," I said, as I got up to go. "You don't deserve all this, but have faith that it will come right in the end. And you've got Mr Cornwell and Mr Bantoft to look after your interests. As you said, they seem to know what they're doing."

Again, this need to keep Charles Cornwell's name close to my lips. Tim glanced at me uncomfortably.

"About Charles Cornwell, Olwen . . ."

"Yes?" I turned sharply, thinking I could guess roughly what he was going to say. But I hadn't, as it turned out, the slightest idea.

"He told me he's ordered a book from you."

I smiled dreamily. "Actually, he bought one book, and he's ordered another. He's called several times."

"Yes. I'm sure he thinks highly of you. He seems a nice enough person, but . . . you do know about him, don't you?"

My smile departed abruptly. "Know what?"

"That he's homosexual."

Chapter 13

When Tim went into more detail, it seemed obvious. Not that he did go into much detail, he merely pointed out the significance of Charles Cornwell and Aubrey Bantoft being *partners*. I was holding onto the door frame, to prevent myself collapsing, as he revealed that they shared the same home address. He didn't say how he knew this, but I knew Tim well enough to know that he hadn't invented it.

"I thought you ought to know, Olwen. I was afraid you might get fond of him, and be disappointed when you found out."

Those were his last words, as he shut the door and I literally staggered down the path.

I had always thought I was pretty broad-minded about homosexuality. I'd met gay couples, occasionally, both male and female. Admittedly, it generally had to be spelled out to me before I noticed anything unusual about them; but once I did know, it took little effort on my part to treat them exactly the same as any other couple. So why did I feel like this about two consenting adults engaging in a private act that, though it diverged from the norm, was neither immoral nor illegal? Why did I suddenly feel like retching?

This was a horror beyond anything I had imagined Tim doing with Craig Dutton. In my worst nightmares, I had never been able to conceive of any physical discomfort being inflicted on Craig by such a gentle man as Tim. Child abuse should have been a far more revolting prospect. Yet it was my present mental picture of two grown men indulging in a sexual act with one another which filled me with an inexplicable disgust, even though compulsion of the weaker by the stronger had no place in this scenario.

My instincts took me into the church. Feeling the need for the closest possible contact with my Maker, I went right down to the front pew, and got on my knees.

"Oh God," I said out loud, "let it not be true! Please!"

It was several moments before I realised that I was not alone in the building. The other occupant was, I hoped, not close enough to have heard exactly what I had said, but I could clearly hear her footsteps at the back of the nave. It was a she; I could tell by the click of high heels. Even Aubrey Bantoft wouldn't have gone out in shoes that made that sound.

"Who's that? Oh, it's you, Miss Harris." The voice was unmistakable. I got to my feet.

"Hello, Mrs Bevan."

She approached, looking confused.

"Did you call me?"

"No, I didn't. I'm sorry if I disturbed you. I was praying."

"Oh." She looked taken aback, as though a church were the last place in the world she would have expected to find someone praying. If I was praying for anything at that moment, it was that she wouldn't ask any more questions.

I was to be disappointed.

"Is anything wrong, my dear?"

Mrs Bevan did, occasionally, call people "my dear", but she had never tried it on with me before. I was Miss Harris, a capable self-employed woman of a certain age, and she sensed that it wouldn't go down well. I was forced to believe that her decision to resort to the epithet at this stage was an indication of her sincerity in wishing to be of assistance.

Adversity has different effects on different people, and Mrs Bevan seemed to be one of those women who, having kept their compassionate side firmly suppressed for donkey's years, suddenly burst out into universal fellow feeling as a result of a single, earth-shattering event. And what could be more earth-shattering, for a woman like Mrs Bevan, than the news that her vicar was being accused of the ultimate in worldly sin?

"N-Nothing really, Mrs Bevan. I just had a bit of bad news, that's all." What caused me to reveal this much to her, I'll never know. I suppose she was simply in the right place at the right time.

"Ah." She was peering into my face, from a height of course, as though trying to tell my fortune from the bumps on my forehead without feeling them.

"The f-flowers are looking lovely," I remarked, hoping that she would go along with the change of subject. "I was admiring the poinsettias last Sunday."

"Gorrrr-geous, aren't they?" She and Aubrey Bantoft would have made a good pair, I thought, had he been so inclined.

"Would you like to come through to the vestry and have a cup of tea with me?" she asked suddenly.

It couldn't have been more unexpected. Perhaps that was what made me accept the invitation, from a woman I'd always detested. It was no more than fifteen minutes since I'd looked into the dregs of my last cup of tea, yet already the idea of a second cup appealed to me. A third cup, actually, as I'd had two with Tim.

The vestry was small, but it had been thoughtfully modernised and equipped with the basics. The electric kettle had originally belonged to Elvis. He had imported it into the church so that he could brew up between rehearsals, but it was used by all and sundry these days. For the flower-arrangers, it was a particular boon, because some of them lived quite a distance away, and at certain times of year – Harvest and the spring flower festival, for example – the arranging of flowers could be a time-consuming activity.

Mrs Bevan, as supervisor of flower-arranging duties, had taken it upon herself to make sure that everyone who used the church in what she would have called "an official capacity" should be well looked after. This included drinking out of proper china cups, with a teapot she had brought from home and a sugar bowl that she kept in a cupboard, neatly protected by clingfilm. There was even a milk jug, though it rarely came out of its hiding place because of the inconvenience of having to empty and wash it after every use.

When there were lots of people wanting refreshment, on an occasion such as a coffee morning or a bring-and-buy sale (or a poetry reading), then the church hall, just up the lane, came into its own; but for a one-off cup of tea, the vestry was the thing. It was also the ideal setting for a confidential chat, which I sensed was what Mrs Bevan and I were about to have.

Like Tim, she took her time about making the tea. I was fascinated by the care she took over the task. Even though she was using teabags, she was meticulous about warming the pot, stirring and leaving it to brew. Then out came the china cups, the sugar bowl, and a packet of custard creams.

"I think I know what's upsetting you," she said, in a voice which, if not exactly quiet, was much reduced in volume from her usual. "It's all this business with the Vicar, isn't it? You were praying for him, weren't you?"

Unable to make up my mind whether to tell a lie or lay myself open to a full-scale interrogation, I stuffed a custard cream into my mouth and cast my eyes modestly downwards.

"You must remember," she continued, almost whispering now, "that God" – she paused mid-sentence and pointed her index finger upwards – "sees everything. He knows the innocent from the guilty, and He will see justice done. Remember what it says in the Bible – 'Blessed art thou when men bear false witness against you for my sake'." I felt sure she was getting her traditional and modern translations mixed up; but I had to admit that she had a point. If that had been the only thing that was troubling me, her words might have been some comfort.

The tea was ready at last, and she was pouring it.

"How do you like your tea, my dear?"

"As it comes," I muttered, through another mouthful of biscuit. Food can be a great source of consolation at times like those.

She began to talk again as she handed me the tea and watched me drink it. No doubt she was convinced that she had rendered a great service to humanity by rescuing me from my lonely act of devotion, and I saw no reason to disabuse her. Perhaps she was even right, because I was beginning to feel better. It had little to do with what she was saying, and a lot to do with the feeling that someone cared enough to want to help me. If she had known what I was really thinking about, how shocked she would have been!

Charles Cornwell and Aubrey Bantoft. Surely not. In my mind, I tried to picture them in bed together, but it was hopeless. I couldn't get as far as imagining Aubrey without his clothes. Had I been able to see them in one another's company, I reasoned, that might have succeeded in putting me off Charles for good. For the moment, all that was happening was that I felt slightly ill.

". . . and I *believe* that it will all come right in the end." Mrs Bevan placed considerable emphasis on the word, "believe", as though to imbue it with some special power that would succeed where all else failed. Perhaps she was right about that too. Her faith was strong, stronger than mine. She could go on loving and believing and trusting through thick and thin. I had loved two men recently. One of them deserved my trust, and hadn't been getting it. The other had never deserved it in the first place.

"Do you feel better now, my dear?" asked Mrs Bevan.

"Yes, thank you."

"And you do have faith, that the truth will come out and the Vicar will be vindicated?"

"Yes, I believe that."

"And is that all that was troubling you?"

She wasn't going to leave it there, I realised. She had seen through me, after all. I hadn't given her enough credit for perceptiveness.

"No," I admitted. "There are other things."

"Oh." She may, or may not, have been surprised; I found it impossible to tell. "Perhaps you'd like to talk about it." There was a certain reluctance in her manner, almost as if she lacked confidence in her ability to deal with the kind of troubles someone like me might turn out to have.

"I'd rather not go into any detail, if you don't mind," I said. "You might be offended by some of the things . . ."

"Oh, my dear, don't worry about that!" Her vehemence took me aback. "You'd be amazed how unshockable I am." This statement was followed by an uncharacteristic hesitation. "I suppose it's something to do with a man. Am I right? No, don't answer that. But I can assure you, I know all about men, and they are rarely worth upsetting oneself over. I cried many a tear over my late husband."

I knew nothing about the late Mr Bevan except that he had been dead for years.

"It must have been terrible for you," I ventured, "when he died."

"Oh, my dear, I'm not talking about when he died! I mean, when he was alive! He led me a merry dance, I can tell you."

I tried, and failed, to picture Mrs Bevan doing a merry dance. Perhaps it was better not to know what she meant by that.

"Let me assure you," she continued, "that there is absolutely no point at all in crying over the opposite sex. They will go their own way in the end. Whatever your young man has been up to, I don't suppose he's any worse than the rest of them."

The description of Charles as a "young man" made me want to laugh, and I knew full well that Mrs Bevan would have found it perfectly possible to be shocked by what I had been told half an hour earlier. Yet there was something reassuring about her refusal to believe in the enormity of his betrayal.

When I had left her, with thanks that were for once sincere, and had begun the walk home, I made an effort to start thinking about Charles in a detached way. There were so many things to "get my head round", as Jessica would have put it.

Gay couples were not outside my experience. I tried to think of specific examples. There had been a lecturer at college, Giles Mulcahy. Giles had a live-in partner, called Sam, whose role was essentially that of a housewife.

Giles had also been a bit of a hunk. Girls newly arrived at the college immediately started to take an interest in him. (That included me, as I now recalled.) It was often a huge disappointment when they discovered the truth, usually from some world-weary second-year student. Undaunted, some of the girls – those not realistic enough to understand that a romance with a lecturer, even a straight one, was virtually a non-starter – would go on trying to attract Giles. Each believed she might be the one to "convert" him to heterosexuality. None of them got anywhere close.

Giles was living proof of the old adage that gay men are often very attractive to women. Look at all those actors and musicians. Rock Hudson, Rudolf Nureyev, Richard Chamberlain . . . It wasn't just his looks that made Giles so desirable, though. Gay men treat women like human beings. Instead of staring at our legs and trying to get their hands on our breasts, they exchange opinions with us and note our personalities.

That was how Charles had been treating me. From the beginning, he had seen that I was worth talking to, worth spending time with. The fact that he wanted to get to know me better didn't automatically mean that he wanted to leap into bed with me. He had thought enough of me to expect me to see that. That was the truth I had to face up to.

There wasn't such a difference between what was happening now with Charles and what had happened with Tim in years gone by. In both cases, I had wilfully misread the signs. In both cases, I was the one who had overstepped the mark of friendship, trying to turn it into something it had never been.

I was trying to put my finger on exactly what it was that bothered me about the idea of Charles being gay. What it came down to, as I was forced to admit in the end, was the feeling that I had made a fool of myself. Naturally, Charles would have assumed that I knew he was gay. He hadn't deliberately tried to lure me into a one-sided relationship in order to make a fool of me. I owed it to him to respond in kind, whatever my instinctive distaste for his private lifestyle.

Chapter 14

He might have been reading my mind again, because he turned up the following Monday.

I was prepared for him. In fact, I had thought about little else in the last forty-eight hours, ever since Tim's revelation. I had even been looking out for him. It was, after all, only to be expected that, once I had found a man I liked, who appeared to like me, once I had found out that the prospect of romance was beyond the realms of possibility, it would flaunt itself before my eyes until it had stretched my powers of tolerance to the absolute limit.

"I was on my way to the vicarage," was his opening line. That figured. He would hardly have gone out of his way to visit me.

"Come in," I mumbled, leaving him to find his own way through the front door as I turned my back.

This wasn't how I wanted it to be – me, grouchy and reluctant, allowing him to make himself pleasant in my living room because I didn't know how to deal with the problem of his sexuality. His bisexuality? I didn't want to look at him, but I couldn't help myself. Objectivity was what was required. I tried to cultivate it while I was making the coffee.

It was obvious that my grudging manner had put him on his guard. He may have thought I was simply in a bad mood, pre-menstrual or something. He may have thought I was still upset about the Sutcliff situation. He certainly couldn't have guessed that I knew his secret.

If it was true. From moment to moment, I would glance at him, hoping for some visual clue, but it failed to present itself. Sometimes, I thought I could see it, that side of him that showed itself in private to Aubrey Bantoft. His well-manicured finger-nails. The neat wave of his hair. The faint scent of expensive after-shave as he stooped to pull out the kitchen stool. At other times, it eluded me. He was entirely masculine in his way of sprawling over the stool, for example, his long legs splayed out for maximum comfort, with the minimum of consideration for anyone who might be trying to edge past him to get out the biscuit barrel.

"No, thank you." He smiled as he declined the offer of a ginger nut, and my heart turned over.

Charm, that was what Charles Cornwell had. Charming Charles. Charles the charming con man, deceiving me, leading me on to destruction.

I wanted to ask him why he was bothering. If he already had someone, there was no excuse for his pursuit of me, and it could hardly be denied that he was, completely and definitely, in pursuit. An exercise in charm, perhaps, to see if he could crack open the brittle shell of this reclusive, intellectual woman, prior to making use of her as a character witness for his client.

"I'm afraid the book hasn't come yet," I said. "It may not come till the end of the week, or even next week."

"That's all right," he replied. "I didn't come for that. I came to see *you*." That kind of blandishment was just crying out to be ignored.

The interest in books might have been genuine. The requirement for a special present for his sister-in-law might even have been genuine. His apparent preference for me could not, possibly, be genuine.

Even while I was telling myself all this, I was believing the opposite. Charles fancied me. I fancied him.

He might, conceivably, feel that a relationship with me was quite compatible with his long-term commitment to Aubrey. He had, I reminded myself, been married. He might have split up with Deirdre because she discovered his dark secret, or because he discovered it himself after years of unsuccessfully trying to form a heterosexual relationship. Deirdre might have decided she couldn't share him with Aubrey, and given him an ultimatum. Charles, despite his other leanings, might have wanted her to stay, but been unable to resist the pull of his charismatic partner.

No matter how I tried, I couldn't see it. Aubrey Bantoft was not, I felt from our brief acquaintance, a very exciting man.

"I met your partner the other day," I said, as I put down a coffee mug in front of Charles. It was mugs, not cups and saucers, today because I didn't feel like going to any trouble to impress him.

"Aubrey? He came over here to see Tim Sutcliff. What did you make of him?" He covered his mouth with the palm of his hand. Was it my imagination, or was he laughing at me?

"He seemed very interested in the church. The architecture, and so on."

"Ah, yes. Aubrey appreciates the finer things in life."

"Does that mean you're not interested in architecture?"

"Far from it. I suppose I should go and have a look around the church myself, one of these days. I don't suppose you'd like to escort me?"

He would never know how seriously tempted I was. I didn't reply, but sat down, taking my mug in both hands in an effort to keep it steady, and tried to use its warmth to stem the creeping coldness that seemed to fill me up every time I started to think about him with Aubrey Bantoft.

He was getting a little edgy now, I could tell. That was, I suppose, what I had wanted, but it seemed to bring me no satisfaction. Once again, I repented of my refusal to be charmed.

"Is there any more word about Tim's case?"

Charles sucked in his lips, doubtless wondering how much he was at liberty to tell a silly, susceptible woman such as myself.

"Not exactly," he said, studying the surface of the breakfast bar. "Things like this . . . I suppose it's difficult for people to understand, but it can take such a long time for anything decisive to happen. In the end, they tend to fizzle out for lack of evidence, or lack of will to pursue them. I'm hoping that's what will happen in this case but, in the meantime, there's a lot of suffering for those involved. My heart goes out to the Sutcliffs, but I can't allow it to cloud my judgement, or I won't be able to help them at all. And I do have other clients." He raised his eyes to my face. "I must sound very callous to you."

I had been thinking quite the opposite.

"No," I said baldly, getting up from my stool and pouring the remaining contents of my mug down the sink. It tasted all wrong. "Another coffee?"

"I haven't quite finished this one."

"No hurry." I turned my back to the draining board, and stood looking at him. If you'd asked me what I was thinking at that moment, I wouldn't have been able to say. My mind seemed to have gone blank.

Recognising my restlessness, Charles stood up, looking uncertain of his ground. "In fact, I suppose I ought to be getting along now."

There was a long pause, while he built up to it.

"I wondered if you'd like to come out for a drink with me, some time soon."

If he'd asked me a couple of days earlier, I would have jumped at the offer. Now I didn't know what to say.

Noticing my confusion, and apparently perplexed by it, he soldiered on. "Nothing formal," he protested. "Just a drink, that's all. Just to say thank you, for finding the book for me."

"That was business." I didn't like the way my voice sounded, but I seemed unable to soften the effect.

"Oh." He couldn't disguise his disappointment. "Would you rather I didn't mention it again?"

"Er . . ." I knew I had turned an unbecoming shade of pink, but I couldn't do anything about that either. "Look, Charles, please don't take this the wrong way, but I . . . I feel . . ."

"Don't try to explain," he interrupted. "All you have to say is that you don't want to go out with me. There's no need for excuses. I've been turned down more times than you've had hot dinners."

"No, it's not like that!" I blurted. "Don't misunderstand. I appreciate your asking me, honestly. It's just that . . . the time's not right."

He regarded me with gravity.

"Does that mean I can ask again, another time?" he said, after a minute.

"Yes." I was being weak. Even my voice sounded weak. But I couldn't bring myself to say no.

He looked at me strangely. "Are you all right?" he asked. "Is there something troubling you? Other than being importuned by a balding, middle-aged man, I mean?"

"You're not balding!" I protested.

"Oh, thank you!" He put one hand up to his head and ran it forward. The smile cracked into his face. "I must remember to tell the hairdresser that, next time he comments on my bald spot."

"I hadn't noticed one, anyway," I said.

After all, why should I have? I had never run my fingers through his hair.

I was thankful that Jessica hadn't been in the house when Charles called. She would have found it difficult to understand my frosty reception of a man I had been praising to the skies. In some ways, though, I would have liked her to meet him. Jessica, even at her tender age, was no pushover when it came to seeing through people, and I valued her opinions.

She returned later, from an afternoon with a friend in Swansea, shopping again. This time she had actually bought something. She showed it to me.

I suppose you could have described it as a dress, except that the amount of material in it was less than I would have required for an apron.

"Very nice," I muttered through clenched teeth, wishing that I had the kind of curveless figure essential to show it off to best advantage.

"Are you in a mood?" she asked, as she put it back in the bag to take upstairs.

"Sorry. I'm not feeling very well."

"Is it that time of the month? You should go and lie down for a while. Shall I get you a hot water bottle?"

I declined the offer of a hot water bottle, but agreed that an hour or so in bed might be a good idea. There was no possibility of going to sleep. I merely lay there, brooding over Charles's most recent visit, wishing I had been nicer to him, and silently crying.

Chapter 15

In an effort to forget Charles, I started thinking about Tim again. The Sutcliffs' problems had always been there, at the back of my mind, however much the exhilaration of meeting Charles had threatened to take over. I wanted to believe that I was cool in the face of this new disaster (if that was what it was), and still capable of logical thinking. Lateral thinking would be more accurate. I had come up with a new theory.

Taking it as read that Tim was innocent of any offence against Craig Dutton, I went on to consider what might have led Craig to concoct such a story. If it were true that Tim recalled no real-life incident that resembled the scenario Craig had described, we needed to look for an explanation outside the context of Tim's acquaintance with the boy. Then it came to me.

Supposing that Craig was telling the truth about what had happened, but the adult in question hadn't been Tim?

At first it seemed an outlandish idea, but the more I thought about it, the more plausible it began to look. Another person, another adult, presumably male, had made Craig do whatever it was he had done. Another man had paid Craig for his services.

Then why accuse Tim? I could think of answers to that one, too. Craig wanted to spill the beans, simply because the memory of his experience was gnawing away at him. He felt dirty and defiled, he felt he had done something wrong. However, he didn't dare point the finger at the man who was really responsible for his shame, either because he was afraid or because it was someone close to him. His father?

There was a sick-making thought. Having seen Dr Dutton in person, I couldn't bring myself to believe it. The man looked absolutely normal. More than that, he looked like a father, and fathers don't do things like that to their own sons. Besides which, if Craig's father himself had been responsible, Craig would never have gone public as he had, and Dr Dutton would have done all he could to sweep it under the carpet rather than going to the police.

Some other male relation, then. Some friend of the family, or someone in a position of authority. A babysitter? A teacher? It had been a teacher to whom Craig had first told the story.

A name came into my mind. I didn't want to hear it, but once it was in there, it wouldn't go away. The name was Elvis Jones.

Not Elvis. No, not Elvis. Elvis wasn't capable of a terrible thing like that. It was Elvis who had gone to the trouble of finding out the whole story from Dr Dutton, simply in order to help Tim formulate his defence. Ah yes, but isn't that precisely what someone would do, in those circumstances? If Elvis were the culprit, he would have acted nonchalantly, as if the whole thing didn't concern him directly. At the same time, he might have felt some guilt, at the idea of Tim being accused in his place. He might have felt obliged to stand up for Tim, to help him defend himself, as long as it didn't mean making a confession of his own.

Of course it wasn't Elvis. These niggling doubts were unbearable. Was there no friend I wasn't prepared to think badly of, no one I trusted without reservation? These past few weeks had been a nightmarish reminder of my own frailty. I hated myself.

My mind automatically switched tracks. Charles Cornwell. That was a different kettle of fish altogether. Charles had never told me he wasn't gay, so he couldn't be blamed if he was. All he had done was to extend the hand of friendship to a lonely woman. He had offered me social activity: "Nothing formal, just a drink." He hadn't even pretended that there was any more to it than that. Men of that sort, as I've observed, appreciate female company, for all the best reasons. There was no reason for me to feel insulted at the idea of being asked out by a gay man.

I dragged my thoughts back to the Sutcliff situation. It wouldn't be long before I had a chance to test out my new theory on Elvis. There hadn't been a Welsh class for weeks, partly as a result of Tim's troubles and partly because of the run-up to Christmas, but I always knew where to find Elvis on a Thursday evening.

"D'you fancy coming to the pub?" I asked Jessica. Considering she was supposed to be my Christmas assistant, she hadn't spent much time in the house lately. She kept borrowing the van and going off to Swansea and Llanelli to see friends. Now she looked up from her magazine with a brightness in her eyes.

"Okay, then!"

It must have been so unusual for unadventurous old Auntie Olwen to want to leave the house at night (I'm not counting the poetry reading, which Jessica wouldn't have regarded as a social activity) that she couldn't resist the opportunity to come with me – if only to keep an eye on me and make sure I didn't get into any trouble.

The Drovers' Arms never got very busy on a weekday evening, not in the winter. Summer was a different thing, when the caravan sites opened up and their residents went out looking for atmospheric village pubs to drink in. The Drovers' wasn't exactly picturesque, but all the nicer pubs were full to bursting.

In winter, there would often be no one in the bar at all. That was one reason why the landlord had been so willing for Elvis to take over a corner for his Thursday Welsh classes. It beat me why they didn't do something to improve the interior, which was shabby, to put it mildly – lino on the floor and nothing much on the walls. No wonder there were rumours about the pub being taken over by one of the big chains. Although it was coming up to Christmas, there wasn't much doing tonight. A few extra people, perhaps, visitors down for the holidays, but still fairly quiet.

"Shwmae!" exclaimed Elvis as we walked in. "Sut wyt ti heddiw?"

"Sut mae, Elvis," I replied, leaving Jessica to find us a seat in his vicinity, while I went up to the bar.

In common with most European languages, Welsh has two distinct forms for the second person of the verb, one familiar (in Welsh, "ti", the form Elvis had just used) and the other formal (in Welsh, "chi"). You have to know someone well before you start calling them "ti". I reflected that, had Charles been a Welsh speaker, I wouldn't have been sure which form to use. It's one of the few areas where English scores over other languages. "You" took over from "thou" centuries ago, thank goodness.

By the time I got to the table with our drinks, Elvis and Jessica were all over one another, figuratively speaking. He was teaching her Welsh phrases, and she was repeating them loudly, rolling her 'r's with rrrelish. You'd never have known she was completely sober.

"Move over." I nudged her little bottom along the seat, so that I could get near enough to talk to Elvis myself, but it was in vain. I should have realised what a mistake it had been, bringing her with me. We would never get onto the subject of the Sutcliff situation now.

My luck was in, however. After half an hour or so, in walked God's gift to women. I'd seen him before. He drove around the village in a van with his name on, but I couldn't remember it. He was a plumber or an electrician, something of that ilk. He was about twenty-five, and even I had to admit he was good-looking.

For a man who fancies himself as much as this one did, he wasn't good at playing hard to get. He took one look at Jessica and . . . took a second look.

"Hiya, Phil!" shouted Elvis, who wasn't slow on the uptake.

"Elvis," said Phil, approaching our table. "How's it going?" He may have been speaking to Elvis, but he wasn't looking at him.

"You know Olwen," said Elvis, "and this is her niece, Jessica. She's down for the Christmas holidays."

"Hello," said the tongue-tied Phil. "Can I get you ladies a drink?"

"Not for me, thanks," I said.

"Thanks, I'll have a Campari and soda," said Jess.

That did it. Sophisticated, or what? The bloke couldn't get back from the bar fast enough, and within minutes he and Jessica were locked in conversation. I wasn't sure whether she was doing it out of consideration for me, because she had (at last) sensed that I wanted to talk to Elvis, or whether she really liked the look of young Phil. Whichever it was, she seemed prepared to continue with the exercise for the rest of the evening. By the time I suggested to Elvis, well before closing time, that he and I go back to my house for a final drink and a private chat, I felt as if *I* was doing *her* a favour.

Over a glass of scotch (for him) and a gin and tonic (for me), I revealed the full intricacies of my latest theory. All, that is, except the bit about Elvis himself being a candidate for the role of the Other Man.

As I talked, he nodded and looked interested. He agreed that there might be something in it. He seemed surprised he hadn't thought of it for himself.

"You see," I expounded, "it's always seemed strange to me that he should have picked on someone like Tim, someone who's so completely beyond the realms of possibility."

"That's the funny thing, you know," agreed Elvis. "Now if Craig had accused *me*, well, that wouldn't have come as quite so much of a shock to everybody."

I had always wondered about Elvis. It wasn't so much that he was effeminate (though I'd heard many ignorant people describe him in that way) as that he seemed somehow sexless. After all, he wasn't much younger than Charles, and he had never married. I realise that doesn't prove a thing, but I had never seen Elvis out with a woman. A single woman, that is. When he came to social events, it was always in a group. The females in the congregation of St Mary's treated him like a kind of pet. Elvis was their tame man, the one who was always available when a male escort was required, but who was quite safe to be with. Their husbands had no reservations about letting them out in his company.

Now that he seemed to be prepared to be open about it, he was presenting me with a good opportunity to pick his brains about that other matter that had been troubling me.

"Elvis," I began. "How easy is it for a man to tell if another man is gay?"

He frowned. "As easy as it is for a woman to tell, I suppose." He thought I was talking about his own case.

"Easier, I would have thought, surely? I mean . . . You know Charles Cornwell?"

"Yeah?" His puzzlement was, if anything, increasing.

"Would you say he was . . . you know?" It was so difficult to find the right words. The last thing I wanted to do was to offend Elvis. He was such a sweet old thing.

"You think Charles Cornwell is gay?" He sounded incredulous. "Isn't he one of your admirers?"

"You make it sound as if there were dozens of them lining up at my door!"

"Don't put yourself down, Olwen. You're an attractive woman. If I was that way disposed myself, you'd be well up my list of desirables, I can assure you." His forthrightness took me by surprise. Evidently, now that he had bitten the bullet, he no longer felt any need to hold back.

"But Charles Cornwell?" he continued. "I don't understand what makes you think that."

"Someone told me."

"Really?" Elvis considered the matter for a moment. "I can't be certain. Of course, it's always possible that he swings both ways. But I wouldn't have thought so. Who told you?"

I hesitated. "I'd rather not say."

Elvis whistled under his breath. "All I can say is, if he is one, he's doing a pretty good job of hiding it. He's never made a pass at *me*, anyway." He grinned, then, seeing my face, wiped the smile away.

"Olwen," he said, "there are different types of gay men, just as there are different types of straight men. Some are open about their sexuality, some are just undecided. The ones who are out-and-out gay tend to send out certain messages, but there's no hard and fast rule. There are places you can go, in Swansea. I've frequented some of them myself in the past, but not since I took up the choir. It's too risky. My music is what's most important to me, you know that. Everything else, including you-know-what, just pales into insignificance.

"I can honestly say that I'd never set eyes on Charles Cornwell before this thing with Tim happened. He doesn't move in gay circles. If he's that way disposed, he must be the kind who deliberately conceals it. That's not uncommon, especially with professional men. But the thing that argues otherwise is . . . If he was so concerned about his reputation, why would he hang out with a screaming woofter like Aubrey Bantoft?"

It struck me as strange that a man who had just admitted to being gay could talk so contemptuously about another gay man. It was as though Elvis regarded himself as outside the norm – if there is a norm – and therefore not subject to that kind of criticism himself. Or perhaps he was getting in first.

"Did you know Aubrey Bantoft before?" I asked.

"Oh, yeah, of course! Known him for years. In fact, we once . . . Well, that's another story. Yes, Aubrey and I go back a long way, but like I said, I'd never seen Charles before he turned up here the other day."

"So you don't think he and Aubrey are . . .?" I was still finding it impossible to say what I was thinking.

"Are what?" Elvis wasn't inclined to let me off lightly.

I inhaled deeply, and let it out. "Do you think they're partners, other than in the business sense?"

Elvis laughed. "See, you can say it when you try! No, Olwen, I don't. I can't make you any guarantees, of course. But it doesn't look like it to me. And in answer to your earlier question, yes, I think I would be able to tell."

I saw Elvis off with a lighter heart. As he had warned, he couldn't give any guarantees that he was right about Charles; but he was as likely to be right as Tim was. More likely.

That left me with a problem. How was I going to explain to Charles what I had thought, without embarrassing both of us terribly? Was I even going to get the chance?

I could telephone him, and invite him round to dinner. It would be very forward, and I wasn't sure I could carry it off. Even if I succeeded, there was the possibility that he would refuse. Furthermore, supposing that I went to all that trouble, and it then turned out that Tim had been right all along? Or supposing that Charles was bisexual, how much would that matter to me?

There was no easy answer to this one. Unable to come to a firm decision, I did what I usually do in these circumstances – nothing.

I didn't sleep a wink that night. That's an exaggeration, as usual. I did sleep, for an hour or two, then I found myself tossing and turning, thinking it all through in my head, wondering how to make it come right. I heard Jessica come home at about midnight, and from the whispers and giggles, I surmised that Phil the plumber had seen her to the door.

She wouldn't let him into the house, I knew that. She only needed to remind him about the puritanical middle-aged auntie, asleep in bed in her high-necked Victorian-style nightie and curlers, but listening out for the slightest noise from downstairs. For her, it was no more than an excuse; she didn't know how close she was to the truth. I had to have someone to care about.

Next day was, if anything, worse. Having scarcely slept, I was in a state of nervous near-exhaustion. I couldn't eat breakfast. I couldn't work. The mail arrived and I found myself looking through the letters without reading a single word. In the end, I had to hand the job over to Jessica.

She herself had had the good sense to remain in bed until ten, pleading a hangover. I took her up a cup of tea, and told her not to worry, but I was certainly glad to see her when she eventually came down.

"The important thing is, did you have a good time?" I asked, trying to give an impression of light-heartedness when in reality I was on the verge of a nervous collapse.

"Great, thanks," she yawned. "That Phil's a head case!"

I wasn't sure I wanted to know what she meant by that. Having asked whether she was planning to see him again and received an inconclusive reply, I got on with my letter-opening. There were also three individual packages – books, of course. I hadn't been expecting the Daphne Du Maurier to turn up so quickly. Other booksellers are busy at Christmas, as well. I recalled that I had asked my supplier to expedite this particular volume. How I wished, now, that I hadn't bothered.

Mentally, I was still climbing the walls. Was Charles gay? Was he bisexual? Was he neither? Did it matter? The point was, I needed to know, one way or the other. Only with all the necessary information at my fingertips could I decide whether it was worth making the effort.

There was only one thing to be done. It was a snap decision, and not one I cared to dwell on. I literally jumped into the van, having reminded Jessica to set the answerphone if she should go out before I got back. Startled by the suddenness of my exit, she nodded and turned up the volume on Sound Wave – to which she had re-tuned my radio the day she arrived.

The single item most often requested by my customers is anything by or about Dylan Thomas. I'm ideally placed to supply such material, since Dylan was born in Swansea and is commemorated on every street corner – mainly by the pubs he drank in. When he described Swansea as an "ugly, lovely town", Dylan was spot on. That's more or less what I was thinking as I waited for the lights to change.

Swansea was hellishly busy. The only parking spaces available were in the High Street multi-storey, unpopular simply because of its distance from the main shopping areas. I had no intention of going anywhere near those. Their sparkly lights and festive garlands were guaranteed to push me further into depression. Not to mention the crowds.

It was only while I was choosing a spot for the van that I realised I didn't know exactly where Charles's office was. I had an idea it would be in Mansel Street or Walter Road, simply because that was where most of the legal firms hung out, but for all I knew it might be in Morriston or Llangyfelach, miles away from my current location. I had visions of ending up at the Central Reference Library in Alexandra Road, leafing frantically through the telephone directory.

Taking a deep breath, I opened my bag and looked in my purse. There it was, sure enough – Charles Cornwell's business card. Bantoft, Cornwell & Wicks, with an address in Mansel Street. I was only yards from their door.

And there he was. My voice disappeared back down my throat, preventing me from uttering the intended greeting as he emerged from the doorway of an anonymous office building and walked directly towards me.

For a few seconds, he didn't notice me. Preoccupied no doubt with work matters, his head was down, his eyes firmly fixed on a point in the distance, somewhere beyond my left shoulder. Seeing him in the street like this gave him a whole new character. Did he always look so dogged, when he went out to snatch his sandwich lunch? Then recognition dawned. The familiar smile cut into his face.

"Olwen!" There was no mistaking his delight. Coming to a halt less than two feet from me, he took a quick look around. "Is this a chance meeting? I can't believe . . ."

"No," I said. "I was going to call and see you – as I was passing. Your book arrived." Opening my bag again, I took out the package and thrust it at him. "Here, take it."

He looked at it, but didn't immediately respond.

"What about payment?"

"There's an invoice inside. You can pay it direct. It's twenty-five pounds. I'm afraid I couldn't get it for less, but it's a good price for what it is. I've checked it over and it's in great condition."

He failed to take the book from my hand. Do it, damn you, I was thinking. Invite me to lunch. Then we can talk. Then I can find out, once and for all.

"Are you on your way out to lunch?" I asked, thinking that I couldn't have been more obvious if I'd tried. "Perhaps you'd prefer me to drop it off at your office?"

"No, it's not that." At last, he accepted the book. "Olwen, I . . . I'd like to be able to . . . But I've got to meet someone for lunch. If you're going shopping, could we meet up later?"

An excuse. I had been misreading him all along. Or perhaps, seeing me in the cold light of day, here in the street, he simply found me uninteresting.

"That's all right," I said. "I haven't got time anyway. I'll see you around. Goodbye." I turned to walk away.

Chapter 16

"Olwen, no! Don't run off!"

I was trying to leave, but found I couldn't because my left hand was firmly clasped in his right. Giving up the struggle, I stood still and looked at him. His eyes held mine.

"I won't let you go until I know when I'm going to see you," he said. Being a solicitor, a man who was used to winning arguments, his determination shouldn't have surprised me.

"If I come to your house tonight," he said, "will you be at home?"

"Come to dinner," I said.

Simultaneously, we both looked down at our linked hands. Simultaneously, we both relaxed our grip.

"What time?"

"About seven, if you can make it."

"I'll be there."

I don't remember walking back to the car, or driving across the common. The next thing I recall was being at home, half an hour or so later, trying to think what I could cook and how I could make sure that Jessica didn't get in the way.

Charles hadn't met Jessica yet. When he saw her, would the contrast between my dowdy middle-aged look and her peachy, youthful glow be too much for him?

"Jess." I knew I had to broach the subject as soon as possible, if only to put her on her guard. "I've invited someone round to dinner this evening."

"Do you want me to go out?"

She was matter-of-fact about it, almost as though she had been expecting it. I laughed nervously. "There's no need to go to those lengths."

"Perhaps you'd like me to cook the meal and serve it, then make myself scarce."

I had to look twice to be sure that she was joking.

"If you like," I smiled.

"I take it you're going to be entertaining a gentleman friend."

"You could call him that. His name's Charles. He's . . ."

"Oh, Tim Sutcliff's solicitor, right?"

For someone who spent half the morning in bed and the entire evening out socialising, Jessica had an amazing knack of picking up information about other people's private lives.

"You don't have to go out," I reiterated. "It's just a meal, that's all. No hanky panky."

"Oh." She pulled a face. "How disappointing! Are you quite sure there won't be any, once I've gone out?"

"I've told you twice, you don't have to go out."

"The more times you say it, the more I know I'm not wanted."

She knew how to aggravate, did Jess, but her very ability to infuriate made me want to laugh.

"Do whatever you like," I said. "Only it would be a help if I knew now, so that I know how many to cook for."

"What are you making?"

"I don't know yet. It depends what's in the freezer."

"I know a really great recipe. You need aubergines and . . ."

"I haven't got any aubergines, so that's out."

"Okay, let me think. What other foods are aphrodisiacs?"

I couldn't help sniggering. "Stop it, Jess, this is no laughing matter. It'll be something simple, chops or something. Now, for the last time, are you going to be eating with us?"

"No. I'll go to the pub with Elvis."

It was difficult to understand what made someone like Elvis so attractive – in the most platonic sense – to a girl like Jessica. It must have been something to do with the fact that he posed no threat. She wasn't short of admirers, but, as she repeatedly told me, they were all after one thing. Whatever Elvis wanted from her, it wasn't that.

"Are you hoping to see Phil?" I asked. That was a mistake.

Jessica's face fell. "No."

I waited for the rest.

"He was supposed to ring me today," she said, after a few moments, "but he didn't. He's probably already forgotten I exist."

I burst out laughing. It must have seemed very unkind, to her, but it was simply that the sight of her sad, beautiful face, betraying the kind of thoughts that normally assailed her fuddy-duddy aunt, seemed highly comical to me at that moment. Fortunately, Jessica understands my sense of humour, and she joined in the laughter.

"I must sound really pathetic!" she said. "Who cares? He's only an electrician, after all!"

"Perhaps he's blown a fuse!" I shrieked, hysterical now.

We fell about the kitchen for a minute or two. I nearly wet myself at my own stupid joke. Jessica strove to maintain the atmosphere of jollity, by continuing with a string of terrible puns about bright sparks and current affairs. By the time I was ready to start thinking about what to cook that evening, she had cheered up no end, and so had I.

I virtually emptied the contents of the freezer onto the kitchen floor, in a desperate search for something suitable, and what do you think I settled on in the end? Pasta. Good old, reliable, easy-to-cook pasta. Never goes wrong, never disappoints, and you can rustle up any kind of sauce to go with it.

Accompaniments were going to be the problem, in winter. Salad wasn't readily to hand. Garlic bread would be asking for trouble. I consulted the oracle.

"Herb bread," decreed Jessica calmly. "And sun-dried tomatoes. I bought a jar the other day. I'll do you a soup for starters, if you like. You can just warm it up when he arrives."

I was gobsmacked. My niece had never been seen to cook at home, and she did the minimum when she was staying with me. Evidently, her university course was teaching her something, even if it wasn't what her parents expected in return for the exorbitant tuition fees.

She went out at six o'clock, and I immediately started to lay the table. I'm like that. I have to be prepared for every eventuality, and the possibility of a single thing not being ready when Charles was ready to eat was more than I could bear to contemplate. On a whim, I brought out some candles I'd had at the back of the cupboard since the last round of power cuts, and looked around for the little brass candlesticks I knew I had somewhere. Then, thinking it might be going just a wee bit too far, I put them away again. It was just as well I did.

The phone rang at ten past six.

"Olwen?" He was on his mobile; I could tell by the feedback. "I'm terribly sorry, but I'm going to have to cancel."

"What?" It wasn't that what he had said wasn't clearly audible, simply that I didn't believe I was hearing it.

"I can't make it. I'm sorry. Something's come up. I have to deal with it. I can't come round, at least not at seven. I might be able to make it later on, if you can wait, but it wouldn't be until about . . ."

"Forget it!" I slammed down the receiver, and immediately burst into tears.

My reaction had been quite unreasonable. Charles was a solicitor. He might have been called to a police station to help some poor bloke who had been wrongfully arrested, or a woman perhaps, who had finally given in and stabbed her violent husband to death after years of provocation. He would hardly have called off our evening together for anything less.

Childishly, I had refused to listen to his apology when he had barely begun it. Perhaps now he would call off whatever it was that was so important, and rush around to try and make amends. That wasn't what I wanted either. Nothing would satisfy me in these circumstances. If my show of temper had caused him to put me first, I wouldn't have respected him. On the other hand, I wanted to know that I was important to him, that I mattered more than work.

That was making the assumption that it was work that had deprived me of my opportunity to talk to him. It might be something else. It might be another woman.

He was bound to have someone, wasn't he? A successful, middle-aged man, like Charles would need to go to lots of functions, parties, that kind of thing; and when he did, he would be expected to turn up with a female companion. If he wasn't gay (and I realised now that I had never really believed Tim's story), he must be the opposite. So there was bound to be someone in his life. There was no doubt in my mind that she was a lot more glamorous than me.

A scenario was playing itself out in my mind. The woman Charles had been to lunch with today had found out about his flirtation with me. She had told him to break off our arrangement so that he could take her out instead. Yes, that would be it.

I unlaid the table. Perhaps I hoped, by that action, to make Fate rebel and send him to me after all. My hopes were in vain. Seven o'clock came and went, half past seven, eight o'clock. I had told him not to bother to come later. He didn't ring again. My fault.

At nine o'clock, bored to tears (or I would have been if I hadn't already cried them all out), I went up and had a bath. I'd had nothing to eat all evening, nor did I feel hungry, just empty. Empty, unloved, and very very sorry for myself. I went and lay down on the bed, turning on the portable TV that stood on the chest of drawers, in search of human company. Michael Parkinson's craggy face smiled out at me. His companions in crime included a top jockey and a foul-mouthed stand-up comedian. The programme had only ten minutes left to run. When it ended, to be replaced by a political discussion, I quickly switched off, but I still didn't get under the duvet. I picked up a book and tried to read.

That *Guide to Gower* was still holding my attention. Every time I opened it, I would find another priceless little snippet. My own village, for example, was described as "remote and unspoiled". There was a whole paragraph on St Mary's, which the author described as being "one of the most interesting churches on the peninsula". Some things, at least, hadn't changed since 1955.

The section on Swansea was equally interesting, for different reasons. The city – or town as it was when the book was published – had been devastated by wartime bombing, so there was no mention of the modern department stores, still less of the Quadrant centre, which had only been completed in the 'eighties. All the places recommended by the book for shopping had long since closed down, many of them before I was born. I would have to remember to ask my mother, when I saw her on Christmas Day.

I heard the rain begin. It started as a light pattering, growing gradually into a heavy battering as the wind caught and whipped it against the window pane. There was something quite comforting about the knowledge that it couldn't get to me, here, inside my home, wrapped up warmly.

Jessica came in at about eleven. I had left the porch light on, so that she could see to get her key in the door, but had turned off all the other downstairs lights before coming up for my bath.

"Auntie Olwen!" I heard her call, as the house was re-illuminated. "Are you here?"

I got up, and came to the top of the stairs. "I'm here!"

Her face was anxious enough, without my coming near enough for her to see that I had been crying.

"Was your dinner a success?"

"It didn't happen. I was stood up."

"Oh, Auntie Olwen, I'm sorry!"

"It's all right," I insisted. "It doesn't matter, really. He phoned to cancel. Apparently something urgent came up. It can't be helped."

From her changes of expression, I could read every thought that was passing through her mind as she looked up at me. The best I could hope for was that she couldn't read mine.

"I'm going to have a mug of chocolate," she said, shaking out her umbrella. "Shall I make you one?"

"Thank you," I said, forcing a smile. "That would be nice. I'll just go and put some slippers on, then I'll come down."

Jessica turned on the television downstairs. It was right underneath my room, which I suppose prevented me from hearing the knock at the front door. Fortunately, Jessica herself heard it.

When I got to the top of the stairs, he was standing just inside the hall, talking to her.

". . . like to join us?" from Jessica, was all I heard of the conversation.

Charles looked up at me, his face a mixture of compassion and concern. From my vantage point, I could see the drops of rain on his hair, glistening under the hall light.

"I'm so sorry, Olwen. As I was passing, I noticed that the lights were on, and I just assumed you were still up. I'd forgotten you had your niece here."

"That's all right." I began to descend the stairs, a little self-consciously because I was in my dressing-gown and slippers. There was no way he was getting away from me again. "I wasn't in bed. Come into the living room, it's warmer."

I had reached the foot of the stairs. He was as close to me as Jessica was.

"I'll make an extra mug of chocolate," she said, hurrying to get out of our space.

I followed her into the living room, and Charles followed me.

"I'm terribly sorry about earlier," he began, without waiting to sit down. "I had a call . . ." He glanced towards the kitchen, to make sure that Jessica wasn't listening, and lowered his voice. ". . . from Tim Sutcliff. I had to go round there, and I've literally only this minute got away."

"You've been there ever since you rang me?"

"Since half past six, yes. I tried to get away after a couple of hours, when the business had been effectively concluded, but Laura wanted me to stay and have something to eat with them. I didn't know how to refuse. I felt I could hardly say I'd been due to have a meal with you. It seemed a little indiscreet."

That was particularly ironic, in view of Tim's willingness to be indiscreet about Charles's big secret. Correction: what Tim *thought* was Charles's big secret. I was ninety-nine point nine per cent sure, by now, that Tim had got it wrong, somehow.

"I tried to ring you on the mobile, to tell you what was happening," he went on, "but I couldn't pick up a signal."

"No one ever can, round here."

"So," said Jessica boldly, advancing into the room with a tray of mugs and setting them down on the coffee table along with a plate of digestive biscuits, "how are you going to make it up to my auntie, for not turning up to dinner?"

I wanted the earth to open and swallow me up. Charles did a double-take. Then that famous smile reappeared, and he laughed loudly.

"I'll do anything to obtain forgiveness," he said. "My best idea so far has been . . . Tomorrow's Saturday. I'm not working, and I assume you're not."

"Well . . ." I started to frame an objection.

"So I thought I'd come and collect you in the car, and we'd go out for the day. I haven't heard a weather forecast, but even if it's chucking it down with rain, we'll find something to do, I'm sure."

"That sounds like the best offer you're going to get, Auntie Olwen," remarked Jessica, without waiting to be asked her opinion. "I should take it, if I were you. Don't worry about the morning post, I'll see to all that."

Charles looked from her to me, with a sheepish smile.

"What time?" I asked.

"Would ten o'clock be too early?"

I shook my head. "Ten o'clock should be fine."

"By the way," said Jessica, as she was clearing away the mugs a little later, "Elvis gave me a message for you, when we were in the pub. I forgot about it, with all the excitement. He said to tell you that he's made enquiries, and the person you were discussing yesterday is in the clear. He wouldn't say any more."

She paused for my reaction. I smiled.

"Does that make sense to you?" she asked, probably thinking that it had something to do with Tim Sutcliff.

"Perfect sense. Good old Elvis. He likes to be mysterious."

Chapter 17

Charles arrived at five to ten, which surprised me. Not that I wasn't ready; I was more than ready. I simply hadn't expected such punctuality from a man who came across as so laid-back and confident.

I had dressed carefully, putting on a cream polo-necked sweater I'd only worn once before, my best jeans, and fleece-lined waterproof boots. It wasn't raining any more, but it wasn't exactly sunny either, and I suspected there would still be a lot of mud around.

Reaching for my anorak, I asked him if he would like a coffee before we went out. He declined, with an air of urgency that suggested he couldn't wait to get out of the house and into the car. It could only be because he wanted us to be alone. Whether that was for the same reasons that I wanted to be alone with him, time would tell.

Jessica saw us off and told us to "have a good time".

"I like your niece," Charles remarked, as I settled into the passenger seat of the silver BMW. "She's very vivacious, isn't she?"

"She doesn't get it from me," I replied coldly. Ridiculous of me, to be jealous of a twenty-year-old girl, but I was.

Charles merely laughed, and started up the engine smoothly. He didn't ask where I wanted to go, but drove purposefully along the narrow lanes, which were evidently well known to him. It didn't take me long to realise where we were going.

"Oxwich?" I asked.

"Is that okay?" For the first time, he looked uncertain of his ground. "I thought we could have a walk along the beach, get a spot of lunch, maybe go up to the castle. Have you been there, since Cadw took it over? It's quite impressive."

"I haven't been up there since I was a child."

"Really? You should. I suppose I'm making a bit of an assumption, that you're interested in history. If there's somewhere else you'd rather go, something else you'd rather do, it's easy enough to change course."

"Oxwich will be fine."

"I should have asked first." He did look, briefly, regretful. Then he flashed me that smile of his. "I'm sorry, I don't get out much."

"I can't believe *that*!"

I was doing it again, making myself sound grumpy and ungrateful when all I really wanted to do was to be with him, soak in his presence, imbibe his personality. I pressed my lips together, determined not to let out any more spiteful remarks, desperate for him to think well of me.

"It's true, actually," he said after a moment, his forehead puckering as he concentrated on easing forward, out of the narrow lane, onto a major road.

I said nothing.

"Would you like some music on?" he asked, having negotiated the corner. He reached across me and flipped open a compartment to reveal a row of neatly-ordered tape cassettes.

"There's hardly time," I commented, cursing myself again as soon as I'd said it. I went through the motions of looking through the tapes. His taste was eclectic, everything from the Doors to Debussy. Also in the glove compartment were two guidebooks.

The Gower is a peninsula, about seventy square miles in area, lying just to the west of the city of Swansea. According to the *Blue Guide to Wales*, it's "a mass of carboniferous limestone". *Michelin*, on the other hand, refers to its "magnificent coastline", but has little to say about the "interior of ancient farmland and commons". However you describe it, it's one of the most scenic parts of Wales. So attractive, in fact, that it was the first place in the whole of Britain to be designated an Area of Outstanding Natural Beauty.

"Since you seem to be a fan of guidebooks," I remarked, "I've got something interesting to show you, back at the house."

"I can't wait," he replied.

When we arrived at Oxwich, he pulled into the car park as though it were very familiar. The ground was uneven; the BMW lurched over it at low speed, coming to a halt in a spot overlooking the grey sea. There was only a scattering of cars; quite a contrast from the height of summer, when you can queue up for an hour just to get to the entrance to the car park and find there aren't any spaces left. One reason why I hadn't been to Oxwich for such a long time.

I was not yet at ease. Typically cack-handed, I fumbled with the child lock until Charles reached across me to release it. He was quiet until we were both outside the car.

"I thought we could take a walk up to the old church," he said, "but if you'd rather do something else . . ."

"I can't think of anything I'd rather do," I interrupted.

On a whim, I took his arm, feeling rather audacious. He looked pleased; at least now I was showing a willingness to meet him halfway. I smiled up at him. He was dressed casually, something new to my eyes. Under his heavy waxed coat, he was wearing a light-coloured polo neck that almost matched my own attire. He had on dark-brown cord trousers and suede ankle boots. The overall effect was one of comfortable bulk.

My arm fitted nicely into his. He was a useful height, about five nine or so. Like most Welsh women, I'm short, and I found his elbow at a point which suited me. I had to remind myself not to get too comfortable. There was no guarantee that his elbow would be available on future excursions.

We walked, in near-silence, past the cluster of buildings that constitutes the village, taking the little path towards the church. There were very few people around. It was a cold day, and so gloomy that the lights in the hotel on the bay were the brightest thing in view. Only when we were well away from civilisation, halfway along the shoreline towards the church, did Charles speak. I was glad he began it, because I wouldn't have known where to start.

"You've been upset with me, Olwen, and I'm not sure I know why. Before last night, I mean. Since I asked you to come out with me. And yet, here you are."

"Yes. Here I am. Here we are." I still didn't know how to go on.

"I wondered if you were trying to tell me that I was being too . . . presumptuous, in trying to turn a business relationship into a personal one."

"Was that what you were trying to do?" Asking questions seemed to come more naturally than answering them, at the moment.

"Are you trying to make me incriminate myself?" He wasn't looking at me.

"It would be rash of me to try that with a solicitor." I hated myself for all these smart-alec remarks, but I still didn't know how to broach the subjects that were closest to my mind.

He inhaled deeply, and I knew it wasn't for the sake of fresh air.

"Look, Olwen," he said, his voice taking on a no-nonsense tone. "If you don't want more than friendship, I can live with that. I admit I'd prefer something more, but this is better than nothing. You're an interesting woman, and an attractive one. From the minute I met you, I . . . Let's just say, I'd like to see more of you. Obviously, it would make life easier if you felt the same way I do. Up until the other night, I was confident that you did. Could you please tell me if I did something wrong? Because for the life of me, I can't think . . ."

"No." Now I rushed to bring matters to a head. "It wasn't anything you did, it was something someone said about you, something which I wasn't sure whether to believe."

We had arrived at the church, and he took my arm out of his, stepping forward to open the rusty little gate. Then he moved aside, so that I could go through it ahead of him. He was showing remarkably little curiosity about my last statement.

"I love this place," he said suddenly. "I love the atmosphere."

"Do you come here often?"

It was only after I'd said it that I realised how stupid it sounded. Charles looked amused; he must have thought I'd intended it as a joke.

"Quite often," he said. "The interior is very interesting, but I don't suppose . . ." He stepped forward and tested the padlock, to check that the church door would not yield to pressure. The iron ring remained stubbornly immovable.

I wished he hadn't done that. There was something symbolic about the church refusing him entry, as though he – or we – had done something wrong and were not fit to be admitted.

"It's a shame they keep so many churches locked," he said, sounding disappointed despite having predicted it. Then he turned to me with a hint of a smile. "We'll just have to come back here in the summer. It'll be open then."

More hidden meanings? He didn't give me much time to dwell on them.

"Now," he said, "are you going to tell me any more, or is this piece of information about me to remain a secret between you and . . . whoever? I should really like to know what it is I'm being accused of, so that I have a chance to defend myself."

Unconsciously, he was making me think of Tim's situation. I probably blushed at that point, but in that day's feeble light, with the shadow of the leafless trees overhead, no one would have been able to tell.

"I'm not sure I have the right to ask this," I said, sitting down on the wall.

Charles sat down beside me, and put an arm around me. The waxy surface of his jacket squeaked against the canvas of my anorak.

"I don't suppose the answer will be any worse than whatever you're imagining," he said.

"Charles, are you gay?"

I couldn't look at him, but I felt his reaction. He tensed, but didn't remove his arm.

"What an extraordinary question! Of course I'm not gay!"

"Not gay, and not . . . bisexual?"

He puffed out air, an indication of annoyance perhaps. "Neither of those things. I can assure you, Olwen, I am completely and utterly and . . . *positively* heterosexual!"

"Thank God!" I said, and promptly started to cry.

Charles didn't say anything, but his hold on me tightened. I took off my glasses, putting my head into the crook of his shoulder, and his other arm came around me. The tears were soon over, but the awkward questions would begin soon enough, and I wasn't sure how much strength I had left, to keep up my end of the conversation.

"I won't ask who's been saying these things about me, Olwen," he said eventually, "but please don't get upset about it, because they're not true. Perhaps someone has seen me with Aubrey, and got the wrong end of the stick. Aubrey, my partner, is a homosexual, as you may be aware, but that doesn't make me one."

"Of course not," I gasped, fighting for breath. "But I was told that you live together."

"We most certainly do not!" he exclaimed. Then he paused, for quite a long time. "I know what's behind this," he said. "I understand now. Phew! You had me really worried there, for a moment."

He relaxed his grip on me, but one arm remained around my shoulders. With his free hand, he took mine and held it, stroking the fingers of my glove as though the wool wasn't there.

"Aubrey's got a long-term partner," he said. "When I say 'partner', I mean partner in the personal sense, not in the way that Aubrey and I are partners. This man – his name's Noel Collins, and you'll probably meet him, sooner or later, if you and I . . . Well, we'll come back to that. Back last summer, Noel and Aubrey had a little falling-out, and Aubrey came and stayed in my spare room for a week or so. That might be how the rumour started. Yes, I'm sure it must be that. Your informant only had half a story. I'm not going to ask who it was . . ." I was thankful for that, at least. ". . . but I would be extremely grateful if you'd set them straight."

He paused. Simultaneously, we exploded into laughter.

"Straight!" he shouted. "Straight! I should say so!"

When I had finished laughing and crying, he pulled me close to him and turned his face towards mine. Another inch and I would have been kissing him, but I didn't mirror his gesture. It was too soon.

"What on earth did you think?" he asked, bemused. "What did you think I was doing, inviting you out, if I was gay?"

"I thought perhaps you liked men *and* women."

"Ah." He was silent for about a minute, considering this. His thoughts must have been moving the same way as mine.

"How much would it have mattered?" he asked.

"I'm not sure. That's what I kept asking myself. But my real fear was that I was imagining that you had any interest in me beyond the professional. You see, I've got used to being on my own, not meeting many new people, not going out much, and I couldn't believe . . ."

It was impossible to finish the sentence, even if I had known which words to use, because I was crying again. This time, Charles was quick to pull me into his embrace, and I just floundered there, against the front of his coat, like a fish that's been hauled out of the water but isn't quite dead yet. Gradually, I regained my senses.

Charles, meanwhile, had unfastened his jacket and pulled it open, so that the soft texture of his sweater lay against my cheek. Putting out my hand, tentatively, towards his waist, I lifted the ribbed edge and felt underneath it. There was something cotton, a tee-shirt rather than a vest, and underneath that, a warmth that comforted.

Charles exhaled noisily. "Careful," he muttered. "I'm not getting any younger, you know."

Whatever he meant by that, it gave me pause for thought about what I was getting myself into, and I made no move to go further. My hand remained pressed against his tee-shirted side. The flab was minimal, for a man of his age, whatever his age was.

Charles wrapped his arms more tightly around me. His hand moved upwards, to caress my hair.

"Was that all it was?" he asked. "You thought I was playing with your feelings? Was that all it was? There wasn't anything else?"

How could I answer that? I made no attempt. After a minute or two of enjoying his warmth, his tenderness, I pulled away, avoiding his eyes in case they led me further into danger.

He was silent, watching me from behind as I stood up and began to roam aimlessly around the churchyard, trying to avoid the muddy patches. The grass hadn't been cut since the end of summer, and it brushed against the hem of my jeans, leaving an uncomfortable dampness. I was glad I had worn something waterproof on my feet.

After a moment's hesitation, Charles got up and joined me.

"I've been behaving very childishly," I said, by way of an apology.

"Not at all!" he protested. "I'm glad you cared enough to be cross with me."

That was a relief, anyhow. Conscious that a whole lot of things remained unsaid, I was content, for the moment, to wander around looking at gravestones with him. No doubt it would remind us both of the necessity of making the most of one's opportunities while one still had the chance.

Charles seemed to like to touch the gravestones. He fingered each one lovingly. All I did was read the inscriptions, as best I could. We progressed gradually around to the back of the church.

Martha Davies had died in 1879, aged thirty-six. Had Martha Davies ever had problems like mine? She probably never had time. Too busy having children and trying to scrape a living. Going to bed at six in winter, by candlelight, getting up at the crack of dawn in summer to see to her huge family.

I laughed quietly to myself. Charles turned his head, quizzically, but didn't ask.

"I was just thinking," I said, "that my notions of history are probably very over-romanticised."

"Aren't everyone's?" I couldn't see his face very well, in the reduced light, but he seemed to be smiling.

"I don't know what's going on in other people's minds. Even yours."

"Probably just as well." He reached out for my hand, and I gave it. "Are you hungry yet? Only the hotel does quite a good bar meal, and I'm starving. It must be the fresh air."

Now that I started to think about it, I found I was ravenous. I'd had no dinner the night before, and only the lightest breakfast. We wended our way back down the path, standing to one side to make way for another couple who were heading towards the church.

"Good morning," they said in unison, as if they knew us, and we responded in like manner.

I wondered what they were thinking, about us. Nothing, probably. Just that we were another middle-aged married couple, out for a winter morning's walk.

"Who was St Illtyd?" asked Charles, as we came close to our destination.

"You don't know?" I didn't want to sound like Anne Robinson, but I was surprised that he could ask that question, as a regular visitor to St Illtyd's Church. "He was one of the early medieval Welsh saints. Fifth, sixth century? He lived around here. He was a sort of hermit."

"Oh." Charles smiled again. "Like someone else I know."

I stopped, and stared into his face, and found myself returning his smile.

The hotel bar was invitingly warm. From a window seat, we had a tremendous view of Oxwich Bay and the Point. Had it been a clearer day, we might have been able to see right across to Devon.

"What would you like to drink?" asked Charles, all devoted attention on this, our first proper date.

I hesitated.

"Let me get you a glass of wine," he urged. "You need something to perk you up a bit."

I accepted the offer, thinking that wine, far from perking me up, would probably send me to sleep. I hadn't had many hours uninterrupted slumber the previous night, thinking about this morning and what it would bring. I had been out of bed at seven thirty, unable to keep myself pegged down any longer.

When he returned with the drinks, I was gazing out at the sea, which looked rougher now than it had when we were walking beside it. The miniature palms and the closed-up beach umbrellas in the hotel gardens rather spoiled the overall effect, reducing what should have been stormy magnificence to a kind of damp pathos.

"There's a similar view from the window of my house," remarked Charles, sliding into the seat opposite. I assumed he meant without the palms and umbrellas, and smiled weakly in response.

"You don't get bored with it?"

He laughed. "I don't see much of it. I always seem to be in the office."

"You shouldn't work too hard. I know I'm a fine one to talk, but at least I can go out and walk around the village whenever I feel like it."

"Yes, that's a plus." There was a slight hesitation before he continued. A stranger wouldn't have noticed, but already I had grown used to the inflection in his voice. I heard it even when he wasn't there.

"I've got a chance of a weekend away before Christmas," he said.

It might have been meant as a hint, or alternatively as a warning. If the former, I was too cowardly to take him up on it. I took a sip from my wine. Then the food arrived, preventing either of us from following up the statement.

Mysteriously, but as predicted, the food and wine had the effect of making me feel, not sleepy, but refreshed. Charles and I kept conversation to a minimum while we ate. He seemed to be enjoying his lasagne, but I couldn't be sure. I really didn't know him well enough to risk making any more assumptions. It wasn't just wine that I drank, either. After the meal, he persuaded me to take a liqueur coffee with him. Its alcoholic warmth penetrated to my boots, and I settled back in my seat to look at him. His dark eyes smiled back at me, over the rim of his glass.

The restaurant, despite the shortage of people out and about, was growing busier by the second, and new arrivals were having difficulty in finding a seat. Most of the patrons seemed to be visitors to the area, down for the Christmas holidays. The companionable atmosphere, pleasant at first, began to cloy, and I became anxious to get out of there, to be alone with Charles again. Once more, we were of like mind, and when I started to shuffle and show signs of restlessness, he asked if I was ready to go and look around the castle.

We walked up the winding road, having agreed that it was unnecessary to take the car for such a short distance. I was out of breath before we were halfway up the hill. Charles, either more used to walking up gradients or simply hardier, laughed and pulled me by the arm, then propelled me in front of him with both hands.

"You're out of condition," he said, still laughing. "I can see I'm going to have to take you in hand."

The satisfaction of hearing a remark like that didn't counteract my growing reluctance to believe that it could be as easy as this. Something was bound to go wrong. Things couldn't go on being this perfect. For a start, there was Charles's other life.

He had said, earlier, that he found me "interesting" and "attractive". More interesting and attractive than the women he met every day in the centre of Swansea? It was hard to believe, hard to accept, not because I doubted Charles's fundamental honesty, but because I had grown up believing myself profoundly undesirable, even on the rare occasions when men told me otherwise. The idea that I might have captured the lasting affection of a man like Charles Cornwell was stretching my credibility to its limits.

With a start, I realised that I had let the morning go by and the afternoon begin without giving a thought to yesterday evening's events. After Charles left my house the night before, besides looking forward to our outing, I had been consumed with curiosity as to the nature of his emergency meeting with Tim and Laura at the vicarage. It had been my intention to raise the subject. Although I knew Charles was unlikely to volunteer any detailed information about "the Sutcliff situation", I had thought that, by a little expedient fishing, I might succeed in extracting the basic facts. A couple of weeks earlier, Tim's welfare would have been first and foremost in my mind. Now I found it was of little concern, by comparison with the question of whether Charles was falling as deeply in love with me as I, I think, already was with him.

I felt guilty, and at the same time glad. If I wasn't thinking of Tim the way I had been, if Charles had already supplanted him in my affections, it could only be to the good. After all, there had never been any future in it. My love for Tim had only ever made me miserable. If this rapid change-about meant I was fickle, well, perhaps that wasn't such a bad thing either; it might save me from getting hurt, if and when Charles himself got tired of me.

We were already inside the castle courtyard, and Charles was getting out his wallet in readiness to pay the entrance fee. Muttering something inane about paying my way, I tried to get my purse out. His hand closed over mine, as I fumbled with the catch of my bag.

"Olwen, this was my idea, and you are not paying for *anything* today," he said firmly.

Masterful men don't normally appeal to me, but I had become like putty in his hands. I simply obeyed, put the purse away again, and followed him, through the ticket office, into the castle itself.

"I don't know when I was last here," I said, wonderingly, gazing around at the range of well-preserved rooms. "I'm not even sure that I ever have been here. Were visitors allowed in? Was it safe, in the past?"

"It was privately owned until 1949," replied Charles, consulting the guidebook. "I'm not sure what happened after that, but I know they were working on it for years. Of course, I wasn't born in 1949, so I couldn't say." He was smirking, his dark eyes twinkling at me, and I couldn't help laughing, even at such a pathetic attempt to raise my spirits. I squeezed his arm, playfully. We were acting like two people who hadn't been born in 1979, let alone 1949.

He handed me the little guide, and I glanced over it as we progressed on our tour. It didn't take long to get around the building, but we lingered, absorbing the atmosphere, making the most of our time together. Whatever came next, I thought, I would always have today, my day with Charles, and I wanted to savour every moment of it.

When we could prolong the visit no more, and the gloom showed signs of transforming itself into real darkness, we walked slowly back down the hill to where we had left the car.

"Do you have any plans for this evening?" asked Charles, when we were back in our leather seats. He wasn't looking at me as he said it. He was leaning across me, flicking through the tapes in their little compartment, studying their backs for something suitable to listen to on the journey home. Perhaps he was bored with my conversation.

"Do you like the Beatles?" he asked, indicating a compilation by the Fab Four. "Music of my childhood," he added.

I approved the choice as suitably neutral, but didn't attempt to answer his previous question.

"I wanted to spend the whole day with you," he said, as he turned the key in the ignition, so that half the sentence was lost under the roar of the engine. Manoeuvring skilfully out of the car park, he appeared completely concentrated on the task in hand, but I sensed he was waiting for some kind of sign from me.

"Would you like to have your evening meal back at the house?" I asked. "I don't know if Jessica will be eating with us, but there's some soup she made, that we were going to have last night, if . . ."

"If I hadn't let you down," he finished neatly. "I hope nothing much went to waste."

"Nothing at all, actually," I admitted. "We were having pasta, so I didn't need to prepare it until the last minute. The soup's in the fridge. All I'd need to do is warm it up. But perhaps you've got other plans."

"I have no other plans."

He didn't seem to feel it was necessary to go on. The Beatles had begun with a quiet ballad, but were about to launch into something louder and more intrusive, so I sat back and listened to them.

Chapter 18

Back at the house, I found, to my inexpressible delight, that Jessica had gone out. Her note said that she wasn't likely to be back before midnight.

"Do you worry about her?" asked Charles, looking over my shoulder as I read it. "Do you feel responsible for her, when she's here in your care?"

"Of course," I said. "But she's twenty years old. And in my heart of hearts, I know she can look after herself. I'm only glad I'm not her mother."

"Are you?" he said softly. "Are you sure about that?"

As usual, I evaded the question, and thought about laying the table.

"It's a bit early to eat yet, isn't it?" I said. "Would you like to watch television?"

"I can't think of anything I'd like less," he replied blandly. "It's your company I want. Couldn't we have a – what do you call it – a conversation?"

I laughed, despite myself. The truth was, I was nervous about the prospect of conversation; we risked getting onto very dangerous ground. It was all very well exchanging confidences when we were out somewhere, with other people around, and I had the option of running away. Letting him loose on my unadorned personality, like this, in the house, was something else.

I managed surprisingly well at first, by the simple expedient of asking him to tell me about himself. He immediately threw me by stating that he had been born in Barnsley, and had only moved to Wales at the age of eight. Hence the local accent; he hadn't a drop of Welsh blood in his veins.

Taking my surprise for disappointment, he added, "I could try a bit harder, if you liked."

He was like that, Charles, always finding little things to do and say, to make me laugh, to get under my skin, to make a hole in the defences I'd built up, so carefully, over the years.

He told me how he'd gone away to study Law, after school in Swansea, and there he had met Aubrey Bantoft, a fellow student. Recognising immediately that Aubrey was gay, he had studiously avoided his company, even though he knew they came from the same part of the country. It was only when they were thrown together, in the same hall of residence, that he had seen beyond the surface.

"Aubrey puts on this camp manner," he remarked. "It's all pretence, a disguise to stop himself getting upset when people say things to him, or about him, about his sexuality. It took him a long time to come to terms with it. It took *me* a long time, come to that. When I got to know him properly, he became my best friend. Other people may choose to misinterpret that, but I don't care. Aubrey's friendship is more important to me than the occasional misunderstanding. He's one of the kindest, gentlest men I've ever met, and frighteningly intelligent. Far cleverer than I'll ever be."

When people say things like that, they don't usually mean them. They want you to contradict them, to give them a boost. Charles didn't need that kind of reassurance. He meant exactly what he said.

Charles and Aubrey had returned to Swansea to serve their articles, and had been lucky enough to be able to buy into a local practice together, a few years later. According to Charles, theirs was an almost perfect business partnership.

"We interface beautifully," was how he put it.

Having heard his life story, I was persuaded to tell my own, which was much shorter and, to my mind, far less interesting. Charles was a practised listener, but to do him justice, I believe he was absolutely genuine in his desire to know more about me. It was getting late when the conversation lapsed for long enough for me to go and start warming up the soup. At his own insistence, I allowed him to lay the table, and told him where to find the herb bread, which had to go into the oven for a few minutes to regain its crustiness.

Jessica's leek and potato soup went down a treat. It was one of the simplest meals I've ever had, but it hit the mark wonderfully well. I could tell Charles thought so, too. Now we were really getting somewhere. A few more hours, a few more confidences, and I wouldn't need to wonder, I wouldn't need to doubt myself any more. After we'd eaten, I offered him a drink, and he accepted a glass of scotch. I poured myself a gin and tonic.

Charles picked up the *Guide to Gower*, which I had left on the sideboard that morning, never imagining that he would share my interest in it.

"Good Lord!" he exclaimed. "Is this what you were going to show me? Where on earth did you find this little gem?"

I told him the story of the family in Limeslade. While I was talking, he leafed through the yellowed pages, being careful not to damage them.

"Nineteen fifty-five," he mused, turning over the fly.

"Had you been born by then?" I asked, almost laughing.

"Just about," he confirmed. "Oh, look, there's something here about the Red Lady of Paviland. We learned about that in school. It's one of the few things I remember. History was my favourite subject."

"All wrong now, of course," I pointed out.

"You'll have to tell me about it some time," he said. "But not now. Why don't you come and sit down?"

The talk we'd had earlier had been, for the most part, light-hearted. We had been finding out more about one another, but on a superficial level. During dinner, I'd felt increasingly guilty about the way Tim and Laura's problems had retreated completely from my mind while I'd been enjoying myself with Charles. Yet I was reluctant to raise the subject now, for obvious reasons.

Just in case they're not as obvious as I think, I might mention that there were several of them. For a start, I was terribly anxious to retain Charles's good opinion; I didn't want him to get the impression that I was thinking of Tim while I was with him. In fact, I *hadn't* been thinking of Tim while I was with Charles. I suppose that was why I felt this strange compulsion to ask about him now – because I felt uncomfortable about going out and having a good time while the Sutcliffs were in such dire straits.

Then there was the matter of not wanting to appear a nosy parker, which also had to do with retaining Charles's respect. I'd already put my foot in it once, letting him know that I'd been gossiping with Elvis. I didn't want to fall into that trap again. It would be unfair, too, when Charles had already made it clear that it would be unprofessional of him to reveal anything that had passed between him and his client. To ask questions would be to put him in an invidious position.

I was on an emotional roller-coaster. Whether Charles noticed anything specific about my behaviour is difficult to say, in retrospect. Clever as he was at recognising my moods, he probably didn't know me well enough – at that time – to read my mind accurately. Perhaps it was the way I had strenuously avoided mentioning Tim all day that gave me away. Even so, he didn't bring up the topic himself until we had finished dinner and were enjoying our drinks.

"I shouldn't ask this," he said, letting me off the hook nicely, "but have you and your friend come up with any further theories about Tim Sutcliff?"

By now I had a pretty shrewd suspicion that Charles knew exactly who my unnamed "friend" was but didn't want to embarrass me by saying so. All the same, the question surprised me. Charles had been at Tim's the previous evening; surely he knew far more about the subject than I did?

"None that hold water. I haven't discussed it with anyone since you told me off the other day."

"Told you off?" His expression combined indignation and amusement. "Would I do that?"

"It felt like it. I was ashamed of myself – and rightly so."

"Oh, Olwen." He was smiling, as his hand came across the table to rest lightly on mine.

I tried to smile back, but failed to convince myself that my mood had lightened. Falling in love was one thing. Being confident of a favourable response was quite another.

"I knew I shouldn't have asked you about it, and I decided to turn over a new leaf. I've been trying hard not to think about Tim and Laura – though I must admit it's not easy."

"Why? Has something happened?"

I couldn't begin to tell him about all the stuff that had come in between his mild reproof, that day in the kitchen, and the present moment – about how I had mistakenly thought Laura was suicidal, about Tim's unusual behaviour, or about the discovery that Laura was in therapy. All that was their private business and not to be shared with a third party, even someone as warm and understanding as Charles. He was the Sutcliffs' solicitor, after all. If they had anything to say that was relevant to the case, they should say it to him voluntarily.

"Charles, I've known Tim and Laura for a long time. I've shared confidences with them more than once, but if there's anything they haven't told you, it can only be because they don't think it would help."

As usual, he seemed to understand. "I'm not pressing you to betray any confidences, Olwen. It's simply that . . . well, I get the feeling that Tim is afraid to be completely open with me – and I don't think it's necessarily because he's got anything very terrible to hide. Frankly, I don't think he quite trusts me."

"So what was all that about, last night? No doubt he called you round there for some reason."

"Of course." He leaned right back in his chair and sat looking at me, and once again I felt I knew what was going through his mind: how much was it safe to tell me? Had I been using my brain to its full capacity, had my head not been stuffed full of silly romantic notions, it might have occurred to me that his uncertainty was a good thing. If, after only a few weeks and a handful of meetings, he was even considering putting this kind of trust in me, it must mean that he felt close to me.

"Without divulging what was said to me last night, Olwen, I have to admit I'm troubled about the whole matter. One of the reasons I've been going to the vicarage in person, instead of just getting Tim to come to my office for consultations, is that I want to see him in a domestic situation, to reassure myself that he's innocent of the charge of indecent assault. Unfortunately, every time I go there, Mrs Sutcliff makes herself scarce. It's almost as though she's afraid of speaking to me, as though . . . as though she fears she might give something away."

I considered this for a moment. "But she asked you to stay to dinner . . ."

"Yes. That was very strange. She was suddenly making an effort to be friendly. Not that she'd precisely been unfriendly before, but suddenly she seemed to want to make a special impression. She evidently knew why I was there, though she wasn't in the room when Tim was telling his story."

So Tim had shared his "version of events" with Charles, at last. I sighed.

"Laura's got a few problems, Charles. I don't feel I should say any more."

"No, I wouldn't ask you to. But thank you for that. Every little helps. There's one specific question I want to ask, which you may not want to answer or may not feel able to answer. May I?"

He was looking at me from under his eyelashes, that little-boy-lost thing again, and I dreaded to think what was coming. I nodded.

"You may as well, now that we've gone this far." Double meanings again.

"In your opinion, is it possible that Tim might lie – or at any rate, invent a story – in order to protect his wife?"

I was dumbfounded. The question didn't make any sense. Tim could hardly be protecting Laura from Craig Dutton. She couldn't possibly have carried out the alleged assault. Charles must mean something else.

"That's a difficult one," I prevaricated. "I can certainly imagine circumstances in which she might need protecting – from herself. And Tim certainly cares deeply for her. As to whether he would tell lies – I suppose that would depend on the likely consequences. I mean, he might tell a white lie, but I can't believe he would accuse Craig of making everything up, if there was any truth in it."

I had it more or less figured out, by now. Tim *had* done something to Craig, something he had reason to be ashamed of. Knowing Tim, I still couldn't believe he had actually intended to make sexual overtures to a child; perhaps he had merely been fooling around, but it was something he knew he shouldn't have done. He was playing the injured innocent because he wanted to spare Laura the ignominy of being seen to be married to a man who had so endangered his reputation. That had to be it.

"I'm sure you're right," replied Charles, and I had no idea which of my statements he was agreeing with. "You're confirming my own thoughts on the matter, for which I'm grateful. I'm still hoping that there may be some way out of all this, without anyone getting hurt."

It should have stopped there. I had discharged my responsibilities towards the Sutcliffs, and Charles had confided in me in a way I'd had no right to expect. It was the subject matter that was the problem. All this talk about husband-wife relationships had unsettled me.

That was when it all started to go wrong because, you see, I couldn't stop myself. All those insidious doubts and niggling worries were playing up again. They had lain dormant only temporarily. The closer we got to intimacy, the harder I found it to shrug them off; and in the end, I simply had to go a step too far. I asked Charles about his divorce.

He didn't seem to mind my asking, not at first. He was matter-of-fact about it. He repeated what he'd said before, that he'd been married for six years and divorced for fourteen. It was what he wasn't saying that troubled me. Perhaps I'd had too much to drink. That's no excuse for the way I gnawed away at the subject like a bone. I didn't see that my determination to get at the truth might be fatal to my own hopes of happiness.

When I started down that conversational path, I had forgotten all about our earlier meetings. It was as though our romance, if you can call it that, had started that very day, that very evening in fact. The things he'd said, when I was showing him the Howard Spring book a few weeks before, and afterwards when I entertained him to coffee, had all flitted out of my memory, only to return at the worst possible moment, looming spectres that threatened my peace of mind.

When I asked him, bluntly, what had caused his divorce, he threw me a look that was almost angry. We hadn't even left the table.

"What you're really asking, if I'm not mistaken, is whether I was unfaithful." Seeing from my reaction that he was right, he went on – which was just as well, because I was speechless. "I won't lie to you. Yes, I did sleep with someone who wasn't my wife. It wasn't the grounds for divorce, but I can't pretend it didn't have an effect on our relationship. I could tell you all about it, if it's important to you."

"I didn't mean to pry . . ."

"No, you've a perfect right to ask, under the circumstances. I know you, Olwen, you set yourself high moral standards, and you expect the same from others. I couldn't look you in the face if I'd not told you the truth, so I may as well get it all out in the open right now.

"Deirdre and I were never really happy, not that I can remember. Ours was a classic college romance, and it should have stayed that way. We were both a bit green. You're considerably younger than me, but you must be aware that things were different in those days, even after all the so-called free love in the 'sixties. I didn't have a proper girlfriend till I was eighteen. Deirdre was equally new to it all. But whereas I saw our relationship merely as an opportunity to sow my wild oats without catching anything nasty, Deirdre saw it as the path to her future.

"I did care for her. I wouldn't exactly say that I was in love with her, but I thought I was, which amounts to the same thing. I had no intention of hurting her. That's why I married her, in the end, not because I actively wanted to, but because it was what would make her happy and, I thought, keep her happy. Her parents weren't keen on us sharing a flat without being married. Neither were mine, come to that. So, to please them and to please her, I married her, thinking that would be the end of it.

"When I was properly launched on my career, I had plenty of things to take my mind off any potential problems. Lawyers can have a good social life, if they so choose. There were meetings, conferences, dinners, sporting events, and there was Deirdre to come home to. For a while, at least, it was enough.

"Enough for me, that is. It wasn't enough for her. She didn't need to go out to work any more, so she stopped bothering. Then she was stuck in that lovely house in West Cross all day, with nothing to do but go to coffee mornings. We had a cleaner, for the housework. It might have been all right, if we'd had children, but, as I think I explained to you before, we didn't seem to be able to manage that.

"I was very slow to notice the change in her. There's no excuse for me. It was Aubrey, funnily enough, who told me that she was seeing someone. Perhaps because of the way he is, he seemed more sensitive to her needs than I ever was. I don't know how far it had gone at that stage. Probably not all the way. She hoped I would notice, and do something about it. I hadn't noticed, and when I was told, I *chose* not to do anything about it. Looking back on it now, I'm not sure what my motivation was."

Charles paused, mid-monologue, to take a sip from his drink.

"There are two possibilities. Either I felt rejected, and didn't want to confront her with it, for fear of making things worse, or . . . I secretly hoped she would leave me, and relieve me of the necessity of ending our marriage myself. I'm still not sure which one of those things it was. Possibly a bit of both."

He seemed to have finished speaking. I was about to make some pointless comment when he started up again suddenly.

"The affair I had – if you can call it an affair – was in response to what Deirdre was doing. It seemed to me that what was sauce for the goose was sauce for the gander, and I saw myself as the wronged one, even though I was fully aware that I had driven her to it. When she found out – as I had intended she would, because by then I *did* want to hurt her – she confronted me, and I revealed that I knew all about what she'd been up to, and we had a huge row. I moved out, for sheer convenience, but at least I had the sense not to move in with the other woman. Who, by the way, is called Gillian Dixon and lives in Kittle, if you want to check my story."

I was totally thrown. "Why should I want to do that?"

"I don't know, but it's obvious that it's important to you. I don't blame you – I know what it's like to place your trust in someone and find that it's been abused. I always knew you'd ask me for the details of my divorce one day, and I'm glad it's come, even if it's a bit sooner than I intended. There shouldn't be any secrets between us."

"Do you still see her? This Gillian?" I wasn't sure why I was asking.

"Occasionally. She was going through marital problems of her own at the time, but she's happily re-married now. How can I explain it, Olwen? It was meaningless. We performed a service for one another. There was no more to it than that. Consequently, we've been able to remain on friendly terms, but when I see her now, I feel . . . nothing. It might as well never have happened."

I got up from the table. I felt numb. Crossing to the drinks cupboard, I poured myself another gin.

"Do you want another one?" I asked, without looking round.

"Am I allowed one? Or would you prefer me to go, now, and leave you to think about things?"

"What things?" Returning to the table, I poured another centimetre of scotch into his glass, wondering vaguely how he was going to get home if he put any more drink inside him.

"Us," he said.

I ignored that. "It's not for me to stand in judgement. I'm sure being married isn't easy. I've never tried it myself, so I can hardly tell you where you went wrong."

"I've never thought of trying it again," he said. "Until recently." He looked directly at me, daring me to ask the question. He was overestimating my ability to risk rejection. Once again, I ignored the invitation.

"If that wasn't the grounds for your divorce," I said slowly, unable to bring myself to use the A-word, "then what was?"

"Separation," he replied. "We stayed apart for the statutory two years. That suited me, because it meant I could have girlfriends without risking commitment. Girlfriends!" He laughed bitterly. "Of course, I was a lot younger then. I enjoyed myself for a while, but it soon wore off. Much the same for Deirdre, I think. At first, she was more than happy to have the house to herself, and the same money coming in that she'd got used to when we were together. I was still paying the mortgage. Then she met someone she could get serious about. Strangely enough, it wasn't the same chap she'd had the fling with. She announced she wanted to get married again, and I did the decent thing. She moved in with him. I got the house back. End of story."

"Was it?"

"No. Of course not. It was only the end of *our* story. And in answer to your unspoken question, yes, I still see Deirdre from time to time, too, and we're on amicable, if distant, terms."

It only struck me then that I loved the way Charles talked. So smooth, so articulate, yet with the odd idiom and figure of speech thrown in to make it completely natural.

"I'm sorry if I seem over-inquisitive," I said, after a few moments' silence. "It's all so much outside my experience."

"Yes, well, be glad of that. I wouldn't wish divorce on my worst enemy. It taught me a thing or two, I can tell you."

"I'm sure."

We lapsed into silence again. Charles continued to sip his drink, while studying my every move. I continued to sip mine, conscious of him watching me. Eventually I got up from the table again. I didn't have his gift for words, and I couldn't say what I wanted to say while he was looking at me so intently. So I turned my back.

"Charles," I said. "You're very important to me, but . . . I'd rather keep your friendship than not have anything at all."

There was no response from Charles. Perhaps he was still trying to puzzle out what I meant.

"Don't let me do anything to put our friendship at risk," I stumbled on. "I want to go on seeing you, whatever else happens."

"Is something else going to happen?" The question surprised me. It was as if he was laying everything at my door, including all the decisions.

"That sort of depends on you."

"Does it? Or does it sort of depend on you?"

I still had my back to him, and I couldn't decide whether he was making fun of me. It was necessary to look at him.

Charles wasn't smiling. He had a gaunt, solemn air about him that I couldn't recall seeing before. He was still holding his whisky tumbler, playing with it, rotating it, pushing it a few millimetres this way and that on the surface of the table. The fidgeting told its own tale.

"I can't say any more," I said.

"Then I'd better go." He stood up. "Thank you for the meal, and the drink. And thank you for listening, and not condemning."

He started to put on his outdoor coat. I wanted to stop him, but I could find neither the words nor the actions. He paused, midway through the act of fastening the coat. Relenting, he moved close to me, and put his hands on my shoulders.

"I hope I'll see you again soon," he said. His hands moved up to my cheeks, and pulled my face into a kiss.

I'd waited so long for this moment, and it was over so quickly. The feel of his mouth on mine, warm, whisky-flavoured and masculine, was enough to make me want to swoon away. Somehow I kept control, and he had drawn back from me again, before I even had time to appreciate his closeness.

"Goodnight, now," he said, opening the front door and leaving me, alone.

Chapter 19

As I turned the van into the lane that led from the main road into the village, I was forced to swing out into the middle to avoid colliding with a vehicle that was standing alongside the hedge, its hazard lights flashing. What a stupid place to park, was my initial thought. Then I saw the young man in a donkey jacket, standing alongside the van, looking desperate. When he spotted me, slowing to a halt ten yards further up the lane, Phil the electrician sprinted up to me, and I wound down the side window.

"Couldn't give me a lift into the village, could you?" he asked. "I can't raise the AA on this sodding mobile. I don't know why I bought it, 'cos I can never get a signal round here."

"You've broken down?"

"Fanbelt's gone. I could fix it if I had the wherewithal. A pair of tights or something." He looked at me hopefully, then his gaze dropped to my legs and observed that I was in jeans.

"You're out of luck, then," I said. "Jessica's not with me."

At the mention of her name, he went quiet. I had half a mind not to give him a lift, in view of the way he'd dropped her without any explanation, but he was already in the passenger seat, strapping on his seat belt.

"I think I've got a spare in the garage at home," he ventured, returning to the original subject of the conversation. "If you can drop me off, I'll have a look for it. Or I'll phone the AA from the house. Same difference."

I cringed at that meaningless expression.

"You'll have to walk back, I'm afraid," I said. "I haven't got time to wait for you."

"That's okay. It's kind of you to stop for me."

He flashed me an engaging smile, the kind designed to have an effect on girls of his own age group. I was made of sterner stuff.

"She's a bit of a goer, your niece."

My fingers tightened on the wheel. "What exactly do you mean by that?" I retorted sharply. If this was his idea of small talk, I was unimpressed.

"N-nothing." He was disconcerted. "She's a nice girl. Good fun. Pity she's in college."

"Most people would say it was a considerable achievement on her part," I snapped. There you go again, Olwen, sounding like your own mother.

"Yeah!" He collected himself quickly. "Yeah, of course it is! Only she's not going to be around here much, so there's no point . . ."

"She meets so many boys at Oxford," I said quickly.

"Oh." The thought evidently hadn't occurred to Phil. "I suppose some blokes don't mind."

"Don't mind what?"

"Well, you know . . . Career woman and all that. When I'm ready to marry someone – or move in with someone . . ." Out of the corner of my eye, I noticed that he had coloured slightly at the embarrassing thought that he had confessed to an intention of ever marrying. "I'd want her to stay home and look after the kids."

"Oh, you would, would you?"

"Well, yeah, of course! It's only right, isn't it?"

"How about your mother? Does she go out to work?"

"She does now," he admitted. "Now that we're all grown up. But not when we were small. She couldn't. My dad's a policeman."

"Really?" Phil didn't coincide with my pre-conceived ideas of what a policeman's son should be like, which I suppose just goes to show how easy it is to be prejudiced.

I'd been thinking about the police quite a lot recently, what with the Sutcliff situation and my own budding relationship with a man who mentioned them in every other sentence. Phil probably wasn't the person to ask about police procedure in child abuse cases, though.

"You weren't inspired to follow in his footsteps?" I asked instead.

"No bloody way! Not with some of the stories I've heard. You'd be amazed what I know about some of the people round here. Some of your friends . . ."

He bit his lip and went quiet all of a sudden. There was no way I was letting him get away with that.

"Such as?"

"Between you and me?"

I nodded assent.

"Mr Jones. You know, the organist."

"You mean Elvis?"

"Yeah. If people round here knew what I know, they wouldn't let him have a job with the church."

"It's not exactly a job, Phil. He gets paid very little. He does it out of love."

"Yeah, well, there's more than one kind of love – if you get my drift."

I didn't ask. Thankfully, we were coming close to Phil's house, or so he said.

"You can let me out here."

My mind was racing. I had half a mind not to stop the van, to make him stay in the passenger seat until he had told me everything. Only that would have made me just as bad as Mrs Hodges and the tomato woman and all the other busybodies.

"Phil!" I called, as he leapt out of the van and prepared to run away. He approached my open window with obvious reluctance and a questioning look.

"I know it's hard, being dumped," I said, feigning sympathy. "But you'll get over it."

I drove away.

Despite deriving a certain amount of spiteful pleasure from my actions, I got to the house in a foul mood. Jessica looked up with concern at my noisy entry. After all these years, she could tell in seconds what kind of temper I was in. I forced myself to smile as I walked past her. My first instinct – to tell her exactly what had just happened – was not a good one. Jess would soon find another boyfriend, a much more suitable one. If she had forgotten Phil, so much the better. If she hadn't, what would have been the point in mentioning his name?

That was all very well, but I couldn't stop thinking about Elvis. I had a pretty good idea of the kind of thing Phil had been hinting at. It might or might not be relevant to the Sutcliff situation. I didn't see how I could possibly find out any more.

Jessica hadn't been slow to notice the change in me, and she was quick to comment on it.

"What's the matter, Auntie Olwen?" she had asked, that morning at breakfast. "Have you and Charles had a row?"

I tried to smile. The idea of Charles rowing with anyone was picturesque – though, from what he had told me, he and Deirdre had managed it.

"Nothing so dramatic," I replied.

"Have you finished with him?"

"I don't think so."

She looked relieved. "Good. He's nice, Charles. He's . . . You know, Auntie Ol, I meet all sorts of people at Oxford."

"Oh, yes?" I couldn't quite see how this was relevant. I pretended to busy myself with the cereal packet, rolling the inner bag carefully back down and fastening it securely with a plastic clip so that the contents wouldn't go soggy.

"Yes. I've got one friend whose father's an earl! Honest to God!"

I smiled thinly, concentrating hard on what was in my bowl.

"The thing is, I don't know whether I'll make a go of it, whether I'll get a good degree . . ."

"Don't worry about that, Jess. You've done wonderfully well to get to Oxford. No one's expecting you to get a First. I was on the phone to your mum the other day, and she said . . ."

"Auntie Olwen!" I looked up, startled by the abruptness of her tone. "I'm trying to tell you something. It's not about my course, I'm not worried about that. It's about . . . people. I'll never regret going to Oxford, because it's taught me something special. Like I said, I meet all kinds of people. Some of them are rolling in dosh, others are from ordinary families like ours. The thing I've learned is to look beyond the surface."

I still wasn't sure what she was getting at, but I made a show of listening.

"You get people who are snobs," she went on, "even though they aren't really well off, and then you get people who are incredibly rich and behave just like anyone else. Some people have a kind of veneer. They've been brought up differently from me, but that doesn't make them stuck-up. When you get to know them, they're really nice, even though they do go hunting and travel first-class on the train and so on.

"What I'm trying to say is, Charles is the kind of person who . . . well, if I didn't know better, I'd think he was a bit flash, you know, with his BMW and his solicitor's manner. But he's not. The way he came in here the other night and drank hot chocolate with us. There's nothing false about him. I suppose what I'm trying to say is, he's genuine. And I'm sure he's not leading you on, if that's what's worrying you."

How could someone so young have so much wisdom? I would have said she had Charles's knack of mind-reading, only she had known me for many more years than Charles had, and had more opportunities to observe my moods.

"He's crazy about you," she added.

The idea seemed so absurd that I started to laugh; then I looked at Jess and understood that she was perfectly serious. After all these years, it shouldn't have come as such a shock to realise that she cared about my happiness.

"I know he doesn't mean to lead me on," I said. "And I know he's a lovely man."

"Then why the long face? Has he done something to upset you?"

"Yes and no. I can't explain, Jess. I daresay it'll sort itself out. Please don't ask me any more." I was afraid I would start to cry. One would have thought, after the way I had saturated my pillow the previous night, that there would be no more tears to come; but there they were, stinging the backs of my eyes, just waiting for the floodgates to open. I'd never cried so much in my life as I had during the last fortnight.

The funniest thing of all was that I knew Jessica wouldn't understand what was holding me back. The idea of a man being divorced was quite a normal run-of-the-mill concept, to someone of her age. In spite of being part of the same family, she hadn't been brought up the way I had, and she didn't have the same hang-ups. If I had told her I was afraid to let myself go with Charles, afraid to go all the way with him in case he changed his mind and lost interest in me as he had lost interest in his ex-wife, Jess would have said I was paranoid. Or perhaps she wouldn't actually have said it, but she would have thought it. I preferred not to lay myself open to ridicule.

I dragged myself through the next couple of days. Charles didn't appear. He didn't ring. There was good reason for me to be the one to make the first move. Yet I continued to hold back. On Tuesday, Jessica asked me again whether I had finished with him. Again, I gave an inconclusive reply.

"You need a bit of a break," she said matter-of-factly. We had certainly been working hard, packing up all those books people had ordered as last-minute Christmas gifts, but that wasn't what she meant. Carefree as she was, she instinctively understood my need for comfort without questions. "Let's go out tonight, you and me. Let's go and paint the town."

I guffawed. "There's no way you're going to get me parading down the Kingsway. I value my life as well as my virtue." It wouldn't have done to admit that I was also concerned for my niece's safety.

"All right, then, let's not go into town. Let's go down to Mumbles. There are a few nice clubs there."

"But it's Tuesday. Nowhere'll be open."

Jessica's mouth fell open. "Auntie Olwen, what planet are you living on? And anyway, it's nearly Christmas. It'll be heaving with people, on their works Christmas dos."

"Don't you think I might stand out a bit, in a club, at my age?"

She made a face. "You're joking! I've seen women in those places who are twenty years older than you, and look it – which you don't. You never know, you might pick yourself up a toy boy."

"I don't think so, Jess."

She looked so disappointed at my outright refusal that I had second thoughts. She was right, for all the wrong reasons. I had barely gone outside the door in the last two days. It would do me good to get out of the house, even if I had a lousy time when I did. At least I wouldn't be brooding over my conversation with Charles, and wondering whether he was ever likely to get in touch with me again.

Jessica was over the moon when I told her I'd changed my mind. Sensibly, she didn't try to advise me as to what to wear. There wasn't a huge range of possible outfits in my wardrobe. In fact, I almost wished I'd bought something, that day she dragged me round the shops in Swansea. What smart clothes I owned were mostly day wear, for attending conferences and special sales events, not for evenings out on the town. There was no point asking for a loan of any of my niece's clothes, because she was much taller than me, and quite a bit slimmer.

Since I was effectively paying for the evening, Jessica insisted that we get a taxi into Mumbles, and I gave in gracefully. It was the only sensible thing to do. For one thing, my niece was wearing that tiny dress she had bought on one of her recent shopping excursions, and I didn't want to send her home to her mother with pneumonia. However, it meant another visit to the cashpoint the moment we arrived; and that was only the start of it. Getting into the club cost nearly a fiver each and, when I paid for the first round of drinks, I nearly had a heart attack. They were charging almost two pounds just for an orange juice. I was beginning to share Jessica's hopes of picking up "a couple of fellers" who would fund the rest of our evening's drinking.

We hadn't been sitting down for two minutes when the first one arrived on the scene. Jessica was a magnet for men of all ages and appearances, but most of them went away again when they caught sight of her companion for the evening. For her part, she stubbornly refused to dance with anyone who couldn't find a partner for her Auntie Olwen.

Eventually we struck lucky. Two men, apparently a father and son, approached tentatively. While the boy was chatting Jessica up, his dad turned reluctantly to me.

"Can I get you a drink?"

"Can you afford it?"

He laughed. "I've taken out a second mortgage to pay for this evening."

"Mmm. I'll have a drink, but later. Sit down." I pointed out the seat next to me.

It was strange that I didn't feel nervous. Evidently, my concern for Jessica's welfare was taking priority over my own anxieties, and I was watching her latest admirer carefully, to make sure he didn't take advantage.

"He's all right, you know," said – or rather, shouted – the man, who was watching me watching them. "He'll look after your daughter. You can relax."

"She's not my daughter!" I shouted back. The corner we had

chosen to sit in was screened from the worst of the disco, but it was still too loud for my liking.

"Oh. Sorry." He peered at me. "It's difficult to tell people's ages, in this light. Or do I mean dark?" He was right the second time. It was pitch-dark but, from what I could make out of his features, he was not unpleasant to look at. A little overweight, perhaps; it comes with age.

"It's okay!" I yelled. "She's my niece. You didn't make a mistake. I *am* old."

He laughed again. "That's all right. So am I. Can I ask your name?"

"Olwen."

"I'm John. Pleased to meet you." He held out his hand for a shake. A bit formal, I thought, but if he wasn't on the pick-up, I was even happier.

I nodded in the boy's direction. "Is he your son?"

He nodded. "Yep. Home from university."

"Same with her." I decided not to mention Oxford. Jessica was always saying that it puts people off. That seemed to have been the problem with Phil.

"And yourself?"

"I'm in business." His awed reaction caused me to elaborate. "I buy and sell books." Cruelly, I wondered whether he had ever read one.

"Chartered surveyor," he responded, pointing to his chest. I wasn't sure whether it was the statement or the chest that I was supposed to be impressed by, so I just did a general impersonation of a person who's been told something fascinating. Out of the corner of my eye, I was still watching Jessica, in conversation with John's son. They got up to dance.

John glanced at me furtively. "Wanna dance?" he asked, without enthusiasm.

"Maybe later." Like maybe when they played a tune I recognised. Or just a tune, full stop. At that point, even Slade's *Merry Christmas, Everybody* would have made a welcome change.

John looked relieved. For a moment, we were stuck for a topic of conversation.

"Where do you live?" He had beaten me to it.

"On Gower. You?"
"Gorseinon."
A bit close for comfort, I thought. The only way he was going to get my phone number was if Jessica gave it to his son. To be brutally honest, though, he didn't look as if he was going to want it.
We had inadvertently slipped into a situation that suited us both, John and I. Rather like Charles and Deirdre, in that marriage that had given them both what they wanted, up to a point, and later in that separation that had also been so mutually convenient.
John had come to this club to keep his son company. He was, as I later discovered, divorced, and didn't see much of the boy, so he felt obliged to make an effort when he got his Christmas visit. His son had no friends in Swansea, and therefore had no alternative, if he wanted to go out, but to go with his father – only marginally preferable to going alone.
This evening he had struck lucky, meeting a girl who was similarly placed except that, in Jessica's case, she was not short of potential company to go clubbing with and was with me only because she had taken pity on my plight. John and I continued to sit there, exchanging the occasional smile and comment. Eventually I allowed him to buy me a drink. It seemed only polite in view of the enormous favour I had done him by bringing along my niece and saving him the embarrassment of attempting to chat up girls who were young enough to be his daughter.
I won't go so far as to say that I enjoyed that evening, but it took me out of myself, to use a favourite phrase of my mother's. It was just as well *she* wasn't there, though. I can't imagine what she would have said, at the sight of her daughter and granddaughter consorting with two strange men, then hobbling out of the club on their far-from-sensible heels, across the Oystermouth Road, looking for a taxi in the wintry dark.
John looked relieved when I turned down his half-hearted offer of a lift home. It would have been considerably out of his way, but in any case I was dubious about his ability to drive a straight line. I hadn't kept an eye on what he was drinking, but I felt sure he'd had more than I had.
We had to wait some time for a taxi. While waiting, we sat on

dirty chairs in the dingy reception area, while teenage boys played the fruit machine and swore a lot. Through the glass we watched passers-by leaving, or being ejected from, other clubs. Someone threw up just outside the window, reminding me why I had never wanted to come here in the first place. I tried to think positive.

We got a cab in the end, finally staggering back into the darkened house at about two in the morning. The prospect of getting up again at eight, to deal with another day's mail, was daunting, but I consoled myself with the thought that business had been unprecedentedly good this Christmas. As a result, I would be able to spend more than I had intended on booze and chocolates to help the celebrations at Sian's go with a swing.

That brought to mind the fact that Charles had asked, at some point during our Saturday outing, what I was doing for Christmas. I had told him that I always spent the actual day at my sister's, but had made a point of telling him that I would be back home on Boxing Day – minus Jessica, who would be remaining with her own family for New Year. He had hinted at the possibility of sharing some kind of special New Year celebration. There were no end of invitations to choose from, he had said, tempting me almost beyond endurance.

And now, probably, it was all over. Charles was, quite reasonably, waiting for some gesture from me, unconscious of the fact that I was waiting for the equivalent from him. He had a right to expect it; I didn't. What I wanted was for him to show some evidence of commitment, some sign that he wasn't going to let me down – too much to expect from a man you've only known for a few weeks. For the sake of that, I was prepared to let my chance of happiness slip away.

Chapter 20

The news finally came through on Wednesday morning. Jessica was still in bed, and I was feeling distinctly fragile after our late night. Deciding that a walk in the fresh air might help to clear my head after opening the mail, I put on my warmest coat and a woolly hat, and headed for the church. My first thought was to walk around the churchyard, but it was even colder than I had thought and, when I noticed one of the choirboys running into the church porch, I followed him inside.

I seemed to be spending a lot of my time in church these days. Too much, perhaps. Solitary contemplation may be good for the soul, but you can overdo it. It probably wasn't healthy to be spending so much time examining my conscience. That knowledge didn't stop me.

As I was about to push open the door, I distinctly heard a voice inside. Elvis's voice.

"Now give it a good suck, Geraint. That's the way!"

I wondered what on earth could be going on. Having no reason to assume the worst, I opened the door and went boldly in.

As I had suspected, Elvis and Geraint were not alone in the church. At least fifteen other members of the choir were present. That was when I remembered that there would be the usual big carol service on Tuesday evening, the night before Christmas Eve. I had wandered in on a major rehearsal. The kids were no longer in school, which was why there was a full turn-out.

As the door closed behind me, Elvis turned his head to see who had come in. Momentary annoyance at the disturbance turned to a smile as he recognised me.

"Olwen, cariad, have you come to join the choir after all these years?"

"I don't think I'd be much use . . ."

"No, you're right, I've got enough problems with this lot. Geraint here's got a sore throat – something chronic it is too. I had to give him a humbug to stop him croaking like a frog!"

There was a titter from some of the girls in the front row.

"Yes, I know he looks like a frog, girls," said Elvis, addressing them directly, "but I don't want him to sing like one. 'Stedda lawr, Olwen. Now let's take it from the top again. 'It was on a starry night . . .' "

For the moment, Elvis was both conducting the choir and accompanying them on the little electric organ that was sometimes used for children's services – not to mention singing along with gusto. On Sunday evening, the deputy organist would play the pipe organ, and Elvis would conduct, but he would be obliged to keep his mouth shut.

Seeing him with the children now, I could understand what made them keep coming to choir practice. It wasn't just the promise of payment. It was Elvis's personality, his drive, his sheer enthusiasm. They might make fun of him behind his back – I'd heard them doing imitations of him in the vestry – but they liked him, they trusted him. He would no more have taken advantage of one of these children than he would have smashed up the organ.

I sat back and enjoyed the rest of the rehearsal. A shaft of sunshine shot in suddenly through one of the high stained-glass windows, turning the interior of the church into a very pretty picture. The holly leaves shone, green and glossy, alongside the latest red-and-white floral decorations – brought in by Mrs Bevan's team that morning, by the look of them. I had been reading, in one of the old books I'd brought back from Limeslade, about the ancient Gower custom of "holly beating" on Boxing Day. Apparently, it was very popular with male chauvinists in the nineteenth century, and involved finding women – usually servants – with bare arms, and chasing them around with large sprigs of holly in an attempt to draw blood.

Given half a chance, I thought, some of the congregation would have been only too ready to revive the practice in the twenty-first century, for the benefit of their own vicar. If they had known what I knew, Elvis might have been in for it as well.

This was no time or place for such unpleasant ideas. I concentrated on the singing, which was over all too soon. When Elvis dismissed the choir and started putting things away, I got up and made a move to leave, but he caught me by the arm and told me to stick around.

"I was coming over your house to fetch you after rehearsal, in any case. You've saved me the walk."

I had seen Tim and Laura at church on the previous Sunday, but hadn't had a chance to ask them how things were going. The thought of Charles rushing round to see them on Friday night was still playing on my curiosity. I had asked Elvis, revealing only that I happened to know that Charles had been to see them and it had been a long session. For once, Elvis was no wiser than I was.

By now, he was evidently back in his usual position of being one up on me, knowledge-wise, but he still wouldn't tell me anything. It was with difficulty that I kept up with his stride, along the lane leading to the vicarage.

"What's happened?" I kept asking.

"All in good time," he kept saying.

When we got to the vicarage, the back door was open and there was lots of noise emanating from the kitchen.

"Look who's here!" cried Tim, as we entered cautiously. "Laura, get Olwen a sherry!"

I sensed that this was more than just a pre-Christmas celebration.

"We've had wonderful news, Olwen," said Laura, handing me a glass. I noticed she was drinking pineapple juice herself. "It's all over. They've decided not to charge Tim."

"You mean, they've cleared you of all suspicion?" I asked, looking at Laura's husband.

A little frown wrinkled Tim's brow. "Tell you all about it later." He winked.

There were several other people in the room, besides Elvis and me and the Sutcliffs. Mr Samuel and his wife stood in a corner, talking with one of Mrs Bevan's flower-arranging team. Mrs Bevan herself was nowhere to be seen. I guessed that Laura had been deliberately selective with the invitations again. Unfairly so, this time.

If there was one thing that made me really happy, it was that the police, or whoever decides these things, had come to their decision before Christmas. It would have been too bad if a family like the Sutcliffs had been forced to go through the most important season of the year with something like that hanging over their heads.

"Have they said what swayed them?" I asked Elvis, when we found ourselves temporarily separated from the main group of well-wishers. What I was really thinking was that Charles's instinct about things "fizzling out" had probably been a reliable one.

Elvis shook his head in reply. "Not that I know of."

I didn't intend to stay at the vicarage for long, just long enough to offer my most sincere congratulations. Tim and Laura would need time to themselves, to absorb the good news. It seemed to me that Charles must have had a pretty good idea that this was going to happen. His urgent visit to the Sutcliffs on Friday must have had something to do with it. I had no right to feel resentful that he hadn't given anything away to me. The Sutcliffs were his clients, paying clients. As for me, I wasn't even his . . . girlfriend.

That word, "girlfriend", the word that Charles found so amusing and so utterly inappropriate for people of his age – *our* age. It haunted me, now, the idea that I might have had the opportunity to become Charles's girlfriend. What I had thrown away, the other night, might have been the chance of a more fulfilling future; or it might merely have been the chance of a fling with a man whose strong point was discretion rather than fidelity.

That didn't stop me thinking about him.

One or two people had started to drift away, it being past their usual time for lunch. I was getting ready to do the same, when Elvis tugged at my sleeve.

"Not yet, bach," he protested. "Tim said he had something to tell me, and I think he meant to include you, too."

Privately, I doubted it. Tim had long since ceased to show me any special favour, and the only thing I had done to merit it lately was to agree to be a character witness – a role I wouldn't now be called on to fulfil.

A few people outstayed their welcome, probably assuming that my continued presence, and Elvis's, entitled them to hang around. Eventually they got the message, and the four of us were left alone in the kitchen.

"I've got a few things to do," said Laura suddenly. "I'll be upstairs if you need me." She nudged Tim in a manner that suggested they had discussed this beforehand.

"There's no need for you to leave us, darling."

Tim was saying one thing, but his body language was saying quite another. I got the distinct impression that he was actively hoping for Laura to disappear off the scene. It reminded me of what Charles had said the other night, about how she always made herself scarce when there was serious talking to be done. Tim relaxed visibly after she had gone out and closed the door.

"I wanted to talk to the two of you, in confidence," he said. He was looking at me as he spoke, but I sensed that whatever was about to come was mostly intended for Elvis's benefit. I was being included only because he knew that Elvis and I were old friends, and that we tended to exchange confidences. Tim was just cutting out the middle man. "I wanted to explain to you why the police have dropped the case."

He looked from me to Elvis and back again, waiting for one of us to ask a question. We disappointed him. In my case, it was purely because I couldn't think of anything to say. In Elvis's case, however, there was something else. When I glanced across at his face, I was surprised at the hardness of his expression. It was almost as though he was preparing himself to disbelieve what Tim said next.

"There was a reason for what Craig did," said Tim. "He didn't understand the significance of what happened. He's a child, he was . . . bewildered. I'm not sure I understood what I was doing, myself."

The silence was almost painful.

"He saw me do something. He didn't know what to make of it, so he tried to tell someone. All he knew was that I had done something wrong. Everyone else just jumped to the wrong conclusion. Craig never told any lies. He was simply misunderstood."

Tim had looked quite cool when he began this explanation, if that was what you could call it; but already he was getting flustered. Elvis's lack of response, in particular, was disconcerting. I felt obliged to help him out.

"What exactly do you mean, Tim? What did you do?"

"I don't know how I can explain it, Olwen. It was to do with Laura. You must have noticed – you must both have noticed – that Laura . . . finds it hard to cope."

For the first time, there was some reaction from Elvis. He nodded slowly, but still said nothing.

"She can't cope with life," Tim went on. "She can't manage the children, she hates the parish, she doesn't even like going outside the door. And then, every so often, when it all gets too much, she hits the bottle."

"There are worse things she could be doing . . ." I began.

"Of course there are. And she's my responsibility. If I hadn't chosen the church as a career, her life would have been very different. She's supported me at every turn, she never tried to dissuade me from becoming a clergyman, but the pressure on her has been tremendous. She was bound to crack, eventually."

"Tim," said Elvis suddenly. "I don't want to sound impatient, bach, but what exactly are you driving at?"

The story, when it came out, was simple enough. It had all happened after the charity concert, just as Craig had alleged, but not at the party, as had been inferred. Tim had been backstage, in a small room set aside for administrative tasks. The takings from the concert were there, and Tim was keeping an eye on things. The money would be checked, later, by Elvis, and by Mr Samuel, who was Treasurer for the fund. They were both still in the main hall, moving chairs.

"It seemed like the best opportunity I was likely to have," said Tim, "to return the money."

It seemed to take me longer to understand than it took Elvis – probably because Elvis, being indirectly involved, had been suspicious all along. It went against the grain, to think Laura a thief, a kleptomaniac, but it certainly explained a lot.

"Let me get this straight," said Elvis, when Tim was well launched into his story. He seemed taken aback at the interruption, as though he had prepared what he was going to say, word for word, and couldn't accommodate any alteration in the order.

Thinking about it, I supposed that was exactly what he had done – prepared a speech to make to us, quite possibly the same speech that he had already made, to Charles and to the police and whoever else needed to be told. I couldn't blame him for that. It must have been very difficult to admit to the world that your wife had a problem obeying the law, especially for a vicar. No wonder Laura had chosen to leave the room.

"You're saying that Laura pinched a few bob out of the takings from the concert," probed Elvis.

"I'm sure she didn't mean to be dishonest. She said she borrowed it because she was short on the housekeeping. You know how strapped we are for cash. It was my own fault, for leaving the ticket money lying around, after Alan Samuel gave it to me. It was just putting temptation in her way." Tim was quite matter of fact about it all, as though no harm had really been done.

"I don't understand, Tim," I said. "Why didn't you just put it back straight away?"

"Because I didn't find out until it was too late. The money had already been banked by the time she confessed to me what she had done. It was the night of the concert, and I was afraid the discrepancy would show up. It was stupid of me to do what I did. I knew she regretted it. I didn't want to cause her any heartache. I saw the opportunity to cover up for her, and that's what I was trying to do."

It was ironic that Tim should have done all this, in an effort to spare Laura's dignity, but ended up dragging Craig Dutton's name through the mud.

"I'm going to sort it all out with the Duttons," he protested, conscious of the apparent inconsistency in his attitude. "I really am. They understand that I was trying to protect Laura. I'll make it up to Craig, somehow."

Elvis shook his head, doubtfully, but didn't say what I guessed he was thinking. "Go on with the story, Tim."

The tickets were two pounds fifty each. Once Tim had put back the money, all he had to do was put a few more ticket stubs on the table so that, when Elvis came to double-check them, the money would tally with the ticket sales. "I had some spare tickets in my pocket. I had lifted up my cassock to get them out, and I started ripping them in half. That's what I was doing when Craig wandered into the room."

"Did he say anything?" I was having difficulty visualising the situation.

"Not at first. He just looked. There was no way he could have failed to see. But he didn't understand. He knew there was something wrong, but he didn't know exactly what. I don't really know what he thought I was doing. He came towards me. He put out his hand to me, like you do with your child, when you know they're trying to hide something in their pocket. Only the roles were reversed." He tried to laugh.

Elvis and I didn't share the joke.

"Believe me," said Tim, serious again all of a sudden, "if I'd had any idea what it was going to lead to, I would never have done what I did. I pulled out the lining of my pocket, to show that it was empty. Craig looked . . . baffled. So I turned around and offered him my other pocket. 'If you can find anything in there, you can have it,' I said. It was a kind of joke.

"I didn't realise I had any money in that pocket, but there was a pound coin. Craig reached into my pocket and took it out. Then he looked at me again. He asked me what I was doing, and I said, 'Nothing'. And I told him to go back into the hall and help put the chairs away. Stupidly, I told him not to say anything to anyone. What I actually meant was that he shouldn't tell anyone I'd given him money. That might have looked a bit off, if anyone had found out. Craig went quietly enough, and I thought that was the last of it."

There was another long silence. I looked at Elvis, half-expecting that he would be looking back at me, but he wasn't. He wasn't looking at Tim, either.

"You've told the police all this, then?" he said, his facial expression unreadable as long as he continued to look down at the floor. "The full story?"

"I've made a clean breast of it," said Tim. "I told Charles Cornwell first, and he was very understanding. He arranged for me to speak to the police, and they saw the Duttons about it. They seem to have accepted it. But I'm sure you can understand why I didn't want it to come out. It was only at Laura's insistence that I told anyone the whole truth, in the end."

It occurred to me that life might have been a lot easier for everyone concerned if Laura had been so insistent in the first place. I dismissed the idea that Tim's reluctance to tell all might have something to do with the loss of credibility a vicar might suffer if anyone found out his wife was a thief. That was too cynical.

There wasn't much more to be said. Elvis and I left the house, in a rather more subdued mood than we had entered. He was saying very little, as we walked down the path, but his uneasiness was only too apparent.

"I'm just glad it's all over," I sighed.

"You believe him, then?"

Despite Elvis's manner, I was astonished by this response.

"Don't you?"

"Come off it, Olwen, his story's got as many holes in it as a bloody sieve! Of course he could have put the money back straight away. There was absolutely no reason. And all that stuff about the ticket stubs – I mean, do me a favour!"

I admit, that part of Tim's story had sounded rather far-fetched. Tearing up unused tickets so as to use the stubs to make sure the money tallied did seem to be going to extremes.

"It's an insult to my intelligence!" exclaimed Elvis, getting into his stride now. "The ticket stubs have got nothing to do with the takings. They're for the tickets that were sold beforehand. People who pay on the door don't get a ticket, so there's no possible way of knowing exactly how many came in. We'd never go to the trouble of counting up the ticket stubs and making sure they tallied with the money we'd already taken. I mean, I know Alan Samuel's a bit of a bloody nit-picker, but even he wouldn't go to those lengths! And even if we did, even if the money didn't tally, we would just have assumed that someone had not turned up or that someone had been given free tickets. It would have been no big deal."

"But Tim didn't know that!" I argued. "That's Tim's trouble, he's not . . . like you and me. He's not practical; he lives on another plane. He's a genuinely good person. Sometimes that makes him overlook the obvious. If you ask me, all that stuff about the tickets is just the kind of thing Tim *would* do."

Elvis gave me a sideways look, but said nothing. I'd never seen him like this.

"Tim's attitude to life makes him do things that another person would regard as . . . inconsiderate," I conceded. "But chwarae teg, Elvis. Isn't what he's just told us a lot easier to believe than the idea that he could have molested Craig?"

Elvis grunted acknowledgement. We walked on in silence, for a minute or two, while I waited for him to simmer down.

"Anyway," I went on, "it's all done and dusted now. If the Duttons can accept what Tim's saying, I don't see why anyone else should argue the point. The main thing is that Laura should get help."

Elvis nodded. I could tell he didn't want to hear any of this. I didn't really understand why.

"Did you get my message, the other night, by the way?" he asked, after a few more moments' silence. "About Charles Cornwell?"

"Oh, yes, thanks. I mean, diolch."

"Did it help?"

"At the time, yes."

Elvis was staring down at the wet surface of the lane, in front of our feet, concentrating on not slipping. There were still a few dead leaves lying around, ground to an unattractive pulp by the traffic, and footsteps, and rain, and time.

"Are you seeing him?" Elvis wasn't one to give up easily.

"I could, if I wanted to."

"Gone off him?"

"No."

"What, then?"

I could see I wasn't going to get away with this evasiveness. I stopped, a few yards from my front door.

"He's sweet. He's wonderful. I like him. And I'm scared."

"Oh." Elvis nodded sagely. "Like that, is it? Now you know he's not *the other way*, you're trying to find some alternative reason for not trusting him with your feelings."

I almost laughed. "I know you're right, Elvis, and I'm being stupid. But I haven't been with a man for years. I hardly know where to start. Charles and I are very different."

"I wouldn't have said so."

The statement surprised me. Sometimes, with Elvis, I thought it was just words. He would say whatever came into his head at the time, for the sake of saying something. It was just luck that he was so often right.

"I don't know how you can think that, Elvis. Can't you see we're from different worlds?"

"No, I can't, actually." Elvis didn't normally use words like "actually". When he did, it was suggestive of irony. "You're both well-educated. You're both self-employed. I don't see why you shouldn't make a go of it. Stranger things have happened."

"I'll bear that in mind. Hwyl, now."

I marched off up the drive. I didn't invite Elvis into the house. I didn't need any more reminding of my own frailty.

When I got back indoors, Jessica was dealing with the mail. I gave her the good news.

"Oh, that's fantastic! Great for Laura, and I'm so happy for the children. Do they know what made the police drop the charges?"

It was the obvious question, exactly the same one I would have asked, and I regretted not being able to tell her the full story. I pretended not to know. Jessica suggested that Elvis, that fount of all knowledge, might be able to tell us, but I was able to put her right on that score.

"Let's go to the pub tonight, and celebrate," she suggested.

I wasn't keen. Then I realised what she was angling for.

"You're hoping to see that Phil again, aren't you?"

"Who?"

That was conclusive enough. We were one as bad as the other. I decided to go along with it, though. There was a lot of work to get through, first. People were still sending in orders and asking me to ensure that their books arrived in time for Christmas, even though the last guaranteed posting date for parcels had already passed. Jess and I set to work with brown paper and jiffy envelopes and cardboard boxes. By six o'clock, we had earned a break.

"Auntie Olwen," said Jessica, coming into the kitchen. "I've finished sorting through the last couple of boxes you brought back from Limeslade, and there are one or two things I'm not sure what to do with. There's a whole set of something, and I think it might be worth a few quid. Will you come and have a look?"

I was intrigued. "Okay," I said, "but let's leave it until we've eaten. How do you fancy a meal in the pub?" Jessica was only too happy to accept that suggestion. There would be nothing in the boxes that couldn't wait.

The Drovers' Arms didn't do a very large range of bar food. It wasn't to be compared with the hotel on the beach at Oxwich. Coming up to Christmas, they were getting a little more custom than usual, so it was as well we had arrived early. We ordered something-and-chips each, and found a good seat in the back bar. Elvis arrived when we were just tucking in.

"Hiya, bach!" he hailed me. "Am I forgiven yet?"

"What's he done?" asked Jessica.

"Nothing. Come over here, Elvis, and sit with us. We've nearly finished eating."

"That's a shame, because I'm just about to start. It would be more companionable if you decided to have some pudding, then I wouldn't feel like the odd one out."

The pub did an even less impressive range of desserts than it did of bar meals. Mass-produced chocolate fudge cake was, in fact, the only thing available, but we accepted it. Comfort eating of the most obvious kind. There had been no sign of Phil, as yet.

When we had almost finished our desiccated fudge cake, and Elvis was wiping the gravy off his chin, after demolishing his steak and kidney pie, a young man walked into the bar. He looked vaguely familiar.

"Damian!" shouted Jessica. Her face was aglow, her eyes sparkling. She almost knocked me over in her haste to get out from behind the table.

"Who's that?" asked Elvis, grinning at her youthful enthusiasm.

"She met him in a club last night." I glanced around anxiously, for fear that Damian's father, John, might have accompanied him once again.

Jessica wasn't playing hard to get this evening. She seemed to have learned her lesson, despite the bad example set by her auntie. The boy must have been equally keen, though, to have come all the way from Gorseinon and hunted around for the village pub. I remembered her taking a break, earlier in the afternoon, to make a phone call. She was a sly one.

"She's a sly one," I said, to Elvis.

"Takes after her Auntie Olwen," he countered.

"Do me one small favour, Elvis. Don't mention Charles Cornwell's name this evening. I want to come at it with a fresh mind, if I ever do."

"'Nuff said. You know me. Discretion is my byword."

"Like when you gave away Craig Dutton's story to Tim, you mean?"

Elvis gave me a reproachful look. "You'd have done the same, I hope. And it's all worked out for the best, hasn't it?"

"Does that mean you've decided to accept Tim's version of events?"

He shrugged. "I was being a bit daft, this morning. You were right, what you said. It's too outlandish to be a made-up story. And it *is* much easier to believe than what was being said before."

It was something to puzzle over, but not for long. Elvis and I got down to some serious drinking. Despite what I had said about not wanting to hear Charles's name, I soon found myself asking Elvis for further details of his acquaintance with Aubrey Bantoft and, from there on, it was downhill all the way. Luckily, I drank so much that night that I can't remember much of what I said to Elvis.

There is one thing I do recall quite clearly, though, and to this day the recollection makes me blush. When we were walking home afterwards, I made my confession.

"You know, Elvis," I said drunkenly, "y're a great bloke!" I don't remember my speech as being slurred, but it must have been. "I never realised, till this week, what a great bloke you are!"

"Really?" Elvis's amused, cynical look is vivid in my memory.

"Yes, y're a great bloke," I repeated, "and I want to tell you something. I've been thinking awful things about you. Y'see, when Tim . . . I mean, I knew it couldn't be Tim, he couldn't do a thing like that, but when I said to you that I wondered if it could have been someone else . . ."

"You thought it might have been me," he concluded.

"Y-e-e-ah," I admitted reluctantly. Drunk as I was, I was already regretting the impulse that had caused me to open my big mouth.

Elvis smiled, but I could see the pain behind his eyes.

"I suppose that's only to be expected."

"I mean," I blustered on, "I didn't really think it could be you. Not *really*. Only I didn't know what to believe, who to trust. I don't know how I could have entert . . ." The word, "entertained", was suddenly giving my tongue difficulty. Actually, I couldn't feel my tongue, or my lips for that matter. "I don't know how I could have thought something like that," I burbled. "I'm so *so* sorry."

"You don't have to explain yourself, bach," said Elvis. "And you don't need to apologise. I don't suppose you're the only person who thought the same. When something like this happens, everyone starts looking over their shoulder. I'd almost started to suspect myself."

I don't remember what I said after that. No doubt I poured my heart out to him, about Charles and goodness knows what else, but he never reminded me about it afterwards. In the morning, with the embarrassment sobriety usually brings, I had a few worries as to whether I had damaged our friendship beyond repair; but when I saw him again, his manner towards me hadn't changed. He was just the same as ever. Good old Elvis.

Unusually, Jessica was first out of bed on Thursday morning. After the evening with Elvis, I had woken with a head that felt rather as if it had been hit by a sledgehammer. Tottering into the bathroom, I took a couple of painkillers and went back to sleep for an extra hour. Jess thought nothing of it. Her rendezvous with Damian seemed to have had the opposite effect. When I came down, in my dressing-gown, to get myself some tea, she was sitting there opening the mail as if these reversed roles were quite normal.

"This was put through the door for you," she said, handing me a slim package in brightly-coloured Christmas paper. "It was lying on the mat when I got up, so I didn't see who dropped it off. I wonder who it's from?"

My first thought was that she was being discreet. There was no way *I* would have picked up a Christmas parcel from the mat without looking to see who had sent it, even if it wasn't addressed to me. Then I saw that the label was in fact an envelope, stuck down by its edges, with the name "Olwen" printed in large neat capitals on the front. Presumably there was a letter or a card inside. Having unstuck the envelope carefully, I toyed with the idea of opening the parcel first.

"Aren't you going to open it?" asked Jessica.

"It's not Christmas Day yet," I objected.

"No. But it might be from someone you haven't sent a card or present to, and if you left it till Christmas Day to open it, it would be too late."

There were all kinds of things wrong with that reasoning, but it gave me the excuse I had been looking for.

The package obviously contained a book. Had it not been for the wrapping, I would have assumed that it was something I had ordered.

"Oh, it's only a book!" exclaimed Jessica in disappointment, as the cover began to reveal itself.

"What do you mean, *only* a book?"

"You've got plenty of those already," she complained.

"As a matter of fact . . ." I began. I had been about to conclude by saying, ". . . this is one of mine", but thought better of it. Jessica simply wouldn't have understood why I found the sight of it so touching.

I opened the letter as carefully as I could, not wishing to show my mounting excitement.

"Dear Olwen," it began.

"This was meant to be your Christmas present, but now I find myself wondering whether there will be an opportunity to give it to you before December 25th. It wasn't easy to think of a personal gift which would neither offend nor embarrass, and I could see you were having difficulty deciding whether to sell it, so I decided to make up your mind for you. Forgive me."

Of course, it was signed, "Charles".

I picked up the book. As I had anticipated, he had signed the fly-leaf. "To Olwen, with love from Charles," followed by the date.

Charlotte Mew's poems had returned to me. How could I ever have thought he would give them to his sister-in-law?

I re-read the note. That "Forgive me" at the end could be read with the previous sentence, but it could equally well be taken as a blanket apology for any and every failure and disappointment he might have felt he had inflicted. A little piece of encouragement which turned out to be all I had needed.

I rang his office immediately, and was devastated when the receptionist told me he was "away". Confused, I asked if she was sure. Yes, he had left, early that morning, for a long weekend in Ireland.

Now I understood. I pictured Charles, making a detour in the cold, dark morning, dropping the book through my letterbox while I was fast asleep, before the milkman had even arrived. I could see what he was doing at this very moment – standing on the deck of a ferry in the Irish Sea, perhaps looking wistfully back towards Wales.

If only he had rung the doorbell. Men are always so quick to take you at your word. Charles couldn't know how little it would have required to make me abandon my Baptist principles and let him carry me away to a weekend of sin.

The receptionist offered to take a message. Under the circumstances, it was the best I could do in the way of a conciliatory gesture, so I asked her to tell him that "Olwen Harris had rung". I wondered how long he would be gone for, and whether, by the time he got the message, it would be too late for it to matter. Christmas was less than a week away.

In another vain effort to cheer myself up, I went into the stock room to have a look at what Jessica had found in the Limeslade boxes. I hadn't been in a fit state to tackle them when we got home from the pub.

When I saw what my niece had unearthed, I was astonished. Evidently, the late owner of the book on Spitfires had been interested in armed conflicts other than the one in which he had personally participated. Jessica had been right in thinking she had found something out of the ordinary. A full set of Oman's *History of the Peninsular War*, the 1902 edition no less. Okay, so they weren't in perfect condition, but they were undoubtedly worth something – possibly even as much as I'd given Mrs Robarts for her dad's whole library.

"Diwedd y byd!" was all I could find to say.

It was one of those difficult moral dilemmas. Mrs Robarts hadn't wanted the books. Left to herself, she would probably have burned them. But what would she have said if she had known that the "dusty old odds and ends" she had found in the attic were the most valuable things in her father's possession? I had given her what I thought was a fair price for everything but, if I'd seen the Oman, it would have been substantially more. On the other hand, it's all part of business, isn't it? It wasn't as if they were worth thousands of pounds. It simply meant a nice little profit for me.

Half-heartedly, I went to the phone and dialled the number Val Robarts had given me the previous week. As I expected, the old man's phone had been disconnected. I had no address for Mr and Mrs Robarts in Wrexham. That decided me. Maybe I would leave it a few weeks before selling the Oman, just in case any of the family got back to me. I didn't think it likely that they would.

"Jessica," I said, "you've just earned yourself a Christmas bonus."

That put her in a good mood, and it made me feel a bit like Santa Claus, which didn't do any harm. When the telephone rang, shortly afterwards, I wasn't thinking of Charles. It was less than two hours since I had left my message. Having abandoned all hope of hearing from him for at least a couple more days, I didn't rush to answer. I left it for Jessica. When she handed me the receiver, silently mouthing, "It's Charles," I was afraid to believe her.

He was on the mobile again.

"Where are you?" I asked, doubting the evidence of my own ears.

"Fishguard. The ferry's been cancelled. Indefinitely. I've got to go home. Can I call and see you en route?"

He hadn't needed to ask.

Chapter 21

Apart from Martha Davies and Val Robarts' father, there are a couple of other interesting people buried in churchyards on Gower. The best known is Petty Officer Edgar Evans, a naval officer who travelled with Captain Scott on what is often described as his "ill-fated expedition" to the South Pole. All Scott's companions perished on the journey home, but Evans was one of the first to go. As well as being a hero, Evans was a hardened drinker, who had fallen overboard in a New Zealand harbour while under the influence, before the expedition ever set off for Antarctica, and had been on the verge of being sent home early. Of course, it doesn't tell you this on his memorial, which is in the parish church at Rhossili.

Another celebrity, buried at Oystermouth, was not a native of these parts, but his surname became a household word in the English language – well, almost. Thomas Bowdler was the man who "bowdlerised" Shakespeare and the Bible, taking out all the naughty bits in order to make great works of literature fit for family consumption. I have no idea what made him come to live at Oystermouth; the book didn't say.

These were two little titbits of information that I picked up from *Curiosities of South Wales*, which I had found in the same pile as the *Guide to Gower*. It wasn't as old as the other book, but it made riveting reading. I needed something like that, right now, to make the waiting bearable. Any constructive work was out of the question, in my present frame of mind.

When Charles arrived, a couple of hours later, looking pale and tired, I didn't know how to greet him. No sooner had I got him into the house than Jessica found some pretext for going out, giving me what she thought was a surreptitious wink on her way through the door.

As the door closed, and we watched her going down the drive, I dared to look at Charles. He was looking at me.

"Very discreet, your niece," he said. "She ought to think about the law as a career, or medicine."

"Or espionage," I concluded. We laughed.

I made coffee, and thanked him for the book. Words seemed inadequate, but I had to try.

"It's a shame about your weekend," I remarked. "I know you'd been looking forward to it."

Charles raised an eyebrow. "You know nothing of the sort. I was dreading it. I've got a feeling it's going to be a much more pleasant weekend than I'd anticipated."

I smiled.

He made a point of telling me he was free for the day, apart from the need to respond to a request from Tim to go and see the Sutcliffs later, to tie up a few loose ends. Charles had made this arrangement as soon as he heard the ferry was cancelled, speaking to Tim not long before he spoke to me on the phone, thinking that it would give him an excuse to return to the village.

He was dressed differently, I noticed, a mix of smart and casual. He was wearing a collar and tie, certainly, but the shirt was dark green and the tie fawn. Instead of the usual suit, he had on a tweedy sports jacket and brownish trousers. It was a homely look, one I felt I could get used to.

"I was so relieved," he said, "when I rang the office for my messages, and they told me you'd already called. I'd been praying that you would. I couldn't bear the thought of not seeing you until after Christmas, or maybe not even then. I thought I would be phoning you from Ireland."

"I nearly didn't open it, you know. Usually I save up all my presents for the big day."

He glanced at the ceiling. "Somebody up there likes me." The smile came on. As I held out the coffee mug towards him, he took it from my hand, set it down on the table beside my own, and put his arms around my waist. I didn't resist. Beneath my fingers, I enjoyed the texture of his green shirt, soft – brushed cotton? – and beneath that, the unmistakable warmth of the human body.

"What shall we do now?" he asked. His dark eyes seemed to glow, in the reflection of the electric fire.

"What would you like to do?"

"I think you know what *I* want," he said. "But *you* need to want it, too."

I wasn't a virgin, before I went to bed with Charles that afternoon. Once, when I was a student, I slept with a boyfriend. Once was enough. It was so painful, so embarrassing an experience, that I was never tempted to repeat it. If that's what sex is like, I thought, you can keep it.

What I wasn't taking into account was the part I had played in making the episode a failure. It wasn't just all those years of being teased by the boys at school, learning to distance myself from my own feelings. My hang-ups were far more extensive than that.

I was brought up a Baptist, with the view that sex outside marriage was, quite simply, wrong. Even the most devout Christians have moderated their views on that subject in the past thirty years. As I got older, I started to realise that sex, in the context of a relationship, is not the most important thing in the world. Having sex with one man doesn't mean you can't, later, fall in love with someone else. Nor does it make it impossible for you to be faithful to anyone in the future; on the contrary, it makes it easier. As I watched my friends get married, have children, and either get divorced or settle into comfortable married middle age, I began to understand more about how relationships between couples work.

Because I believed I was doing wrong when I had sex with my boyfriend, my body rebelled. I was so uptight, so nervous and anxious, that there was never any hope of it being an enjoyable experience. It was just as bad for the boy – his name was Dave, and I was deeply, genuinely in love with him – as it was for me, because I left him wondering what he had done wrong. He was, before that night, a virgin too. I hope my performance didn't put him off women for life.

Believe it or not, I couldn't even keep quiet about the fact that I hadn't enjoyed it. In the morning, I did nothing but cry, repeating, over and over, that I had sinned and it served me right. Dave left in confusion, and we never spoke to one another again.

By the time I was thirty-five, I no longer took the view that it was wrong to have sex with someone you weren't married to. I was perfectly prepared to give it another try. The trouble was that, by that time, there was no one available to give it a try with. I was well and truly on the shelf.

No doubt I could have found someone. I could have made a desperate tour of the bars and night-clubs in Swansea, which are always full of men, of all age groups, looking for a casual pick-up. There was always a John to be found. The trouble was that I was looking for a relationship. There was no point otherwise. So I lived with my frustrations.

What Charles and I did, that December afternoon, in my bedroom, was so completely different from my previous experience that afterwards I simply wanted to cry with happiness. There's no need for me to go into detail. Suffice it to say that Charles made me feel wanted and – yes – loved. He was experienced with women, I could have told that even if I hadn't known, but the knowledge didn't make me feel cheap and nasty. On the contrary, if he was willing to make the effort to break through the defences I'd set up around myself, I knew he must really care for me.

So comfortable and relaxed did I feel, after the event, that I dozed off, to be woken some time later by a fully-dressed Charles, offering me a cup of tea.

"Oh, no!" I exclaimed, sitting up so quickly that I nearly knocked the cup out of his hand. "What time is it?"

He smiled, and for the millionth time I thought how much I liked his narrow, earnest face.

"Don't panic," he said. "Jessica's not home yet. There's time for you to get dressed. Have a bath or something. I've showered, by the way. I'm afraid I'll have to go soon. I've got an appointment with the Sutcliffs, in case you'd forgotten."

He had changed out of the dark green shirt and sports jacket, and was now in his habitual white shirt and business suit. For a moment I wondered how he had managed it; then I remembered that he must have had an assortment of clothes packed away in his car for the weekend. It gave me a little frisson of pleasure to think of the old lady next door watching him fetch his things from the car and seeing him emerge, later, dressed differently. Changing your clothes in someone else's house implies a level of intimacy that she would undoubtedly take note of. Just because I didn't want anyone else in the house while we were engaged in making love, it didn't follow that I didn't want the whole world to know about it – eventually.

"Will you come back?" I asked, taking the tea but not meeting his eyes. My expectations were high. I was aware that I was just asking to be disappointed.

"Do you want me to?" He sat down on the bed and put his arm around me.

"Only if *you* want to."

He laughed. "This conversation is getting very delicate. I didn't think all this pussyfooting around would still be necessary. Not between us. Not now."

I put the cup back in the saucer, and looked up at him.

"Charles, I'm sorry. I don't know what to expect. This situation is quite unfamiliar to me."

He gave me a little squeeze. "Supposing I were to take you out to dinner tonight?"

I nodded, smiling. "That would be . . . lovely."

"And afterwards, we could do any one of a number of things."

I waited for him to enumerate them, but he chose not to.

"Shall we play it by ear?" he asked.

I nodded again. He had taken away my power of coherent thought, let alone sensible speech. Kissing me lightly on the forehead, he stood up and walked to the door. Framed in the doorway, he turned around.

"Don't forget," he said. "I love you."

The first time he said it, an hour earlier, I had thought it was just the heat of the moment.

When I had heard the front door close, I did as he had suggested and ran myself a bath. I could see that Charles had used the shower, but he had folded the damp towel neatly and put it back on the rail, and had opened a window to prevent condensation. The air was freezing, and I closed the window again before turning on the bath taps.

Jessica came back when I was just about to get out of the bath.

"I'm back!" she called. "Hello? Auntie Olwen? Are you there?"

"I'm in the bath," I shouted back. "I'll be out in a minute!"

Jessica didn't seem surprised when I walked into the living room dressed in a towelling robe and slippers. I half-expected her to ask why I was having a bath in the middle of the day, and was preparing some extravagantly complicated explanation. Then it dawned on me that, not only did she think nothing of my appearance, but she probably wouldn't have raised an eyebrow if I had told her that I had just spent the entire afternoon in bed with a lover. It came as such a relief to realise that I hadn't done anything wrong and I didn't need to explain myself to anyone.

Jessica asked if I had any plans about what to have for dinner. Taking a deep breath, I announced that I might be going out to eat. She didn't ask where, or who with; she simply said that, in that case, if I didn't mind, she would make herself an omelette.

Time went on, and insecurity started to get the better of me again. It was six thirty, and I had almost made up my mind that Charles wasn't coming back when I heard his car pull up outside and saw him, through the front window, getting out and coming up the drive. I thought he looked a little harassed.

I hadn't changed yet. I was wearing an old track suit, in the paranoid belief that, if I went to the trouble of dolling myself up, I was bound to be left looking stupid and rejected. Now I found myself torn between dashing upstairs, leaving Jessica to answer the door, or being there to greet Charles in person. While I was still thinking about it, he spotted me through the window, dropped the harassed look, and waved.

As I opened the door, I was hesitant about my best course of action. Should I reach for him impulsively, hug him and kiss him? Jessica was in the kitchen; she wouldn't see. That wasn't my concern, in any case. What I feared was making a fool of myself in front of Charles.

I opened the door as slowly as I could, simply to give myself time to absorb the sight of him. He smiled anxiously as I revealed myself gradually.

"All right?" he asked, unwilling to step over the threshold without an invitation.

I stood back to let him in. "How did it go?" It was the best compromise remark that I could think of.

"Fine. Nothing to worry about. What have you been doing with yourself?" His voice was quiet. Like me, he was fully aware of Jessica's proximity, and equally concerned not to be indiscreet.

"Nothing, really. Just looking out for you." Damn, that was a mistake. I hadn't meant him to think my whole life revolved around him.

He was smiling again. "Sorry it took so long. Just a couple of things to be ironed out. Have you decided where you'd like to go this evening?"

"I hadn't thought." It wasn't quite true. I had mentally run through all the restaurants I could think of, wondering which would be most conducive to relaxed conversation and what degree of dressing up each would require.

"Fibber!" he said, releasing the tight rein of formality and leaning over to kiss me. "Is there anywhere you particularly fancy, or would you prefer me to surprise you?"

"Surprise me," I said. "But I'll have to get changed first."

"If you like," he replied, as though I could go anywhere the way I was dressed.

Jessica came back into the living room at that point, looking unsurprised to see Charles. Greeting him briefly, she began to lay the table for her solitary tea.

"I won't be long," I said, and rushed up to my room, where I had laid out a selection of possible outfits on the bed. I chose the simplest dress of all, a long-sleeved thing in midnight blue which I felt would blend in anywhere. Throwing it on, I made myself up, very lightly, and examined myself in the mirror as I brushed my hair into some sort of shape.

Radiant. That was how I looked. It shouldn't have come as a surprise. After all, today was the day I had graduated from middle-aged spinster to youthful, attractive, desirable woman. Nevertheless, it was quite a shock to witness the change in my appearance. I wondered if Jessica would notice.

"You look nice," she remarked, as soon as I walked back into the room. "Going anywhere special?"

Charles had got up from the sofa and was looking at me in awe.

"My, don't you scrub up well!" he laughed. Then, observing my nervousness, he held out his hands to me. "Don't wait up, Jessica," he said, without looking at her. "We may be out quite late. In fact, we may not come home at all."

"Have a good time!" said Jessica, without turning a hair.

"Do you think she knows?" I asked, when we were safely in the car and Charles was starting up the engine.

"Knows what?" he chuckled.

I must have sounded incredibly stupid. Charles didn't seem to mind, though. He drove across Fairwood Common, into the outskirts of Swansea, and turned down towards Mumbles, where there are several very expensive, very good restaurants.

"I think we'll try Patrick's," he said, "if that's all right with you."

I said nothing; I had never been to Patrick's.

It was obvious, when we arrived, that Charles had made a reservation. The hostess seemed to be expecting us, and Charles was clearly a regular customer. Besides, this close to Christmas, we would never have got in on spec. I wondered why he had gone to the trouble of pretending to leave the choice up to me; presumably to avoid a repeat of the conversation we'd had on the way to Oxwich. Perhaps he had booked tables at a dozen restaurants, just to be on the safe side.

It was almost a week since we had been to Oxwich together. In the intervening period, I had barely seen him, yet already it seemed years ago.

The restaurant Charles had selected was small and intimate. The food was amazingly good, too – we chose the special Christmas menu – but that wasn't the reason why I enjoyed the evening so much. It was Charles himself, his unforced bonhomie, his thoughtfulness, his tenderness, the way he walked me back to the car afterwards and almost tucked me into my seat. Getting in beside me, he leaned across to kiss me.

It began gently, growing more passionate by the second, until he pulled away.

"We'll have to go somewhere," he said, running a finger round the inside of his collar to relieve the tension.

I was already trembling with anticipation.

"My house isn't too far," he added.

I let myself be carried along on the tide. When we got to the Cornwell residence, I was too far gone to notice anything about my surroundings. We didn't even bother to go upstairs. Charles closed all the curtains, and turned on some subtle lighting. Then we made love, on the sofa, by the gas fire.

It was gone midnight when I came to my senses and thought about Jessica.

"Charles," I murmured, rousing him from his half-sleep. Raising his tousled head from my shoulder, he looked drowsily into my eyes.

"What's the matter? Is something wrong?"

"I don't know what to do about Jessica. If I'm going home . . ."

"No, no, no." He began to sit up. "No, please don't go. I want you to stay. Please. If you're concerned about Jessica, we can ring her and let her know you're all right."

"It's a bit late to ring now. She may be in bed."

Charles levered himself upright. "If she's asleep, she won't be worrying about you."

It was true.

"You know your trouble?" he added. "You're always thinking about other people. Why don't you consider your own convenience for a change?"

Just as it crossed my mind that he didn't want to get up from his comfortable position to get dressed and drive me home, he added, "But if you really feel you must go home, I'll take you myself. I'm not entrusting you to any taxi driver."

He started to pull on his underpants. That was all the encouragement I needed, to stay with him.

I rang Jessica, first thing in the morning, to try to explain.

"I was a bit anxious," she conceded, "when I got up this morning and you weren't here. But I just assumed you'd stayed at Charles's house."

"Yes, I did." I was astonished at how easy she found it to accept that her Auntie Olwen should stay out all night. "I'll be back before lunchtime."

"I should think so too," she laughed. "Dirty stop-out! I take it you took my advice and had a good time."

"I had a wonderful time."

"Well, don't worry about anything. If there are any calls, I'll deal with them. When I've finished my breakfast, I'll make a start on those last few parcels."

As I put the phone down, I sighed. Charles, who was over on the other side of the bedroom, putting on his socks, looked up from the task.

"Well? Was she worried?"

"Not really. Obviously I'm not as indispensable as I thought."

"You are, to me." The smile cracked his face open again. "Come here and give me a kiss."

"*Another* one?"

This new intimacy felt so good. I couldn't believe my own stupidity, having allowed myself to wait so long for the happiness that had landed, literally, on my doorstep.

Chapter 22

It almost goes without saying that later, back at home, my doubts began to rise to the surface again. Charles had dropped me off at the house, saying that he would return later. He couldn't promise lunch, but he could promise dinner. I was about to invite him to have it with me and Jessica. He forestalled me by insisting that *he* would cook, in his own kitchen, and I would be his guest. Of course, I could bring my niece if I *liked*, but somehow he didn't think she would feel comfortable, being a gooseberry.

When I had stopped laughing, kissed him, and gone inside, I found a message from Jessica, who had evidently finished the parcels and gone out in my van. Damian? I didn't mind, as long as she remembered to take the parcels to the post office on the way. Damian wasn't as much to look at as Phil, but I thought he would suit her better in the long run. At this precise moment, I wanted everyone in the world to be as happy as I was.

"The Vicar phoned," said Jessica's note. "Please ring him back ASAP."

I hadn't expected Tim to be in touch again so soon. He should have been out celebrating with his family, now that his ordeal was over. How had Charles put it? "It's all been ironed out." Perhaps that was what the call was about. Perhaps Tim and Laura were intending to throw a big party for their supporters.

No. That would be insensitive. The Duttons wouldn't be celebrating. Their good name had been dragged through the mud; their son was still branded a liar in the eyes of the world. The best the Sutcliffs could do in the way of rejoicing was to have a quiet drink at home with a few neighbours. Perhaps they would be better off just going into the church, next door, and saying a quiet word of thanks to the One who had brought them safely through their troubles. That was what I intended to do.

How my attitudes had changed, with age! There had been a

time when I would have been prepared to condemn both Charles and myself to everlasting unhappiness, simply because I believed divorce was wrong. Of course divorce is wrong, by comparison with a happy marriage. Compared with the shared misery of an incompatible couple, however, it's nothing. I had spent all these years looking for a perfect man, never thinking that I could, perhaps, do more good by finding myself an imperfect one and setting about the business of restoring his faith in humanity.

Not that Charles had ever lost his faith in human nature. I was the one who was imperfect, I saw that now. I was the one who had needed repairing. It was Charles who had healed *my* wounds.

I wasted no more time in setting out for the vicarage. I could have rung Tim, but since I intended to go into the church anyway, there was hardly any point. If, when I arrived, the Sutcliffs were out, it didn't matter. I could always go back again later.

The church, as usual, wasn't locked. I went down to the front pew, where I could see the altar properly from my seat. I found the sight of it encouraging. It reminded me of all the other people who worshipped here on a Sunday, and who had done so, every Sunday, over the past couple of hundred years. That's what a church is: the people, not the building.

Yet there can be some consolation in physical objects, like my books, as long as we consider their spiritual associations rather than their material value. While I was thinking along those lines, I said a little prayer for Val Robarts and her husband, and the other members of her family, whom I had never met.

All those fellow-worshippers of mine, over the years, had looked at that altar, the way I was looking now, and seen it as a representation of something which, though beyond human understanding, was capable of giving comfort to those in pain. To me it was an object, nothing more, but an object endowed by time with special powers of grace. The rather threadbare altar-cloth had layers of meaning for me that its grander equivalent in Westminster Abbey could never have. And Mrs Bevan had probably spent all yesterday morning arranging those flowers. She had turned out to be a bit of a brick, on the quiet, had Mrs Bevan.

After I had said my prayers, I closed the church door carefully behind me and walked down the little winding path, past the back of the building, towards the vicarage. It was a dull morning, and there was a light glimmering in the kitchen. Someone was at home, so I hadn't had a wasted journey.

Tim answered the door in person.

"Olwen!" The spontaneous hug was unexpected. I was getting ready to congratulate him for about the tenth time, but when he pulled back from me, he wasn't smiling. "I'm glad you came," was all he said, before ushering me into the kitchen.

There was no one else around.

"Where's Laura?" I asked automatically.

"Gone to her mother's, in Gloucester, with the children. She thought I needed a bit of space." Before I had time to speculate on the significance of that remark, he went on: "I left a message for you, with Jessica."

"Yes, I got it. That's why I'm here."

"Been out on the tiles, I gather." His little laugh was forced.

"I was out with Charles Cornwell," I said. "You know, your solicitor. The man you told me was gay."

He looked slightly ashamed. "I think I may have been mistaken about that."

"It's all water under the bridge now. Anyway, you can hardly be blamed if you weren't thinking straight, with all that's been happening to you recently. I'm so glad it's all been sorted."

"Mmm." He hesitated. "Would you sit down, Olwen? Can I get you some tea, or coffee?"

I accepted the offer, simply because it would give Tim something to do with his hands. He seemed to be in a state of extreme nervous anticipation.

We made small talk while the kettle was coming to the boil. He asked where I had been with Charles, and I told him we had been out to dinner in Mumbles. I didn't mention what had come afterwards. He may have guessed; but my instincts told me he wasn't very interested. He was saving up all his energy for something else.

"Everything *is* all right, isn't it, Tim?"

He had filled my cup, and was sitting opposite me, stirring his own brew as if it were the only thing in the world that mattered at that moment.

"N-no, not exactly. I want to talk to you, about a decision I've come to. There are a few people in the world whose opinions matter to me, Olwen, and you're one of them."

He looked up from his cup. I tried to smile. Another day, I might have been flattered.

"The thing is," he continued, staring back down into the steaming liquid, "I've decided to leave the clergy."

In the past, I'd had the occasional experience of being able to guess what Tim was about to say, before he said it. This wasn't one of those occasions.

"Am I hearing right?" I asked, rhetorically.

"I'm afraid so. I haven't come to the decision lightly. In fact, I've been thinking about it for some time." He paused, waiting for me to ask the question, partly because he couldn't get the words out.

"Why?" My voice sounded far away. "Why now, just when everything's coming right?"

He was close to tears. So was I.

"Have you lost your faith, Tim? Is that what it is?"

"You might say that." He was terribly hoarse. "But not in the way you mean."

I had no choice but to wait. He took some time to gulp back his feelings, enough to be able to continue the explanation. For the sake of sparing his embarrassment, I concentrated on my own tea.

"I've done something terrible," he said.

My breath had become very uneven, I noticed, and my mouth was dry.

"Not . . . You're not going to tell me that you were guilty all along?"

"No, not of that."

The tension drained away from me, but only momentarily. He lost his words again, and I waited, again.

"The story I told you before, about Laura. It wasn't true. It was close to the truth, in a way, but it wasn't true, and I should never have let her talk me into it." It was painful to watch him, gasping for the breath to go on.

"Then what . . . ?"

A tear dropped from one of his lower eyelashes, into his tea. He was so far gone, he didn't even notice.

This was a moment I had dreamed of for years, a moment when I could reach out to Tim, help him through a difficult time. It was so different from the situation I had imagined, a whole world away. Tim was helpless enough. Unfortunately, so was I. What I wanted more than anything, at that moment, was for someone to walk in through the door and make everything all right. Specifically, Charles.

I did what I thought was right, rather than what I wanted to do. I reached out my hand, across the table, and rested it on Tim's. The gesture seemed to have the desired effect. He sat up a little straighter, and began to collect himself.

"What I told you the other day," he croaked, "was an attempt to avoid carrying the can for what I did. What *I* did. Not Laura. Me."

"You're telling me it had nothing to do with Laura?"

"Oh, it had something to do with her, all right. I mean, the things I said about her, to you and Elvis, all those things are true. I'm not trying to make excuses for myself. And I do love her. It's just that I worry about her. Somehow, while I was worrying about her, I took it into my head to act in a way that wasn't exactly . . ."

"What did you do?" I hadn't meant it to come out sounding so sharp, but Tim was gathering his wits now. He was prepared for the question.

"I stole."

It took a moment for it to sink in.

"Do you mean, from the concert takings?"

He nodded, still looking down into his tea. I watched him, with an almost superhuman effort, raise his head, so slowly, until he met my eye.

"That's right," he said. "It was me that took the money. When Craig caught me in the act, I wasn't putting the money back. I was taking it. Now do you understand?"

"No. I'm afraid I don't." It couldn't be as straightforward as he was implying. It simply couldn't. "What exactly did you do, Tim, and – more importantly – why?"

He sighed deeply, and pushed his chair back from the table,

with a grating sound. He leaned backwards, looking at the ceiling while bracing himself against the edge of the table with both hands. Then he looked at me again. "Like I said, it started with Laura. I wasn't lying when I said she was always short of money for the housekeeping. The old chestnut about vicars being poor as church mice. I mean, look at this place!"

Mechanically, I obeyed, taking in the dingy walls and the bare floor, the elderly furniture and the peeling paintwork.

"But you don't have to pay for your heating and lighting," I said stupidly.

"No. You know why? Because I don't get paid enough to cover it! I can barely afford shoes for the kids, let alone luxuries like heating and lighting. And in case you hadn't noticed, there *isn't* any heating to speak of, only a few electric fires. In a place this size. I ask you!"

Curiously, I felt little sympathy. "So you're saying you stole because you couldn't afford to keep your family?"

"No. I'm not saying that. If it had been that, there might have been some excuse for what I did. But then, if it had been that, I could have got help. There are all kinds of charities and welfare funds and so on. No, it wasn't that."

"Then . . . what?" I had the feeling I had already asked this question, about a hundred years ago.

"Evil."

"Evil?" The word sounds so strange, in your own mouth, almost an archaism. It's probably because the connotations are so powerful that we're afraid to use it nowadays.

"That's the only explanation I can think of. I *was* worried about Laura, I *was* worried about how we were going to live, and while I was preoccupied with those . . . worldly things, Evil got the better of me."

I sat there, struggling with my feelings, while Tim finished his story. Just as he had told us, a few days before, the incident involving Craig had taken place in the back room at the church hall, after the concert. The takings were all there. No one would have thought of not trusting the Vicar to be on his own in that room, with that money.

Tim had decided, on impulse, to do a preliminary count. Not

the kind of thing he would normally have done. He had picked up a stack of pound coins, and weighed it in his hand. Ten pound coins. Ten pounds.

"It just occurred to me," he said, "how easy it would be . . ."

For the sake of ten pounds. For the sake of a sum of money that wouldn't have bought his kids one shoe between them, Tim had put his whole career on the line.

"I'll never know what would have happened," he added. "I think – I hope – I would have put the money back but, once Craig had seen me, I didn't have a choice. He'd come into the room so quietly. I still don't know what he was doing there.

"After I'd taken the money and put it in my pocket, I panicked. I picked up some of the ticket stubs, and started fidgeting with them. I thought they might somehow give me away. My mind was in turmoil, trying to think what to do. Suddenly, I looked up and there was Craig, standing by the door. I wasn't completely sure whether he'd watched me take the money off the table and put it in my pocket, so I tried to bluff it out. He held out his hand, just as I described."

"My other hand was still in my pocket – I was that close to putting the money back. I took it out, empty, in the hope Craig would think he'd been mistaken. But he wouldn't let it go. He asked what was in my pocket, and I just stood there, holding up my cassock, while he felt around in there. Believe me, there was nothing sexual about it. It never entered my head. Craig pulled out a handful of coins and just . . . stared at them. Some part of me wanted him to accuse me of stealing them, but of course he didn't dare. I took the coins back from him, I pressed one into his hand, and pushed him away. Then I let my cassock down quickly, and told him to go back into the other room."

"Oh, Tim." My voice sounded strange to myself. It was as well that I was sitting down, because I could feel the weakness overcoming my whole body, and that quivering in my legs that you get at a moment like this.

"The rest was like I said. I told him not to say anything. That was the giveaway. If I'd said nothing, he might not have realised there was something really wrong. I might have got away with it."

"Did you put the money back on the table, afterwards?" It was a question I felt I shouldn't have needed to ask.

Tim shook his head. "But not for the reasons you're thinking," he protested. "I was afraid someone else would come in, Elvis or Alan Samuel. Then I would have been in even more of a mess."

The room had gone quiet. Outside in the garden, I could hear a cat mewing. A fanbelt squealed, out on the main road, giving me a sudden mental image of Phil's beaten-up van.

"Why did you lie, Tim? Why didn't you tell the truth, from the beginning?"

He made an awkward little shrug, tipping his head to one side and pursing his lips.

"I don't know. I suppose I thought it would all blow over. Because I knew I hadn't done what I was being accused of, it was easy to deny it. I thought if I just kept saying that nothing had happened, everyone would believe me, and they would just think Craig had been mistaken. Only it wasn't like that. It got more difficult, as time went on, not easier. I wanted you to know, Olwen, you and one or two other people, because I couldn't go on with this pretence of innocence any more. I've already told Craig's father."

"Dr Dutton?" The image of the man's appearance, the only time I had ever seen him, in a Swansea shopping centre, was vivid in my memory. "What did he . . .? How did he . . .?"

"He was surprisingly understanding about the whole thing," said Tim. "You might say he heaped burning coals on my head, by being so forgiving. And he doesn't even consider himself to be a Christian!"

"Was it his idea, that you should give up the clergy?"

"Oh, no. Give me some credit, Olwen. That was my own decision. Dr Dutton actually said he didn't care one way or the other about that, but he admitted he would prefer it if I removed myself from the village. Craig's been through hell over this. His father will be only too happy if none of the family ever has to set eyes on me again."

If I had ever felt sorry for the Duttons, my heart went out to them at this moment.

"How many other people know?" Even now, even in this extremity, I was thinking about myself, and wondering where I came in the pecking order.

"In telling Dr Dutton, I've had to accept that he will tell other people. Though he did say, when I talked to him, that he hadn't yet made up his mind whether to make it generally known. He wasn't even sure that it would be a good thing to tell his wife. He wants the slate wiped clean, including the memory of what's happened."

"Laura?"

"I told Laura first, of course, before anyone else. I may appear to be a cold-blooded liar, but I've always had difficulty concealing anything from her. Believe it or not . . ." He paused, and a furtive glance told me his real fear – the fear that no one would ever believe anything he said, ever again. "Believe it or not, it was Laura's idea to make up that stupid story, about her having stolen the money, and me trying to put it back. We put in the bit about the ticket stubs because I knew Craig had seen me with them. If he had mentioned that, my story would sound more plausible. Laura said that people would find it easy to believe that she was the guilty one, and easy to excuse simply because everyone knew she was in a bit of a state, psychologically speaking."

I'd always known that Tim didn't understand women. He was about to confirm it.

"The odd thing was, once it was done, once I had said what she wanted me to say, to get myself off the hook, she didn't want to know me. She almost seemed upset to find that it had worked, so easily, that the police were prepared to accept my story. That's why she went away. I think she'll come round eventually. I hope so. I p-pray . . ."

The tears came, like a flood. Tim put his head down on the table, and sobbed loudly.

It's at moments like these that women come into their own. That's what we're supposed to be good at, comforting others, and we usually come through. I like to think of myself as a normal woman, and I did what I thought was expected of me. Getting up and coming around the table, I put my hand on Tim's shoulder and made soothing noises.

"You can't turn the clock back, Tim. It's done now. If the Duttons can forgive you, then it's not for me to stand in judgement."

"I . . ." Tim muttered something through his tears. It was totally unintelligible, and it was pointless.

"I'll get you some more tea." It was the only thing I could think of doing. There was no wife to minister to him, so I might as well stand in her place.

I didn't like to think of Laura. Mechanically, I rinsed out Tim's mug and replenished it with a fresh one from the teapot, adding milk and sugar. Tim didn't normally take sugar, but it seemed to me that he might need it on this occasion. Hot, sweet tea is supposed to be a remedy for shock; or so I remember learning when I was in Brownies. I was biting my lip to stop myself coming out with one of my mother's favourite little sayings, the one she used to repeat whenever she caught one of us out in a lie.

Oh, what a tangled web we weave . . .

"Let it all out, Tim," I said tritely, pushing the unadulterated tea in front of him. "There's no shame in crying. You're sorry for what you did. That's what's important to . . . to God."

It was the kind of thing Mrs Bevan might have said. She had stood by Tim and Laura in their hour of need, but I wondered how she would react when she heard that her faith in her vicar had been misplaced, right from the beginning.

There was no question in my mind that I was finally hearing the truth from Tim. The story was simply too bizarre to have been made up. Other aspects of the situation were still bothering me.

"Does Ch-Charles know about this?" I asked.

"Yes. When he came here, last Friday, I told him I remembered something happening at the concert. I repeated all that stuff about the ticket stubs. Laura and I had rehearsed it together but, when it came to the crunch, she wasn't able to face it out. She wanted me to speak to him alone. I'm not sure that Charles believed any of it, but he said he would act as an intermediary between me and the Duttons, and he would try to prevent Laura having to answer to anyone. It seemed Craig's parents, and the police, were only too willing to accept an explanation of that sort. They thought they were sparing Laura from humiliation.

"The funny thing is . . ." He raised bloodshot eyes to look into my face. "It was the whole business of the police dropping the charges that made me realise I had to confess. I prayed. I thanked God for letting me off so lightly. But the answer I got from Him wasn't quite the one I'd expected. Ironic, isn't it? I spent all that time denying that anything had happened, partly for the sake of my family, and now I've gone and made things worse for them than ever."

"It's not surprising, though," I said, sitting down again. "You couldn't let Laura take the rap, any more than you could let Craig be called a liar, when he wasn't. You've got more decency."

We sat there, for a while. Tim gradually came round, drank his tea, stopped crying and generally quietened down.

"When Charles came round here yesterday," he said, his voice dull with spent emotion, "I took my courage in both hands, and told him the whole truth".

"What did he think you should do?" I asked. Perhaps I shouldn't have been talking about Charles, at a moment like this, but I was curious to know how he would tackle this moral dilemma.

"He didn't seem surprised," said Tim. "I think he'd always suspected that there was more to it than met the eye. After all, there's no smoke without fire. But you know solicitors. They operate according to a different moral code from the rest of us."

My first thought was that Tim didn't mean to upset me, saying a thing like that about a man he knew I was fond of. Then I recalled how eager he had been to tell me that Charles was gay. I didn't suspect him of having made all that up. Obviously, he had genuinely believed it at the time. It was his motive for telling me that was questionable. I was beginning to suspect that Tim had always known I adored him, and had got used to being adored. Now that I was taking an interest in someone else, he was, to put it bluntly, jealous.

Maybe Tim was right; maybe Charles did operate according to a different moral code from me. It would take time to find out. The possibility that he operated according to a different code from Tim, on the other hand, was almost a welcome thought. I still felt sorry for Tim. I understood his feelings. I didn't, however, intend to let him wallow in my sympathy.

"Tim," I said. "You've got to get it together. You can't just mope around telling everyone how useless and wicked you are. What are you going to do if you leave the clergy?"

"I don't know. I haven't really thought. It depends on a lot of things."

"Have you actually handed in your notice yet? Have you told the Bishop?"

"No, and yes. I've spoken to him on the phone. I've told him the bare facts. He said I ought to consider my position. He didn't tell me to resign."

"Then do me a favour, Tim, don't do it yet. Take time to think about it. There are other people to be considered."

He looked surprised at this idea. "It's for the sake of other people that I'm . . ."

"Yes, I know," I interrupted. "But think a bit more carefully. Consider the congregation of St Mary's. Some of those people have stood by you. They've stuck their necks out for you. I don't just mean me and Elvis, now, I mean people like . . . Mrs Bevan and Mr Samuel. What is this revelation going to do to their faith in the church?"

He looked at me as if I'd said something outrageous. "I don't see how that is relevant," he said, after a moment. "I've done wrong, I don't deserve to be a vicar."

"Then what do you deserve to be?"

He hesitated. "A teacher, I thought."

"A teacher?" I exploded. "Tim, what are you thinking of? A teacher, in charge of impressionable children? If you're not fit to be a vicar, how on earth can you consider going into a profession like teaching?"

He looked abashed. "Then what are you suggesting I do, Olwen, go on the dole? What about Laura and the kids?"

"Yes, what about Laura and the kids? What does it do to your position in the context of the family if you turn around to them and say that you're not fit to do the job you've been doing for the last fifteen years? Do you want them labelled as the family of a man who had to leave the clergy because he didn't tell the truth?"

"I don't see any way round it. Laura will leave me, no doubt, and go back to her parents . . ." He was so steeped in self-pity that my sympathy was ebbing away by the minute.

"Tim, this is your opportunity to make amends! Okay, so you've done wrong. But it's not as if you robbed a bank, or killed someone, or had an affair!" I wasn't sure where that last bit had come from, but I suppose I was just starting to see things in perspective.

"Why not make the best of things? Use this opportunity to show people that it was a one-off, that you can be deserving of the cloth. I'm not saying it'll be easy. But if the Bishop is willing to give you a second chance, take it. At the very least, your parishioners ought to have some say in the matter!"

"I'm not sure I can face them. Any of them, apart from you and Elvis."

"Leave me out of it! I'm a Baptist, remember? I go to St Mary's for convenience, and I daresay I'll go on going there, whoever the vicar happens to be. Elvis will do the same."

Tim nodded a grudging acceptance of the truth of what I'd said. "I don't know, Olwen. I can't think. I'm a mess. I'm grateful to you for believing in me, after I've let you down so badly . . ."

"Cut the crap, Tim!" I said sharply. "Start using your brain."

I picked up my coat from the chair. "I'm going now. Please, Tim, think about what I've said. And pray for guidance. I'll call and see you again. Don't do anything . . . you'll regret."

Had I thought there was any danger of Tim being suicidal, I wouldn't have left him at that moment. Tim's faith was strong. He had never shown any signs of slipping into agnosticism. On the contrary, hadn't he told me that Evil was responsible for his actions after the charity concert? And that God had personally instructed him to set the record straight?

Chapter 23

Elvis met me in the lane, as I was walking home. From his mournful expression, I suspected he already knew what I had just been told.

"You look as if you've had bad news," he observed.

I was determined not to give anything away until I was sure that he was in on the secret.

"Fancy a drink?" he asked, jerking his head in the direction of the Drovers' Arms.

I looked at my watch. It was ten past twelve.

"I could do with some lunch," I remarked. "Let's go."

We sat miserably in the back bar, waiting for our toasted sandwiches to turn up.

"How much did he tell you?" asked Elvis.

"I don't know whether I should say."

"He told me he was going to confide in you."

"He didn't tell me he'd already confided in *you*." I don't know why I should have resented Elvis knowing. Some vestige of my old feelings for Tim, perhaps.

"Oh, come on, Ol! He didn't have much choice. I always knew there was something fishy. After all, the kid was in my care, I was partly responsible if anything *had* happened. And despite what I said to you the other night, I never believed the expurgated version."

The sandwiches arrived, and we tucked in. I took another swig of my gin and tonic, between mouthfuls.

"Do you think the church can survive this?" I asked.

Elvis stared into his beer. "Stuff the church!" he said dramatically. "Can the Sutcliffs survive?"

"How would I know? I've never even been married."

"Doesn't look as if it'll be long now, though."

I searched his face for a clue to his opinions on that subject.

"It's a bit late for me, Elvis."

"Rubbish! It's never too late."

"I don't know." His words pleased me, in spite of the doubts. I was voicing them only in fear of being disappointed by Charles, as I'd always been disappointed by the few men I'd known intimately in the past.

"Have you ever thought of getting married, Elvis?" I was trying to change the subject; I hardly expected an affirmative reply.

"As a matter of fact, yes. When I was in my twenties, I really thought I would. It seemed the *decent* thing to do, if you understand me. I was brought up chapel, like you were. I started going out with a girl called Billie Mainwaring."

"Billy?"

"No, *Billie*. Her parents were very into country and western. It was funny, because there used to be a rugby international called Billy Mainwaring."

He didn't say so, but I hazarded a guess that their peculiar Christian names were one of the things that had brought Elvis and Billie together.

"Anyway," he continued, "*Billie* and I went out together for about eighteen months. I was quite smitten with her, in my way, though we never . . . you know. I was on the verge of popping the question. Then I looked at her one day, so pretty and so cute, and I thought to myself, 'Do you really want to make this woman's life a misery by marrying her?' So I didn't."

"Did she know why? Did she mind?"

"I think so. It was a shame, because I lost her friendship, in the end, as well as her companionship. I've never made the mistake of getting too close to a woman since then."

"You don't see her, now?"

Echoes of my conversations with Charles.

"No, she moved away. Stoke-on-Trent. I had a Christmas card from her the other day. She's married now, of course."

Elvis stared into his drink. The memory of Billie Mainwaring had made an impression on him. I reproved myself for thinking it strange that he should have the same kind of regrets as Charles, about the past. After all, they were both men, albeit different varieties of man. Perhaps they weren't as different as I had once thought –

except that it would never be possible for me to get as close to Elvis as I had to Charles.

"Who do you think we'll get instead of Tim?" I asked, changing the subject successfully this time. "Assuming he does what he's threatening to."

"Someone young, I hope."

I expressed surprise. "Really? I'd have thought you'd have preferred someone middle-aged. Young people always want to change things, don't they?"

"That's a popular misconception. I prefer them to older people. After a certain age, you get set in your ways, you stop being adaptable, you expect everybody else to change to suit *your* preferences." He laughed. "I should know."

I pondered on this. Unintentionally, Elvis had given me a reason to shy away from the prospect of deeper involvement with Charles. Not that it could get much deeper than it already was. It wouldn't have been easy to extricate myself now, even if I had wanted to; and I didn't want to. I turned the conversation down the route I preferred.

"There's one good thing. The church is thriving, or at least it was before this problem with Tim, and the congregation will soon build up again. I hope the replacement won't be long in coming. If we're lucky and get someone young, it'll be even more of an attraction."

"Hmph!" Elvis looked unenthusiastic about the prospect. "I don't care who he is, as long as he leaves me to get on with my job."

"He or she," I corrected.

"Oh, God, no, you don't think they'll send us a woman, do you?" He laughed at my shocked expression. "Only joking. Come to think of it, a woman might be the best thing of all. I get on well with women."

Now it was my turn to laugh. "Elvis, you're incorrigible!"

We talked on, and the gin worked its way through my insides, warming me up. When I looked at my watch and saw that it was nearly two o'clock, I leapt to my feet.

"Is that the time? I'll have to get back. Jess will be wondering what's happened to me."

When I said "Jess", of course I meant Charles. The silver BMW was parked outside the house, alongside my van. I wasn't surprised, when I opened the front door, to hear the unmistakable sounds of my niece flirting with my . . . "boyfriend".

"Excellent!" he was saying. "Don't rush into any career decisions. You should take a leaf out of your aunt's book, if you'll forgive the pun. She's recognised that what's important is doing something you enjoy. It's not a question of money. She's a very sensible woman."

I knew he had heard my entry, so I wasn't taken in for a moment.

"Flattery will get you nowhere," I remarked. "And what are you doing here anyway? You said you wouldn't be able to make lunch."

"I said I couldn't promise," he corrected, glancing at his watch as he stood up. "But I take it you've had yours, by now." He leaned towards me, and kissed me. Over his shoulder, I caught sight of Jessica's smug expression.

"I'm sorry," I said. "If I'd known you were coming, I wouldn't have let Elvis drag me into the pub. I bumped into him on the way back from the vicarage."

At the mention of the vicarage, Charles stiffened, and pulled back to look into my face.

"Did Tim tell you?" he asked, lowering his voice in the hope that Jessica wouldn't overhear.

"Yes," I said shortly, and went into the kitchen.

Charles followed me, and stood, leaning against the door, watching me in his usual way. "I hope you understand why I couldn't say anything."

"Of course." My voice still sounded harsh and uncompromising. He was bound to think my resentment was directed at him.

He crossed the kitchen, and wrapped his arms around me, from behind. "I love you," he murmured, into my ear. "I know I can't make it come right, but I love you just the same."

I paused before commencing my task, resting my hands on his linked arms. "I love you, too." It was the first time I had been able to find the courage to say it. "And I know it's not your fault."

I pointed to the stool by the breakfast bar, and he dutifully sat down while I started making coffee.

"I want to take you out this afternoon," he said. "It's not a bad day. We could drive up over Cefn Bryn, and have a little walk to Arthur's Stone."

The prospect of standing on a windy plateau admiring a pile of prehistoric rocks, even with Charles at my side, didn't hold much appeal at that particular moment. I shrugged. "I'm not sure I feel like it, Charles. Can't we just stay in and watch the horse racing or something?"

He laughed. "Oh my, we are down in the dumps, aren't we? Never mind. Come to Charlie." He held out his arms to me, and I walked into them.

"Charlie?" I queried. "Is that what people call you?"

"It has been known. But I must admit, there are things I prefer to be called. Such as 'darling'."

There he went, making me laugh again, slipping inside my defences. I lowered my head onto his shoulder.

"I used to think so much of Tim," I said. "And I still do, in a way. It's heartbreaking."

"We all make mistakes." A cliché, but one which seemed particularly apt at that moment.

"Sometimes," I mused, "we don't do the things we really want to do, just because we're afraid of making mistakes."

"Very true," he agreed, and I knew his thoughts were in tune with mine. They usually were.

The kettle came to the boil, and I pulled away from him again. Glancing towards the open door, I saw that Jessica had left the living room, presumably to save herself the embarrassment of watching the two old fogeys get on with their pitiful little romance.

"How do you reconcile yourself with something like that, Charles?" I asked. "And what did you advise Tim?"

"Oh, Lord!" He put his elbows on the breakfast bar, and his head into his hands. "I wish I had the answer. To your first question, it's 'with difficulty'. To your second, nothing. I offered no advice. As far as I was concerned, my duties as his solicitor were completed when the police decided not to charge him. To be fair, I don't think he wanted to consult me, merely to do me the courtesy of telling me the truth. What did he have to say about it, this morning?"

"He said that solicitors operate according to a different moral code from the rest of us."

Charles looked up at me. "Did he now? Hmm. I suppose he

has a point. Or at least, I can see why he would think that. Believe me, Olwen, it's not that I don't have a set of morals of my own. You might think they're rather on the flimsy side, but I can assure you they exist. I don't know if you'll understand this, but . . ."

He held out his hand to me. I took it in my own, which he promptly kissed and laid against his cheek.

"I always suspected that there was something a little disingenuous about your friend Tim's denials. Being a vicar, there might well have been something he was choosing to conceal. However, it was my job to try to help him defend himself, and the evidence against him was really very slight. If I had thought he was guilty of the assault, then I would have advised him to come clean and tried to help him get off lightly. But I had no reason to think that, so I tried to bring things to a head.

"When he told me, last week, that he'd remembered something, I admit I didn't delve too deeply into it. Enough people had suffered. The police, I think, always knew that the case against him wasn't likely to stand up in court, and I pressed for a quick decision because of the factors involved – the families, the children, Christmas coming, and so on. We got lucky. It's not up to me to hold a post mortem. You see . . ."

He pulled me close, and buried his face in my jumper, so that his voice was muffled.

"I take on all sorts of cases. I help, or try to help, all kinds of people. The law is a funny thing. It's there to protect people, but it's not always about right and wrong. I've tried, over the years, not to get hardened to it. But it's not easy. I have to try and look at things dispassionately, objectively. My career as a solicitor is quite separate from my life with you."

The words were saturated with additional significance, for him as for me. I put my arms around his head. Looking down, I stroked his hair.

"You know," I said. "I was wrong. You *have* got a bald patch."

Chapter 24

We went out that evening, and enjoyed ourselves. Charles cooked dinner in his beautiful house. Oh yes, it was beautiful, with a view right out over Swansea Bay. It was immaculate, too. He employed a cleaner and, since he spent very little time there, she wasn't exactly overworked. Before dinner, I stood in the living room, martini in hand, looking out into the Channel. It was a lovely evening, for the time of year. Cold, naturally, but there had been some late sunshine, and the sky was clear, the stars twinkling. There would be no need to worry about adverse weather conditions over the Christmas holiday. We don't get a lot of snow on Gower, because of the sea. Floods, yes; snow, no.

A friend of mine emigrated to America about twenty years ago, and now lives in the San Francisco Bay area. From her bedroom window, she has a magnificent view out across the bay, dominated by the Golden Gate Bridge. In every other letter, my friend tells me how much she misses "home", and how the scenery around her is not a patch on Gower.

It's a truism that we always want what we can't have, that the other person's grass is always greener. Maybe I'm an exception to the rule, because I appreciate what I have. I consider myself lucky to live in such stunning surroundings. My friend is right, you see. Gower *is* one of the most beautiful places in the world.

Charles was in the kitchen, making what he called his "speciality". It turned out to be pasta, in a pesto sauce, and I have to admit it was delicious. I was rather glad, now, that I had missed the opportunity to make that pasta dish for him, at my house. The comparison wouldn't have done me any favours.

After dinner, we walked along the road to the nearest pub, which was packed with Christmas revellers. Charles went to the bar, while I settled into a seat by the big open fireplace. Such was the queue to be served that he was gone for some time. I didn't mind, because it gave me a chance to watch him operate. He didn't know that my eyes were on him all the time. Like most men, he was thinking of something else while he waited his turn, and only glanced in my direction once, to check that I was still there. I was pleased to see that he *did* wait his turn, not try to push in. The bar staff seemed to know him, and exchanged greetings. I heard one of them call him "Mr Cornwell" and remembered that this was his local.

We didn't stay long. A couple of drinks later, we walked back to Charles's house, hand in hand. My life seemed to have changed beyond recognition, in these last few days. I had warned Jessica that I probably wouldn't see her till Sunday, whereupon she had asked me if it would be okay for Damian to stay the night in my house, adding that he would "of course" sleep on the settee. I wondered how long he would stay there.

It couldn't go on indefinitely, all this wining and dining, but we made the most of it, Charles and I, while it lasted. Sooner or later, as we both knew, our relationship would pass into another phase, and that would be crunch time. For the moment, we concentrated on finding out about one another, and loving every minute of it.

Spending the night with someone is a whole different thing from going to bed with them for an hour or two in the afternoon. For a start, there are the little practicalities: which side of the bed will you sleep on; and does either of you snore?

It was a new departure for me. The last time I'd shared a bed with anyone was with Jessica, when she was a toddler and there were lots of visitors in the house. She was what you'd call an "active sleeper". In other words, she tossed and turned and kicked so much that I hardly slept all night. I hadn't, until now, looked forward to repeating the experience.

Charles had a water bed! It was fairly new; he'd only owned it for a year or so. That got rid of any subconscious fears I may have had about occupying another woman's territory. Making love on the water bed was interesting; sleeping in it was out of this world. For me, there were other new experiences. Not needing a hot water bottle, in the depths of winter, was one. Charles gave off enough heat in bed to power the Number One blast furnace in Port Talbot steelworks.

On my second visit to his house, I had come equipped with basic overnight things, including pyjamas!

"You won't be needing *those*," chuckled Charles, taking them from me, gently but firmly, and folding them neatly into a drawer. "We'll leave them there, in case of emergencies," he added.

After all the years I had spent on my own, waking up beside him had a naturalness about it that was unexpected. It was, quite simply, as though we had always been together. Looking back over the past few weeks, I recognised that it had been like that throughout our brief friendship, from the moment I first saw him standing at my front door.

"I've been lonely too, you know," he said, when I looked into his eyes that morning, snuggling up to him for comfort.

It was something of a revelation. Up to that point, I had veered between thinking myself unworthy and thinking Charles superficial. It had never occurred to me that we might be equal partners in this relationship, each giving, each accepting.

We hadn't heard the last of the Sutcliff situation, either. My thoughts kept going back to Tim and Laura, sometimes with irritation that I had been so easily taken in, sometimes with pity for the suffering of a young family – two young families. There were many cruel things I could have said about Tim, but I couldn't have denied that he was suffering at least as much as his wife and children.

On Sunday evening, after a day spent lazing around half-dressed at Charles's house, I returned to the village, in time to attend church. I didn't ask Charles to come with me. He offered, but I knew it wasn't his scene, and I didn't want to make him uncomfortable. He was only offering because he thought I might need support – and, I supposed, because he didn't like to be out of my company for a moment.

We had our Christmas arrangements planned, down to the finest detail. Charles had to work on Monday and Tuesday. There was no way round that. Wednesday was Christmas Eve, and he was insistent on taking us both out for a celebratory lunch, before I set off for my sister's with Jessica. On Boxing Day, I would return, without Jessica, and he would be around in the evening. We would take it from there.

The Fourth Sunday in Advent. There were whispers, among the congregation, about the outcome of the Dutton case, but it was clear that most people had very little idea what had really happened. Tim looked a lot better than the last time I had seen him, and made no reference to recent events. He hadn't, as I feared he would, announced his decision to leave the clergy. That gave cause for optimism.

On the way out of the church, I shook hands with Tim in the usual way. He acted as if nothing had happened, looking past me at the next parishioner. That was only to be expected.

On Monday afternoon, I heard (from Elvis) that Laura had returned from Gloucester. Jessica went over to see her, and reported back that she seemed much as ever. "Normal" wouldn't quite be the right word.

Jessica, of course, still knew nothing of the true story behind Laura's recent ordeal. In any case, she was so wrapped up in young Damian – who seemed to have taken up semi-permanent residence in my living room over the weekend – that she wouldn't have noticed any difference in Laura's behaviour.

Chapter 25

The next time I set foot in the vicarage was on Tuesday evening, the day before Christmas Eve. I had knocked off early, leaving Jessica to finish off what little remained in the form of correspondence and phone calls – mostly apologies for not being able to dispatch late orders in time for Christmas. It was the customers' own fault for leaving it so late, but I still felt obliged to let them know. Mostly, they appreciated the thought, and didn't cancel the orders. You could almost hear them preparing the excuses for their loved ones: "I've ordered the most *marvellous* Christmas present for you, darling, but they phoned me at the *very last minute* to say they couldn't deliver before Christmas! I hope you're not *too* disappointed!"

My reason for finishing at lunchtime was that I wanted to do some cooking. I hadn't, as yet, given Charles anything in the way of a Christmas present. There was nothing I could think of that would come anywhere near his romantic gesture of the Charlotte Mew book. The best idea I'd had was to make some miniature mince pies with marzipan topping, and put them in a little box tied up with ribbon. It was a personal kind of gift, and a suitable one for someone living alone. For the past few years, since before his mother died, I'd been doing them for Elvis at Christmas. I would drop his off in the morning, on my way out.

It was the night of the big carol service. When I saw the note that had been put through the door, inviting me to drop in at the vicarage after the service, I thought of asking Jessica to come with me, but she was frantically trying to complete the jobs I'd left her. The minute I was out of the door, I knew she would be on the phone to Damian, making arrangements for future assignations. I was half-expecting him to turn up in Newport on Boxing Day. Not wishing to interfere with the course of young love, I set off alone for the service.

It went off well. The order of service at these events seldom varied, but tonight there seemed to be a special sparkle about the whole proceedings. It showed up most of all in the choir's performance. We had all the old faithfuls: *Tawel Nos* (or *Silent Night*, if you prefer), *Hark! The Herald Angels Sing*, and my own particular favourite, *O Little Town of Bethlehem*. Young Geraint, his sore throat a thing of the past, sang a solo during *It was on a Starry Night*, a modern carol that all the children seemed to know well.

Tim was looking better than ever, more relaxed, beaming at everyone as he linked the lessons and the music with a few well-chosen words. Perhaps he had changed his mind. Elvis would have been the first to know, I guessed. He too was on top form, coaxing out the sentimentality in the choir's tear-jerking rendition of *In the Bleak Midwinter*, then swinging his arms about lustily when it came to the grand finale: *O Come, All Ye Faithful*.

Afterwards, I hung back, waiting for him to pack up his music so that we could walk over to the vicarage together, but I didn't ask him the obvious question, because I knew he wouldn't give me a straight answer.

Everyone was there. Laura was smiling, passing round the mince pies and sausage rolls, but there was visible strain behind the smile. Not everyone noticed. They were too busy wondering what this evening was all about. There was bound to be a reason why we had been invited here, instead of to the church hall where the children were. Tim had another announcement to make.

It wasn't the one I had been expecting. My heart thumped so loudly, when he called for silence in the big kitchen, that I thought everyone in the room must be able to hear it. The occasion reminded me vividly of that other evening, only a few weeks earlier, when Tim had told us the terrible news about Craig Dutton. Tonight, Tim was smiling. It wasn't such a false smile as Laura's. I dared to hope he might have come to terms with what he had done.

"Could I have everyone's attention, please? I've got some news for you all. There is good news and bad news, but mostly good. At least, I hope you'll think it's good news." He said this with a little laugh, and the audience took its cue and joined in. It was Christmas, after all, and it would have taken a lot to throw a damper on the celebrations.

"As you've all heard by now, the police have decided not to charge me with any offence as a result of the little . . . er, problem I told you about a few weeks ago. But I want you all to know the story behind it, and I want you to know the outcome of it all. I hope you won't think too badly of me, when I've told you.

"I never thought Craig Dutton was a liar. I always thought there must have been some misunderstanding. However, in the beginning the police and Social Services wouldn't tell me exactly what Craig had supposedly accused me of. Apparently that's quite usual in these cases, but it made it difficult for me to issue a firm denial. At last I found out what Craig had actually said, and once I knew that, it was easy for me to remember the circumstances and explain how the whole thing had got . . . twisted.

"I won't go into the full detail here, it's not necessary. Suffice it to say that there was an incident, which Craig misinterpreted. When I explained things to Dr and Mrs Dutton, they accepted my side of the story. I've also spoken to the Bishop, and I've made him aware of how the misunderstanding occurred. So that's that, all sorted. I would like to say that I bear no ill will against Craig and his family, and I hope they bear none against me. In particular, Craig is not to blame. It was all a big mix-up, and it's best forgotten.

"Which brings me to the bad news. These past few weeks have been very trying for my family. I owe them a lot, especially Laura, for their understanding and tolerance. The time has come to repay their faith in me."

He took a huge breath.

"The best way to do that, in my belief, is for us to make a fresh start. So I've called you here tonight to tell you that I've asked the Bishop for a transfer to another parish, and he's agreed."

At this news, there was a general "awww" from most of the guests.

"No!" protested Tim. "Let's have none of this awing. All good things must come to an end. We've been here for six and a half years, six and a half very happy, fulfilling years. But the time has come for a change. In fact, the transfer will be to another diocese. We're going to North Wales, to a rural community, not dissimilar to this one in its way, except that the Welsh lessons will be more important from now on."

There was some laughter. Elvis grinned around at everyone and gave Tim a thumbs-up sign.

"Will we be getting another vicar?" asked someone, anxiously.

"Of course you will!" Tim smiled. "I can't actually tell you his name yet – though I know it – because he's still serving as a curate elsewhere in the diocese, and the transfer arrangements have to be finalised. But he's a young man" – here, Elvis looked at me and winked – "and he's very highly thought of in his present parish. They'll be sorry to see him go, but their loss is your gain."

"We'll be sorry to see *you* go," pointed out Mr Samuel, who, I suspected, had not been honoured with Tim's confidence, despite having been the one who had found him a good solicitor at an opportune moment. It had only just occurred to me what a debt of gratitude I personally owed our verger.

After Tim had finished his speech, while most of the assembled company were still discussing it in little groups of two and three, Laura came over to me and Elvis.

"I'll really miss you two," she said, and turned to me. "Is there any chance of Jessica coming over to see the children in the morning?" she asked. "It'll probably be the last time they ever see her, and they are so fond of her."

"Of course she will," I reassured, "but please don't say it's the last time. You'll be coming back to visit us, I'm sure, and your visits might coincide with Jess's."

At that precise moment, Tim arrived at Laura's shoulder, and slipped his arm around her waist. She glanced up at him, anxious and (it seemed to me) reproachful.

"I'm glad you changed your mind," I said, assuming the comment was ambiguous enough to be understood by both of them and simultaneously unintelligible to any third party, excepting Elvis.

"That was entirely thanks to Laura," said Tim, gazing down at her fondly. "She made me see how important it was to carry on. I owe her everything. More than you know."

Thanks a lot, Tim, I thought. In view of the sacrifice his wife had been prepared to make to spare his reputation, it was only fair that her advice should have carried more weight than mine; nevertheless, the words hurt. I did him the courtesy of believing that they hadn't been designed to.

"There's one more thing, Olwen," added Tim suddenly. "I'm not going to be able to finish that village history now, and I was wondering if you'd be willing to take it on. Laura never had time to do any work on it, and I know the new chap isn't interested in that kind of thing. If you're agreeable, I'll drop all the material off at your house some time over the Christmas break."

I nodded, unable to find the right words.

"You'll be the ideal person to do it," said Laura, leaning over to touch my hand. "I told Tim, he should have asked you in the first place."

Tim smiled indulgently at her. Before they turned away, I saw him put his hand over her womb, and then I understood. I glanced at Elvis, but he was giving nothing away. I just hoped Laura would be able to lay off the booze for the next few months.

Elvis and I left together, long before the vicarage revels had ended. I wanted to get to bed at a reasonable time, so as to be up early to look through any last-minute mail (not that I could do anything about any late orders, but I might at least manage to phone people and let them know) before Charles arrived to take us out to lunch. Then there would be the long drive to Sian's, followed by the Christmas festivities, and then – the rest of my life. To my surprise, I realised that I was quite looking forward to it.

"Jessica's love life coming up to scratch these days, is it?" asked Elvis. Suspecting that he was leading up to asking a few apposite questions about my own affairs, I tried to distract him.

"I'm glad it didn't come to anything with that Phil," I remarked. "By the way, is it true his father's a policeman?"

"Mmm. A fact I've had cause to be grateful for, in the past."

I tried not to look at him, though in the dark his expression probably wouldn't have given anything away.

"What do you mean, Elvis?"

"Oh, something and nothing. It was years ago. I got into a bit of trouble, in town. Not long after I split up with Billie. Phil's dad caught me with my trousers down, so to speak. Luckily, he knew me, he knew Mam was a widow, and he knew I was hoping to become a professional musician, so he let me off with a warning."

"I see." Another mystery solved.

"I kept out of trouble after that," added Elvis matter-of-factly.

As for me, I kept quiet.

Elvis kissed me goodnight at the end of the lane, and wished me a merry Christmas, or rather a "Nadolig Llawen". As an afterthought, he took something from his pocket – an envelope, containing my Christmas card. Elvis was always last minute with his personal preparations for the festive season, considering how organised he was with the church services.

After we had parted company, I started to think again, and that's fatal for someone like me. Besieged by doubts, I went over in my mind all the things Tim had said, and that only made me feel worse.

I should have been elated that he had decided to remain in the clergy after all; but what preyed on me was the fact that it was Laura, not me, who had persuaded him. Laura, combined perhaps with the prospect of becoming a father for the third time, with all the responsibilities, financial and otherwise, that the role entails.

Even the thought of becoming co-author of the village history didn't prevent me from starting to feel a bit down. As I put my key in the lock, I reminded myself that, in twelve hours' time, I would be seeing Charles again. It went some way towards cheering me up. I wondered if he had rung while I had been out.

If he had, he probably wouldn't have been able to get through. Jessica was on the telephone when I came into the living room. She didn't seem to have heard me.

". . . very well. And Auntie Olwen's got this sort of boyfriend."

"*Boyfriend*?" My sister's voice, at the other end of the line, was so loud that I could hear the word clearly, from the other side of the room.

It was at that moment that Jessica turned around, saw me, and went a lovely shade of red.

"Don't mind me," I said, walking past her into the kitchen. I made a show of switching on the kettle, in the hope that she would continue with this line of conversation. Jessica was on her guard now, but she didn't dare give her mother any warning that I was listening in. That would have been as good as an admission that they had been getting ready to gossip about me.

While I was waiting for the kettle to boil, I opened the envelope

Elvis had given me. The card was a conventional one, sold in aid of a national charity. Elvis had simply signed it with his name – he didn't go in for endearments – but on the left-hand side, in his usual florid hand, he had added a few bars of music. I spent a moment or two working out the tune in my mind. Recognising it as the introductory bars of Mendelssohn's Wedding March, I allowed myself to smile.

My niece was still on the phone. Continuing to listen, I began filling in Sian's questions, between Jessica's answers.

"Nice," I heard her say. Sian had obviously asked what Charles was like.

"Er . . . Charles." (What's his name?)

"Oh, I don't know. Forties, I suppose." (How old is he?)

"Um . . . a solicitor." (What does he do for a living?)

"I'm not sure." That last one wasn't so easy, but I made a stab at it. "How did she meet him?" Sian was probably asking. They were all the same questions I would have asked.

"Tell your mother I can look after myself, thanks!" I called out from the kitchen.

"She said she can look after herself."

(Blankety blank!)

"Yes, she's here. She's just come in. Do you want to talk to her?"

I came back into the living room, and took the receiver out of my niece's hand.

"I thought you were out," said Sian.

"Yes, I've just come in. In good time to hear the character assassination."

"Don't be daft. Just tell me all about him."

"Not now. It's too soon."

"Is it serious?"

I sighed. "I'm sorry, I don't really want to talk about it at this stage. Don't worry about me. I know what I'm doing. Besides, Jess has been here to keep an eye on me."

"Hmm. From what I've heard, she hasn't seen much of you lately."

We laughed together. There wasn't much I couldn't say to Sian, or she to me.

"Don't worry," I repeated. "I haven't led your daughter astray."

Jessica had left the room while I was talking. When I had put down the receiver, she returned, looking a little sheepish.

"It's okay, Jess," I said. "I don't mind people talking about me behind my back. I just didn't realise I was that interesting."

She came over and put her arm around me. "You know, Auntie Olwen, I really hope it'll work out, between you and Charles. You look so right together, if you know what I mean."

Was it flattery, or youthful inexperience, or – just conceivably – the truth?

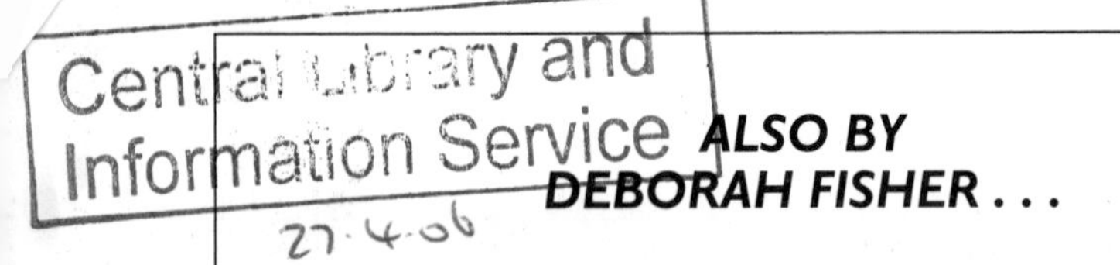

ALSO BY DEBORAH FISHER . . .

A BROAD CHURCH

Rosemary Gardner has friends, an interesting job, and a lovely home. Give or take a few romantic complications, life is running smoothly.

Wealthy Valerie Farmer wants to put a stop to that. She has plans for Rose's village, and no one dare's stand up to her – until the arrival of distinguished historian, Professor Nathan Pendragon. With assistance from the charismatic Pendragon and his "Re-enactment Society", Rose and her neighbours battle (literally) to preserve a historic landmark in the heart of England.

In the course of the campaign, Rose will discover that friends can be deceitful, and enemies can become friends.

A Broad Church
published by Unlimited Publishing,
Bloomington, Indiana, USA, 2001.
ISBN 1-58832-009-X